Simmer

Simmer

Midnight Fire Book Two

Kaitlyn Davis

All Works By Kaitlyn Davis

Midnight Fire
Ignite
Simmer
Blaze
Scorch

A Dance of Dragons
The Shadow Soul
The Spirit Heir
The Phoenix Born

A Dance of Dragons – The Novellas
The Golden Cage
The Silver Key

To my family for their unconditional love,
my friends for their overwhelming support,
and my fans for their incredible enthusiasm.
Thank you from the bottom of my heart.

Chapter One

"I hate packing," Kira whined and collapsed onto the heap of clothes piled high on her bed. She did not want to move another muscle.

"Just pick out some outfits." Tristan chuckled, not looking up from the pad of paper he was scribbling on.

Kira arched her head, glancing in his direction. He sat with one leg outstretched and one knee bent, leaning against her headboard in relaxed concentration. With squinted eyes, he focused on rubbing in the graphite pencil marks he had just made with his already blackened fingers. If she wasn't so tired, Kira would have crawled a little closer to see what he was drawing, but instead she dropped her head with a sigh.

"Easy for you to say. You just have to sit on my bed looking all artistic and mysterious while I run around like a crazy person trying to get ready for two months at conduit boot camp."

"Then my plan is working perfectly." He smirked and finally put the sketchbook down. Kira peeked over at the pages, wondering what image of her he was crafting, but saw the last thing she ever expected—a self-portrait. Fighting her exhaustion, Kira jumped up in curiosity.

"What are you doing?" She spun the image to look at it closer, noting the strong cheekbones and crystal eyes he had drawn perfectly. The hairs that always threatened to fall over his eyes seemed just ready to spill, and Kira saw the faint outline of her own features. She realized he had been sketching both of them.

"Just something for you to take to Sonnyville, to carry around and show everyone, especially any guys ages eighteen to twenty-two."

Kira rolled her eyes. "You know I don't date men who are younger than a hundred. I can't stand the immaturity level."

Tristan grabbed her hand and pulled her against his chest, making her giggle. With her arms wrapped around his waist, she let her breath slow to the pace of his heartbeat. Tristan's strong arms encircled her, hugging her as tightly against his body as he could, and he sighed.

"I'm going to miss you," he whispered, and Kira's mouth widened into a smile. She rested her chin on his chest so she could look into his face, taking in each hair on his head and memorizing the features she already knew better than her own.

"I'm going to miss you, too." She leaned up and kissed him quickly, her thoughts already wandering to what lay ahead.

A few months had passed since Kira had woken up from the coma. Luke had convinced the council to let her recuperate before forcing her to go to Sonnyville, and they all agreed that the day after graduation would be, what Kira liked to call, doomsday. Just this morning, she and her friends had all donned their robes and received their diplomas. And before she knew it, time had all but slipped away. But more than anything, Kira dreaded saying goodbye to Tristan. Luke had promised to sneak him into Sonnyville at least once, but Kira wasn't sure if it would even be a good idea to bring Tristan around so many conduits. Tomorrow morning they would have to say goodbye, and even though Kira knew it wasn't goodbye forever, two months was starting to seem like an impossibly long time apart.

"It's going to be fine," Tristan said and kissed her forehead. "And you'll be safe there, which is the most important thing."

"I know. I just wish it wasn't for so long. Do you think you'll be able to find Diana soon?" Kira questioned, bringing up the topic they had skirted around for the past few weeks.

Tristan knew Diana was still a threat. She had come back to Charleston multiple times while Kira had still been in a coma. She managed to evade Tristan, but he still sensed her presence and both of them knew that she was planning something. But neither Kira nor Tristan had known what, until about a week ago when a pack of vampires came to Charleston after hearing a rumor that a mixed breed conduit was alive and in the neighborhood. Tristan had managed to persuade them, forcefully, to leave but more would come. The safest place for Kira was with the conduits, not with her vampire boyfriend, especially since Tristan would be off hunting Diana while Kira was away.

"I know where to look. She can only run for so long." Tristan tried to reassure Kira. He ran his hand along her arm in a soothing motion. Kira relaxed into his touch.

"And you'll find out about my mother?"

"I'll try," Tristan said, but he wouldn't look her in the eye. They had had this conversation before, with Luke too, and Kira was the only one with hope that her mother was still alive. Luke and Tristan agreed that Diana had used it as a dirty trick to shock Kira, giving her the chance to escape, but Kira felt something deep inside, a gut instinct urging her to believe that her mother was living and breathing somewhere on this earth.

Kira opened her mouth to say so, but decided against it. She was too comfortable resting in his arms to bother fighting, and the last thing Kira wanted was to argue with Tristan on their last night together. Instead, she inched up his chest, noting the glint in his eye and leaned in for a kiss.

He slid his hand up her back to cup the base of her

neck and pulled her face into his, letting her know he was thinking the same thing. After a teasing moment of stillness, Kira leaned the extra centimeter forward and their lips met.

Instantly, her pulse quickened and her heart began to race as she lost herself in the sensation. The butterflies flying in her stomach seemed specifically tuned to Tristan, appearing every time he touched her. A warm feeling spread from her fingers to her toes, creating a titillating contrast as his cool fingers brushed over her skin.

With heavy breaths, Tristan grabbed her around the waist, easily flipping her over and pressing her body down into the soft bed as he took charge. A familiar twinge of excitement ran up Kira's spine, but she felt something else too, almost like a hint of anger stirring distantly in her mind. And then she heard a cough in the doorway.

"Sorry to interrupt," Luke said with a smile on his face and a steely look aimed at Tristan. Kira sighed and pulled back, trying to scoot out from underneath Tristan. For his part, Kira noted wryly, Tristan made no move to help her escape and instead let his weight hold her down. After a few seconds, which seemed like a few hours, Kira freed herself from Tristan's arms.

"Hi Luke." She smiled and sat up, trying to fix her hair. Yes, she was happy to see her friend, but who wouldn't be slightly annoyed at the interruption and very annoyed at his obviously smug face? Yup, Kira mused, the coma hadn't really changed a thing. Their mutual fear for her health had allowed Luke and Tristan to stand in the same room once in a while, but they were a long way away from friendship.

"Clearly, you're almost ready to go. Now, if we could just find a way to teleport your room to Sonnyville..." He surveyed the empty suitcases and piles of clothes all over the floor. Kira threw a small pillow at him for the sarcastic remark, and he jumped out of its path, holding his hands up in surrender.

"All right, all right, but in all honesty...what the heck happened in here? It looks slightly like the Tasmanian devil tore this place apart."

Kira shrugged. "This is just how I pack."

"So, there's a method to the madness?"

"No, trust me," Tristan spoke up and turned over to lean against Kira's pillows. *Traitor*, she thought, *your hair is still rumpled from our make-out session and you're siding with Luke.*

"So, it's a little messy. I'll be ready by tomorrow, don't worry."

Luke copiously surveyed the room again, eyes wide in doubt. "It's not like you're going to see the queen—"

"There's a conduit queen?" Kira interrupted, ready to freak out.

"No, the Queen of England. Did you hit your head again?" Luke questioned, barely able to contain his laughter.

"No," Kira huffed and picked up the closest thing she could find, which happened to be a dress. She looked at it and debated if she would need sundresses in Sonnyville. It wasn't like she would be trying to land a date; she was going there to learn how to fight. Kira cocked her head to the side, going back and forth between the options.

"What's the big deal? Just put it in your suitcase," Luke said, exasperated.

"That's what I said," Tristan chimed in again, and Kira dropped her hands to her side giving him a stern look. It seemed they had no trouble ganging up against her, but when she wanted everyone to get along they were enemies again. *I mean really*, Kira thought, *this is absurd.*

A beep sounded from the street, and Kira threw the dress back onto the floor, excited for the escape. Their whole gang was going out together, one last hurrah before Luke and Kira left, which meant she could put off packing for a few more blissful hours.

"Time to go!" Kira chirped and raced from the room, not waiting for either of the boys. Her parents were gone for the night, at a preschool summer event for her little sister Chloe, so she walked right out the door and into Emma's car. Luke appeared a minute later and hopped into the backseat.

Kira suspected that Tristan had already slipped away. Her friends liked him, but the tension with Luke was always obvious, and Kira and Tristan had both decided it was not worth the battle, at least not on her last night in Charleston.

"So, where to?" Kira looked around, eyeing her friends. As per usual, Emma drove and Kira sat in the front seat while the boys piled in the back. She took in Emma's short jean skirt and professionally applied makeup, then looked back at the boys again, seeing that Miles had replaced his usual comic book T-shirt for a button-down. It seemed as though everyone had gone fancy for their last night.

It suddenly dawned on Kira how strange it was that this would be the last time the five of them could hang out, at least for a while. They were sort of her family, especially after helping with her recovery. But with Miles going to Harvard, Emma and Dave both going to Texas, and she and Luke "taking a year off," things would definitely be changing. Kira wasn't sure what she thought about it yet, but decided to just try to enjoy this night. She needed to have fun, because even though Luke hadn't said so, Sonnyville would be far more work than pleasure.

"Well," Emma began, and Kira knew there was a saga of a story about to begin. "I wanted to go out to a fancy dinner, and the boys wanted to play video games. So we decided that we needed to meet in the middle. You know, not go too fancy but still have fun. So, we thought about it and thought about it—"

"We're going to my place," Miles voiced up, knowing Emma could have easily talked for another ten minutes without reaching the point. She shot daggers at him through the rearview mirror.

"So, yes, we're going to Miles's house. His parents had to leave right after graduation, so we'll have the place to ourselves. And not that we really need to, but we thought about it and—"

"Now we can throw that rager we've always wanted to!" Luke cheered. Kira rolled her eyes when she heard the slap of a high five. Dave and Luke were clearly excited by the idea. Kira, not so much.

"Wait, you threw a party?" She turned to look at the three boys in the back seat, each with a goofy smile plastered on his face. She had been hoping they would have some time with just the five of them, not a crazy high school party.

"Not my idea." Emma threw an apologetic look in Kira's direction.

"C'mon. It'll be awesome. We'll be leaving with a bang," Luke said. His hand landed on Kira's shoulder and he shook her a little, trying, she assumed, to shake her into the idea.

"So, where's Tristan?" Emma asked, clearly trying to change the topic. Kira knew Emma was on her side. She could already envision the two of them chatting by the punch bowl, watching Luke and Dave try to convince Miles to talk to some girl, knowing that it would fail miserably. Kira hoped he would have better luck at Harvard; a fellow nerd would really love him, much more than the cheerleaders or Goths that Luke and Dave antagonized him into asking out.

"I didn't realize we were having a party, so I told him

to go home for a while. He has some packing to do. You know he leaves for his backpacking trip around Europe tomorrow," Kira said, ending with the cover story she, Luke, and Tristan had all decided on—Tristan was spending the summer in Europe, while, totally randomly, Kira got a job at a restaurant in Orlando, and Luke was working at Disney World.

"Don't worry, I told him before we left. He's going to stop by, I think," Luke said quietly from the back seat.

Kira turned around, shocked, and heard Dave mutter "dude" under his breath.

"What, what? I'm a nice guy," Luke said and shrugged. Kira turned back around in her seat, stunned. It was no secret that Luke hated Tristan—it meant a lot to her that he made the gesture. Maybe, she thought ruefully, he was only being nice because he knew she would be with him and not Tristan for the next two months.

By the time Emma pulled over outside of Miles's house, the party was already in full swing. His house had been closed off, but his family owned an old plantation, so their backyard was gigantic. With one look at the parked cars on his yard and ring of headlights, all Kira could think was that his parents would freak out when they got home. She couldn't imagine those tire tracks would go away very fast. And it looked as though their entire class was there, dancing on the grass to music blaring from a ton of cars set to the same radio station. Plastic cups already spotted the ground, and Kira saw that the football team had set up multiple kegs in the beds of their pickup trucks. She almost felt strange as they approached the house she had visited so many times before.

"We barely know these people," she whispered to Emma. The two of them were arm in arm, a few feet behind the boys who were rushing to join the fun.

"I know, but it'll be fun! And now, we'll be the people who everyone remembers for throwing an awesome party after graduation." Emma grinned at the thought. Kira started to smile too; she could get on board with this. It would be far better to be known as a member of the party-throwing brigade than the weird coma girl.

Yeah, the last few weeks of school had been fantastic with her friends and Tristan, but everyone gave her strange looks. No one in the school really knew what happened on the night of the eclipse except for Kira, Luke, and Tristan. When Tristan had rushed her to the hospital, Luke stayed behind to clean up as much of the blood on her yard as possible. The cops still came to her house, and they had found traces of human blood despite Luke's attempts, so they started investigating. There were rumors that Tristan had beaten her up and Luke had to stop him, or that Tristan and Luke tried to kill each other. The three of them had tried to play it off as an animal attack, but it was still the town gossip for weeks. After a while, it became old news, but in high school, old news almost never disappeared completely. Going out with a bang suddenly didn't seem half bad, and Kira let Emma lead her forward to the party.

They both grabbed diet sodas and walked over to the boys who were stationed on Miles's porch, looking out over the party, surveying whom they could get him to dance with.

"I say Susie Harp." Luke pointed at the small, pixie-like girl with brown hair. Kira slapped his hand down when she and Emma got closer.

"Stop pointing," she chastised and rolled her eyes. Maybe Miles wasn't the problem; Dave and Luke could easily be holding him back.

Luke ignored her and pointed at Susie again. "Come on, she's cute and this is the last night I get to watch you in action."

"No way man." Dave put his arm around Miles's shoulder, steering him in the opposite direction. "Amy MacDougall, she's the girl you should go for."

All five of them looked over at Amy, who was dancing on the hood of a car while one of the basketball players stood at the ready in case she fell over. Her dress had wet spots from where she spilled her own drink all over herself, as Kira had witnessed five minutes before. They all looked back at Dave—he was clearly going for the "she's drunk so she'll definitely dance with you" approach.

"David," Emma started, pulling him away to reprimand him for sort of telling the group that Miles's only hope was someone who had no control over her senses.

"So, I win. Susie it is," Luke said, pushing Miles forward. He shrugged his shoulders as if to say okay, shook his head to get in the zone, and then straightened his glasses before walking over.

"This is going to be good." Luke put his arm around Kira so they could watch together.

"Why? What do you know?" Kira asked, not liking the mischievous glint in Luke's eye.

"Nothing, nothing," Luke shushed her.

"Luke," Kira said harshly. He looked over at her, slightly deflated, as though Kira were totally ruining his fun.

"Okay, so I might have already told Susie that Miles had a crush on her, and she might have already told me she would love to get to know him better, if you know what I mean." He wiggled his eyebrows and they watched as Miles led Susie to the pseudo dance floor that the circle of cars created. He shot both of them a not-so-discrete thumbs up, and Kira silently prayed he didn't screw it up.

"You're quite the matchmaker." She laughed.

"I do what I can," Luke said and looked over at her. Their faces were close together, and Kira could almost feel his pulse quicken. Not for the first time, she thought maybe she was reading his mind, because Kira knew before Luke even made a move where his thoughts were going. She broke his gaze, pulling away, and Luke released his hold on her arm to step a few feet backward. When she heard his shuffling feet pause, Kira turned her eyes around to face him and eased her body back to rest against the railing. The small space between them might as well have been miles.

"So, what about you?" she asked, trying to break the tension. "Amy's up for grabs, you can always try for one last high school hurrah before we leave tomorrow."

Luke grinned at the joke, trying to ignore the fact that Kira had very clearly just blown him off. She wondered what would happen when they went to Sonnyville. He had not been overtly obvious about his feelings for her, and sometimes Kira thought she was making it up in her head, but at moments like this, when she caught a glimpse of his small tendrils of longing, Kira wondered what really went on behind his goofy exterior.

"So, are you excited for tomorrow?" he asked, crossing his arms and leaning against the wall opposite her. Under the porch lights, Kira thought his bleach-blond hair seemed to glow, and she realized she would be the only person for the next few weeks who didn't have almost white locks.

"It's strange to think about being surrounded by conduits. I'm excited, but it's a little nerve-racking too," she said honestly.

"Everyone will love you, don't worry. My little brother can't wait. I think he thinks you're a shiny new toy for him to play with."

Kira smiled, already picturing a miniature version of Luke running around with a wide smile on his face, fascinated by everything around him. Luke's family would be interesting to finally meet. Kira wondered what his sister and parents would think. Had he told them about Tristan?

"And," Luke continued talking, recognizing that Kira still needed reassurance, "the council really isn't that bad. Everything is going to be great, you'll see."

"I hope so," she said and glanced back out at the party. Miles and Susie were still dancing, getting friendlier and friendlier Kira thought, and Dave and Emma had disappeared. So much for the five of them hanging out. Everywhere she looked, she saw her classmates, but they seemed more like strangers to her now than ever before. She wasn't sad to be leaving this town, just the few amazing friends she had made there.

Kira looked back at Luke, ready to ask more questions about their travel arrangements for tomorrow, when she saw him focus on something beyond her shoulder. The muscles in his face tensed, his usual laugh lines disappeared, and Kira saw his whole body stiffen. It could only mean one thing.

"Lover boy is here," he said.

Kira turned to see Tristan weaving his way through the crowd. Like a shadow sneaking between the rays of the headlights, he molded into the dark. Every part of him was hidden except for his pearly skin. Kira tried to smother the smile threatening to spread across her face and turned back to Luke to silently let him know she wouldn't abandon him to spend time with her boyfriend.

"I'll leave you two alone," Luke said, pushing against the wall to straighten his body and prepare to walk away.

"Luke, stay. I want to hang out with both of you."

He shrugged, as if to say *that's not possible*, and started to leave. Kira heard the porch steps creak behind her, knowing it was Tristan, and spun around.

"We need to talk," Tristan said, his voice full of concern. Luke stopped walking and looked back, alert.

"What's going on?" he asked. Kira could tell he had transitioned to business mode and had let the personal drama go for the moment.

"Privately. Can we get inside?"

Luke nodded and walked over to the door. Reaching above the doorframe, he pulled out a spare key that Miles must have told him about and opened the locked door.

Tristan grabbed Kira's hand, entwining their fingers, and quickly kissed the top of her head before following Luke inside.

Luke shut the door behind them. The kitchen was eerily dark and the soundproof glass dulled the strains of music coming from the party. Heavy shadows crept around the lines of light peeking through the windows, making the three of them seem very alone. Kira shivered with a sense of foreboding and dropped Tristan's hand to lift herself onto the granite countertop. She knew she would need a seat to hear the news Tristan clearly felt was urgent.

"What's going on, Tristan?" she asked.

With traces of sadness lining his clear blue eyes, Tristan looked at her and responded, "You and Luke need to leave now. Immediately. I brought Luke's car and packed your stuff." He ended quietly, as if not wanting to believe the truth in his words. Kira reached out to grab his arm, pulling him closer. There was something else, something he didn't want to tell her. In the corner of her eye, Kira could see Luke pacing around the kitchen, thinking.

"They're here, aren't they?" Luke stopped walking and faced Tristan, who just nodded.

"What?" Kira asked, feeling left out, before realizing Tristan of course meant vampires. "Wait? They're here? As in Charleston or the backyard?"

Tristan ran his free hand through his hair and turned to Luke in full protection mode. Kira had seen this act before, and she didn't like it. "The pack of vampires I sent away last time, they're back. We have five, maybe ten minutes before they reach the party and tear this place apart. You both need to leave now."

"But what about everyone else?" Kira jumped from the countertop, not allowing them to ignore her. She could not leave these people to fend for themselves.

"We need to do something," Luke said, walking closer to the two of them in order to figure out a plan. Tristan nodded in agreement. "Okay, Kira and I will just have to face them. We're powerful enough to bring down a few vampires, this will all be fine."

"No, that's way too risky," Tristan said, looking Kira in the eye. "You have to leave. You and Luke get in the car and start driving. I'm going to lure the vampires away, pretend I'm with them and that I saw you leave. Hopefully, I can lead them in the wrong direction for a while so you and Luke have a chance to escape."

"Oh, and your plan is totally foolproof," Kira smarmily replied. "I would rather fight them. It's what, eight or nine vampires? Luke and I can handle it. You can't do this on your own, Tristan." She reached her palm up to cup his face, letting her finger brush against his hair. She wouldn't let him do this alone.

"No, Kira," Luke spoke forcefully. "Tristan's right. He needs to do this. It's the best way to make sure you don't get caught."

Kira turned to Luke angrily. "It's not like you wouldn't gladly watch him die," she hissed, then looked away, instantly sorry for the remark. Luke was better than that—she knew he was better than that.

"This isn't about that, okay?" Luke replied softly, staring at the ground to hide his involuntary wince. "Everyone at this party is at risk right now, and you being here only amplifies that. Tristan's plan is the best way to keep everyone safe. So, let's go." He grabbed her hand and started pulling her from the kitchen toward the front door of the house.

"Wait, Luke. Wait!" She tugged against his hold and stopped walking to glance back at Tristan. Drenched in shadow, he stood in the kitchen alone, turned slightly away from her and Luke as though he knew this was goodbye but couldn't bring himself to say it.

"Meet me at the car," Luke said and dropped Kira's hand to leave the two of them alone. He disappeared out the door, and before Kira could blink, Tristan was by her side. His hands gently cupped her face while he stared into her fire-laced eyes.

"It's going to be all right," he said, urging her to believe him. Kira tried to quell her racing heart and believe his words, but even if it was all right tonight, neither one of them knew what the future would hold in these next two months apart. He would be chasing down Diana, and though Kira knew he could take care of himself, even vampires could die.

Kira rested her forehead against his, enjoying the brush of his cool breath on her cheek in this one moment of peace.

"I love you," she whispered.

He leaned in to kiss her, and Kira pulled him closer, not wanting to let go and lose the touch of his soft lips on hers. Tristan lifted her off the ground, hugging her close to his body, and she wrapped her arms around his neck. Everything felt perfect, at least for an instant before his body stiffened. He broke their kiss, pulled her in even tighter for a final hug, and then set her back down, still holding her.

Kira stared into his sapphire eyes, reading the sadness-tinted longing in his irises and knew the vampires were here. Tristan let her go and stared, moving his eyes so he could take in every inch of her face. She ran her hand through his hair, pushing the ebony locks off of his forehead one last time, breathing in the moment.

In the time it took for Kira to blink away a tear, Tristan had vanished, leaving just a memory, and she was left alone holding only the air.

Chapter Two

Kira dashed through the house, sprinting out the front door and down the driveway, racing to beat not only the vampires but also her own emotions, which threatened to burst forth.

Before she rounded the street corner, Kira saw headlights and heard the familiar rumble of Luke's pickup truck. *Really*, she thought, *the truck?*

"Let's go, Kira," Luke yelled from the driver's seat and the passenger door popped open. Kira jumped inside and slammed it closed while Luke pushed the gas pedal all the way down, throwing her back against the seat with the force.

"Where are we going? Do we even have a plan?" Kira dragged her seatbelt around and clicked it into place.

"Yes," Luke said, not looking away from the road. His hands were white from gripping the steering wheel so tightly. "All we need to do is get to the airport. No vampires would dare attack us there, not in front of an audience and security cameras."

"How far away is it?"

"About half an hour."

Thirty minutes, Kira thought. It didn't seem like a long time, especially not with Luke zipping through the empty, fog-filled roads as he was now. And after five minutes, Kira was beginning to think they were in the clear. Tristan must have diverted the pack, or, she thought darkly, they had reached the party and decided to drop their chase. Kira searched the night for the sound of sirens. Twisting in her seat, she looked out the back window, just in time to see the faint outline of a body rapidly approaching.

"Luke!" she yelled, grabbing his shoulder. He flicked his eyes to the rearview mirror, and his brows tightened into a frown.

"They're here," he said, like a sigh, as if a faint hope had been denied. "Okay, Kira, listen. I want you to kick out the back window—"

"What!" She jerked her head to the side and knew her eyes were just about popping out of her skull.

"Okay...that might have been a bit drastic, but it would have been really awesome." He smiled. She rolled her eyes.

"Luke, be serious!" She wanted to shake him, but she looked out the window instead. The vampire was gaining speed and fast.

Luke reached back with his arm, unlatched the window, and slid it open. "Kira, you're going to have to fight them. Remember to keep moving quickly and, whatever you do, don't lose control. You need to make speedy movements. Do not concentrate on just one vampire because we're probably already surrounded."

Kira nodded and stuck her head out the opened window. The wind whipped her hair around and the trees swooshed by quicker than her eyes could follow. Of all the ideas they had had, this was probably high on the list of the worst, she mused and started pulling herself through the tight space. The vampire disappeared from the road, but Kira wasn't stupid enough to think they had lost him.

Finally, Kira made it through the window. She tried to stand but got knocked over by the wind and slammed against the metal bed of the truck. There was no way she would be able to stay up when every bump in the road sent her flying. She noticed a rope in the back and crawled over on her stomach, grabbing the string. She looped it around her waist and tied it to a hoop in the bed of the truck. At least she couldn't be sent flying over the edge.

The wind still whistled in her ears, making it hard for her to hear anything else, and she was so concentrated on not toppling over that she didn't see the vampire jump through the trees until Luke shouted her name.

Blindly flinging her hand to the side, Kira shot flames into the night.

"Control!" Luke screamed from inside the car. Kira could only just hear him over the crackling of her fire. But she stopped, realizing the vampire was long gone and she had been wasting energy on open space. *Think*, she chided and leaned against the back of the truck for stabilization. Finally adjusting to the rhythm of the road, Kira scanned the trees, waiting for something to jump out.

She saw a blur of blonde hair before registering the female vampire that jumped out from the right side, and she shot a short, controlled flame right at her face, sending the vamp in somersaults back into the trees. To her left, another blur, and Kira fired again. She watched as the vamp circled in the air only to land on stable feet. He kept charging from the road, and Kira concentrated again, putting a killing force behind the blow. He retreated to the woods.

A tingle in the back of her neck made Kira turn around seconds before Luke bellowed, "In front!"

The blonde female stood in the middle of the road with her hands outstretched, ready to stop their car. Kira sent a stream of light arching over to encase the female from above. She put all of her concentration into the kill, and by the time Luke and Kira had reached the spot, all that remained was a pile of dust that scattered in the wind.

Kira was amazed at her own power. She had never been this accurate or this fast before. It might have been the extra adrenaline, but she took a moment to look at her own hands. The scars glowed in the darkness like coals still cooling on the grill.

The sound of boots slamming against metal jerked Kira awake. She stuck her hand toward the sound, letting her power go, and only saw the glowing blue eyes of the vamp as it flew off of the car.

Another jumped from the left and she shot it. One more from the right, and Kira knocked it down. Next, two vampires planned an attack together, and she threw her arms wide to the sides, shooting both at once. But hands grabbed her neck from behind, and the tightly knotted rope slipped free from her waist. Kira swung her hands back and latched onto the vampire's head, burning it. A high-pitched scream pierced her ears, but she refused to let go. Soon, the squeal came to a halt, and Kira's own hands slammed together. A cloud of dust swooshed in front of her, and she knew the vampire had imploded.

Something howled from the forest and before she could process, Kira had been lifted up and thrown down against the bed of the truck. A brown-haired vampire with blood dripping from his lips stared down at her, growling. He was crouching, ready to pounce, when the truck came screeching to a halt.

Before Luke had time to turn around in his seat and fire, a new blurred figure slammed into the huge vampire, sending him over the side and into the thick trunk of a tree with a slap.

"Go, Luke! Drive!" Tristan shouted and smacked his

hand down on the roof of the car. Kira looked him over, noting the rips in his shirt and the blood seeping out of fresh wounds. He met her eyes and winked. Then a smile rose on his lips causing his dimples to appear.

"Love you," Tristan shouted over his shoulder as he jumped from the speeding truck and slammed into yet another vampire that had come flying from the trees. *He's enjoying this*, Kira thought, flabbergasted.

But Kira still felt her heart sink when she scrambled to her knees and watched Tristan disappear from her sight, locked in a death grip. She couldn't shoot the other vamp without risking Tristan, and before long, the two vampires had disappeared altogether.

The faint sound of beeps and rumbling engines caused Kira to turn around, and she saw the highway ahead. She and Luke were finally free from the country roads. They had made it.

"Get inside," Luke said and slowed the car to make it easier for Kira to crawl through the window and slip back in.

"Are you all right?" Luke asked when Kira was safely seated and buckled in. She took a moment to survey the damage, and besides a bump on the head and a few scrapes, she was fine, just tired. She raised her hand, and let her palm glow, sending the light inward to heal herself. Almost instantly, Kira felt revived. She sighed and rested her head against the back of her seat.

"So, let's agree to never do that again," Kira said.

"I don't know. You were pretty awesome up there. That move where you twisted your arms and burned that vampire chick's head apart. I mean, that was like comic book amazing."

Kira smiled. "That was pretty badass."

"Kira, the Vampire Slayer...no...Kira, the Avenger...nah, still not right...Kira, the Human Flame Thrower...eh, maybe—"

"Luke?"

"Yes?"

"Stop."

"Okay."

Kira looked over to see that his lips were still moving. "Luke, you are not giving me some fancy nickname. Stop."

"Oh, come on. I just thought of something amazing."

"No." She laughed at his persistence.

"Please?"

"No." She stood strong.

"Pretty please with a cherry on top...?" Kira finally looked him in the eyes, meeting his puppy-dog pout, and couldn't resist.

"Okay, fine, but keep your eyes on the road."

"All right, here goes," Luke said, adding a dramatic pause for effect. "Kira...the Flaming Tomato." He grinned widely, super proud of himself. Kira snorted almost against her will.

"Luke, that stinks. That is actually the worst superhero name I have ever heard. I prefer the Human Flame Thrower."

"Too late," he cheered. "Kira Dawson, the Flaming Tomato. I think it has a nice ring to it. You have red hair like Shaun White, but you flame while he flies. It's perfect."

"It's terrible. If you ever call me that again, I may have to hurt you."

"You, hurt me? Never." Luke was doubtful, clearly.

Kira turned to look at Luke, grinning, and finally gave in. "Hey, I'm the Flaming Tomato, mister. I could kill you with the simplest flick of my finger."

He smiled triumphantly, and Kira let the conversation fall away as she noticed the exit sign for the airport. In an hour or two, they would probably be seated with their seats up and tray tables secure, flying off into the night sky, away from everything...and everyone.

"Do you think he's okay?" Kira didn't have to clarify.

"Yeah, you have nothing to worry about," Luke said as he switched lanes onto the exit ramp.

They rode in silence for the next five minutes, enjoying the peace, until the lights from the parking lot came into view.

They had arrived.

The clicking of the turn signal filled the silence as Luke made his way through long rows of empty spaces speckled here and there with a car. He pulled his truck to a halt in the last space of the longest row, the spot closest to the garage exit.

"Do you think they followed us?" Kira asked while peering around the fluorescent lamps and through the slight fog that stilled danced along the ground.

"I'm not sure," Luke responded. He reached for the handle on his door, and then hesitated. "On the count of three, we make a run for it, okay?"

Kira nodded. The entrance to the airport was maybe fifty yards away. They could definitely make it. She reached back for the duffle Tristan had stuffed full of her clothes and saw Luke take hold of his. She fixed the strap over her shoulder and met Luke's waiting eyes.

"One," Luke started.

"Two," Kira added.

"Three," they said simultaneously. Kira flipped the handle, shoved the door open, and jumped out. Luke had already rounded the car, and Kira sprinted forward, keeping pace with him. They made it out of the dark parking lot and were greeted with the bright lights of the airport entrance. Neither one of them slowed for a second until they were at the automatic door, panting and out of breath, but alive.

Kira sucked air into her lungs. The distance hadn't been far, but fear had made her heart race even faster than the running. When she straightened and walked through the sliding door, Kira noticed the security guard for the first time. He looked at Kira and Luke with clear suspicion.

"Nice night for a sprint through the parking lot, don't you think?" Luke said as they walked by, and Kira elbowed him in the ribs. That taunt would not help anything. Luke shrugged and made his way to the ticket counter. Kira waited with their bags, looking up at the arrivals and departures board. It was almost one in the morning, and while Kira loved Charleston, the small, two terminal airport was not exactly hopping at the moment.

She scanned the names, searching for Orlando or something in Florida, but there were barely any planes flying for the rest of the night, and the flights for the next morning had already been listed. Sighing, Kira walked over to Luke, dragging both of their bags behind her.

"There aren't any more flights tonight, we need to find something for tomorrow," she said when she got closer. Luke turned with two tickets in hand and grinned.

"Don't worry. We're not flying commercial."

"What? What are we flying?" Kira went for the tickets, but Luke moved faster, keeping them just out of reach.

"You'll see."

Kira didn't like the smirk on his face, but she followed as he walked past her, picked up his bag, and made for the security check.

They walked silently through the brown, carpeted hallways. The last time Kira had been there, she remembered judging the quaint decor, thinking it provincial compared to the vast, open space of New York's LaGuardia Airport. But now, Kira appreciated the hand-painted murals of herons on the marsh and Carolina gators. The personal touches of the smaller city were welcome, and she realized that soon she would be downsized to an even tinier town, which brought her thoughts right back to the conduits and the mysterious transportation they had provided.

Luke strode confidently through the airport and politely waved to the workers they passed as though old friends. Kira stepped more meekly behind, afraid of what she approached.

When they reached the terminal, Luke showed a flight attendant their tickets and she opened the exit door, signaling both of them to follow. Kira had no idea what to expect as she walked through the opening into breezy air, but the streamlined five window private jet that greeted her was the last thing she imagined.

"Luke, is this a joke? That can't be our ride."

"No joke. Conduits fly in style," he whispered in her ear and used his finger to close her jaw, which had dropped straight to the floor.

"How is this possible?" Kira asked, still not convinced.

"Just follow me." Luke laughed and looped his arm through hers, tugging her down the steps and over to the plane. Kira followed him up the entrance, ducking her head to fit through the ovular door, and almost couldn't believe what she saw. Eight cream-colored leather seats, large enough to fit two people each, filled the space. One long couch stretched below the windows on the left side of the plane, and two flat-screens graced the front and back walls of the space. The cup holders and foldout tables were made of mahogany, and Kira thought even the carpeted floor looked luxurious. Her mouth dropped open again and she moved to close it as a man stood up from one of those comfy seats that Kira couldn't wait to collapse into.

"Luke! How have you been?" the man asked, stretching his arm out to shake Luke's hand. Kira took note of his tailored suit and sandy blond hair, before reaching out to shake the hand he now focused on her. "And you must be Miss Dawson. It's an honor to meet you."

"My pleasure," Kira said, still not totally trusting the wide smile he presented her.

"Kira, this is Councilman Andrews," Luke said, but something in the way he looked at her made Kira even warier. She remained silent, letting the tension build into an awkward silence. For some reason, Kira couldn't bring herself to trust this council or its members.

"Well, now that introductions are out of the way, we have business to discuss. Luke, come sit with me?" The councilman asked, breaking up the moment. Luke nodded and picked up his suitcase.

"Wait." Kira touched Luke's arm. "Mr. Andrews, can I please talk to him first?"

"Of course," the councilman said, flashing that smile again, one that was slightly too wide to be real.

Kira sat down, sinking into the chair that was even more comfortable than she could have imagined. Luke sat across from her.

"Pretty nice, right?" he said, gazing around the small room.

"Well, yeah. You said you would explain this little surprise?"

"I can't go into details right now." Luke nodded his head in the councilman's general area, letting Kira know the councilman was listening in on them. "But let me put it this way—Area 51 is real, it's just not about aliens. In exchange for our help, the government keeps our secret and gives us military funding. And a fancy way to fly was at the top of our list."

"So, what? You're saying that the government has some secret lab where they study vampires?"

"Basically, yes—vampires, among other things. We've heard rumors of were-creatures or faeries, but I've never seen any." Kira leaned back, processing. She guessed there had to be other things out there. But still, actually hearing it was just bizarre.

"Luke?" Councilman Andrews called out. He sighed under his breath.

"Look, I have to go talk to him. I need to brief him on what happened and let him know why we arrived so much sooner than planned."

Kira nodded in understanding. "Before you go, I just want to say thanks. If you hadn't been yelling instructions to me, we probably wouldn't have made it here. I never even saw that vampire in front of the car until you screamed at me."

Luke smiled slightly. "I don't even remember screaming. Must have been too caught up in the action. Anyway, there's a phone in the armrest, I thought you might want to call your parents once we get in the air."

"Thanks," Kira said and watched as he retreated to the rear end of the plane to talk to Mr. Andrews. *It's amazing*, Kira thought, *how he thinks of everything*. He had saved her life again that night without even realizing it.

The plane vibrated as the engine started, and she looked out the window to watch as they moved closer and closer to the runway. After they rounded the last corner, the plane picked up speed, and she held on as it lifted off the ground, defying gravity in a way that still amazed her. The forest below started shrinking, and the cars racing down the highway began to look more like toys than anything else.

Kira wished it were daylight so she could catch one last glimpse of the Ashley River in memory of one of her favorite afternoons. She searched for the lights of Charleston but saw only the black stretch of the ocean. Folly Pier would be out there somewhere, she realized, as she stared out at the eastern horizon.

Leaving things behind was always hard, but leaving the place where she had discovered so much about herself was more difficult than she had realized. In the past year, almost everything about her life had changed, but South Carolina had been a constant. The humid air that clung to her skin, the tangy smell of salt in the wind, or the rustle of a palmetto in a chilly winter's breeze—all of it had become comforting to her. Sonnyville, home of an ancient society she had only just scratched the surface of, would be completely new. She would miss the sand, the beach, the hot sun, and the low-country attitude where enjoying life was the most important thing.

Kira stopped searching the darkness for her home and reached inside the armrest for the phone instead. She dialed and it rang once before it clicked.

"Hello?" It was her mother, and Kira felt sorry for the obvious panic in her voice.

"Mom, it's me. I'm—"

"Oh, thank god. What happened? Are you all right?"

"I'm fine," Kira said loudly, halting her mother before her questioning got out of control. "I'm on my way to Sonnyville with Luke. We had to leave a little earlier than expected." She didn't want to frighten her mother, so she kept silent about the reason for their leaving early.

"I know. Tristan came over and told your father and me about the council summoning you a day early. We didn't even get to say goodbye."

Kira smiled, silently thanking Tristan for knowing her well enough to understand that she wouldn't want her mother to worry. It also meant that he had made it and that the vampires had fled after their car chase.

"Honestly, maybe it's better this way. Now we won't have to go through that whole bawling in each other's arms sort of goodbye." She heard a sniffle on the other end of the receiver. "Mom, stop crying. Seriously, I'm only leaving for two months. I'll be back to annoy you and Dad in no time."

"I know." She sniffled again. *Mothers*, Kira sighed. "Your father wants to talk to you."

"Kira?"

She smiled at the deep rumble of her father's voice. "Hi, Dad."

"Hi, honey. We're so happy you're all right. Luke better be treating you like a lady." Kira rolled her eyes.

"Dad, relax. I'm staying with Luke and his family, and my boyfriend is in Europe for the next two months. You have nothing to worry about."

"Well, that's a father job, we—"

A high-pitched, barely understandable squeal sounded through the phone, cutting her father off.

"Chloe!" Kira chirped, excited.

"Kira, where are you?"

Kira smirked. She could easily envision the pout on her sister's face. "I had to go away for a little while, but I'll be back soon."

"Can you make pancakes when you get back?"

"Of course." Kira chuckled. Her sister would miss her food more than she missed her.

"Yay! Here's Mommy."

"Call us when you land, okay sweetie?"

"Yes, Mom."

"We love you."

"I love you, too," Kira said and hung up the phone. Maybe two months away wouldn't be so bad. It would be an adventure, like going to camp for a summer. She would come back with enough stories to enthrall her sister and enough skills that her mother might stop worrying a little bit. Maybe she would learn more about who and what she was, and why the council had decided to keep her alive even though her life supposedly meant the end of the modern world.

And maybe, Kira thought as she pulled the chain holding her locket and ring out from underneath her shirt, maybe she would come back with a few more memories of her real parents. Maybe, she finally let herself dream, she would come back with her real mother.

Kira leaned her head against the window and watched the sky change with the rising sun. At first, the deep ebony sky lightened to a vivid indigo, slowly turning from a dark violet to a light pink, until wispy tendrils of cerulean poked through the painterly scene. Even the clouds seemed fluffier than usual.

Before long, Kira dozed off. She didn't notice as the bright sun scattered the clouds and enlivened the ground below. She didn't notice the warm glow on her cheeks and how her skin naturally reacted to the brilliant rays. She didn't even notice when the plane started to descend on the sleepy town below, one that had just started buzzing with the morning's events.

She did notice when Luke lightly touched her shoulder and shook her awake.

"Kira," he whispered, his lips slightly closer to her ear than necessary. In her groggy state, she welcomed the warmth of his breath. "Kira, we're here."

Her eyes shot open.

Chapter Three

Kira jerked awake and moved to stand up, promptly smacking her forehead against Luke's chin.

"Ow." Kira brought her hand to her head, rubbing the now aching spot. "Luke, there is this little thing called personal space..." He cupped his jaw, moving it around to fix the slight displacement Kira had caused.

"Hey, I was just trying to wake you up. How was I supposed to know you'd shoot up like the Energizer Bunny?"

Kira ignored him and stood up gently this time, easing out of her seat. She grabbed her things and followed Luke off the plane, realizing the councilman had already left the two of them alone.

The first thing Kira noticed when she exited was that it was hot, scorching hot. Almost instantly, a slight sweat rose on her arms. There was no breeze, just the heaviness of still air letting the sun bake her.

After she let the temperature go, Kira looked around at the small landing strip. The airport was almost nonexistent. There was only one runway, one building, and two of these small planes resting in the open air. And then she noticed the car that was waiting a few yards away. She assumed it was the one that would take her and Luke to Sonnyville, and started walking over.

"Are you excited to be home?" Kira asked when Luke sat beside her in the backseat and closed the door.

"More than you know," he replied, and Kira could almost feel his excitement sizzle in the air.

A driver sat down in front of them and revved the engine.

"Where to, Mr. Bowrey?"

"The town square, please," Luke responded, reaching in his bag for a few papers. Kira was taken aback by the formal use of Luke's last name. To her, he was the slightly cocky, mostly goofy best friend. But here, Luke was treated with the utmost respect. It was strange to see him so grown up, Kira thought as she studied his concentrated features.

"What?" Luke asked, turning and catching Kira's stare.

"Nothing," she said and flipped her attention to the world outside of her window.

For a few minutes, nothing seemed different. Trees flashed by, a blue sky danced above them, the road was made of gravel and it was painted with striped yellow lines—nothing unusual. But then, they pulled to a halt outside two large, scroll-topped, cast iron gates. Kira watched as the driver lifted a remote and pressed a button. The gates slowly creaked open, and the car inched through them.

For some reason unknown to her, Kira expected something crazy to happen when they entered the town. But the deeper in they drove, the more normal it looked, like the perfect picture of suburbia. They passed white-picket fences, shingled roofs, mowed front lawns, and there was nothing out of the ordinary at all. In fact, if anything, it was eerily silent. She didn't see people anywhere, despite the sunny day. There were no children hopping through sprinklers or parents watching over them from a shady porch. The longer they drove, the more spooked Kira became. Where were all the people?

"We're almost there," Luke said, tucking all of his things back inside his bag. Kira shifted her attention from the ghost town to her friend.

"Where is everyone?" Kira asked.

"They're waiting for you." Luke laughed.

"Me? Why?"

"Kira, you're the only mixed breed anyone has heard about in modern history. Believe it or not, you're a huge deal."

A knot of butterflies grew in her stomach. Being the

center of attention was never something that had crossed her mind when coming to Sonnyville. Training? Yes. The council watching? Yes. Children gawking? Definitely not. *Stupid*, she chastised herself, *of course my being here is a big deal.*

"Here we are," Luke said. A wide smile lit up his features and crinkled the corner of his eyes.

The first thing Kira noticed when Luke opened the door was the cacophony of voices in the air. When she looked outside, she understood why. Every citizen of Sonnyville must have been in that town square. The grassy park looked more like a sea of blond hair as Protectors of all ages spoke excitedly to one another. Every so often, Kira saw a streak of fire soar through the air only to land in someone's open palm to be absorbed back into his or her skin. Happy, was what she first thought. All of these people looked happy and content with their lives.

Luke stepped out of the car first, and the crowd started to quiet down. With slight hesitation, Kira emerged, greeted only by a deafening silence. She had never felt so self-conscious in her life. Between the yellow hair, the blue sky, and the green trees, her red curly hair stood out like never before. Her flame-tinted eyes were the same as everyone else's, but that similarity seemed far too small for Kira to notice at the moment.

"Well, you sure know how to make an entrance," Luke whispered, taking her hand. "Follow me."

Kira couldn't speak. She just let Luke lead her

through the crowd, which parted like the red sea as she approached. When she met someone's eyes, they looked away. She saw little children cling to their parents, afraid to approach. *Are they scared of me?* Kira wondered. But she didn't have time to complete the thought because she bumped into Luke who had stopped walking. He dropped her hand and moved aside, so Kira could see the council waiting for her.

They sat overlooking the crowd on a raised wooden platform, each man resting on a large carved throne. She assumed this was the space where they held town meetings, but after the completely modern airplane, this archaic arena was the last thing Kira had expected. There were seven people on the council. All of them were men, all of them wore suits, and all of them were intimidating. She approached the platform and slowly walked up the steps, all the while fearing her legs would give out before she reached the top.

"Luke Bowrey." Kira jumped at the loud, booming voice and glanced at the older man who spoke. His hair was pure white, almost blinding to look at, and he sat in the center seat. "Won't you join us?"

Kira looked back at Luke, who smiled as if he were the picture of serenity and walked up to stand beside her.

"Councilmen," Luke greeted them with a bow.

There is no way I'm curtsying in front of this crowd, Kira thought. She didn't want to let on how scared she was when all of these people had different expectations of her.

"Hello. Nice to meet you all," Kira said in the strongest voice she could muster, which seemed almost like a squeak to her, but clearly was not what they had expected. Luke looked over at her with eyes brimming in annoyance.

"Miss Dawson, we're aware you are not familiar with our customs, but when the council is in session, do not address us so informally. We are a society built on traditions, and though you don't know them yet, we expect you to respect them."

Kira stared at the man who spoke, her eyes wide in shock. He stared right back, looking down on her—not at her, but on her, as if she was a bug that needed to be squashed. His hair was perfectly coifed, pulled back to hide a gleaming bald spot. Slight wrinkles framed his eyes and his skin was leathery from too much time spent in the sun. His voice was loud and commanding.

Who are you, she thought, *to sit up on your throne and judge me?*

Her fear had been replaced with anger. These were the men who were responsible for keeping her entire life a secret and a lie. They sat on their daises, overlooking the crowd and were content to be there. They were comfortable, too comfortable, and Kira thought it was time for a change.

Almost as if sensing her altered mood, Luke reached out for her hand. Kira swatted him away. Her neck tingled with the sensation of Luke's frustration. It was palpable, but she wouldn't be the docile girl these men could push around.

"I meant no disrespect," Kira said, starting off politely, before continuing, "but seeing as I had no idea that any of you even existed for the first seventeen years of my life, I hope you'll be a little patient with me...councilmen." She finished by crossing her arms over her chest and cocking her hip to the side so all of her weight rested on one foot.

The older man shook his head and shifted his eyes to look at Luke. "We expected more from you, Mr. Bowrey, much more." Luke shifted his weight from one foot to the other and opened his mouth to respond. Kira knew he would apologize for her, but that wasn't what she wanted. Sure, the council could make her life horrible for the next few weeks if they wanted to, but they didn't own her.

"Leave Luke out of this. He—"

"He can't be left out of this, Miss Dawson. Luke was supposed to train you. Luke was supposed to teach you about our ways. Luke was supposed to get you ready for this life. Instead, he befriended you. He let too much slip because he cared about you. Twice, you have almost been captured because you have not been trained properly."

How dare you, Kira thought, *how dare you blame the one person who's been there for me when I had no idea who or what I was.* Even when she had no one to trust, not Tristan and not her parents, Luke had been there for her.

"Don't you understand?" Kira stepped forward, leaving the shamefaced Luke behind her and hating this man in front of her for speaking to him that way. The six other men on the council disappeared. The silent crowd slipped away. Even the trees and sky seemed to fade until all she focused on was the nameless man before her. "You were the ones who failed. You were the ones who never told me who I was. You were the ones who kept everything secret from me. And you are the reason I wasn't prepared when Diana and the others decided I would be their next meal. Luke was the one who saved me. He told me what I am and made me trust myself again. Luke kept me alive. He saved me from your mistakes."

When she stopped to breathe, a sense of happiness and pride broke through her anger. She wasn't sure where it came from, but it burst into her chest, blossoming like a flower. Her tunnel vision receded, and she suddenly remembered where she was...smack dab in the middle of a mass of people she had probably just royally offended. The councilmen glared at her. She looked past them at the crowd behind, not daring to turn her head to look at Luke or the people behind him. All of them looked shocked. No one moved, and no one shifted his or her eyes away from the platform. Even the breeze had stopped.

Kira gazed around the sea of statue-like bodies, searching for one friendly expression, until she saw a woman whose face held a small smile. She was old with sun-kissed skin and white hair that gleamed in the sun. As she gazed in that woman's face, Kira's anger calmed. The woman was somehow familiar and comforting. But the moment was ruined when she saw the man start to stand.

He eased out of his chair, pushing his hands against his knees for the extra strength. Kira watched as he reached behind his chair to grab a long stick she hadn't noticed before. One end was topped with a gold ball and the rest was smooth and polished, and she realized it was a cane. Placing the tip of the cane on the ground before him, he stepped down from his raised chair and ambled over to her.

No longer angry, Kira took in the situation from a different angle. Off of his throne, this man no longer scared her. She saw him for what he was—an old man afraid of change.

The wood creaked with his steps. And Kira saw now that his eyes held the strength his frail body clearly didn't have. Maybe the council didn't rule with fear like she had expected. *Maybe these people really do love these men*, she thought.

He stopped in front of her, straightening his body to its full height, trying to regain some of the composure Kira could tell he had lost.

"You remind me of my daughter," he said at last, after staring at her face in silence for a few moments. Kira exhaled, releasing a breath she hadn't even realized she had been holding. "She too struggled with following rules and it killed her. I saved your life seventeen years ago despite knowing that the fate of our world would rest on your shoulders. Do not make me regret it."

His eyes seemed about to water as he walked past Kira, not looking back. Shuffling tired feet, he reached the edge of the stage and used his cane for balance as he walked down the steps. The woman who had smiled at Kira made her way over to the bottom stair and hooked her arm through his. The gesture looked more like reflex for the elderly couple, and the crowd parted for them as they walked away.

Kira watched until they disappeared from sight into a car that slowly pulled away from the curb.

"Luke, were they...?" she asked quietly, turning to look at her friend. He gazed back at her sadly and nodded—those were her grandparents. Kira's legs grew weak and, almost in slow motion, she plopped down onto the wooden floor. The locket felt heavy around her neck, and she reached into her shirt to grab it. After opening it, Kira wondered how she hadn't realized they were her family. The old woman looked so much like her mother—eyes slightly too large with a reserved smile that seemed full of secrets. The look she had been giving Kira was the exact same one her mother held in the photo. It was obvious now.

Kira heard a cough and looked up to find the source of the noise. Councilman Andrews looked over at her with impatience, but Kira also thought she noticed a bit of concern in his expression.

"Miss Dawson, if we could resume the meeting."

She glanced at Luke, who shrugged apologetically and offered her a hand. She took it and tucked the locket back under her shirt. There would be more time for ruminating later. After taking a deep breath and pushing the hair out of her face with both hands, Kira was ready to hear what the council had to say.

"On behalf of everyone, I would like to first apologize for what just passed between Councilman Peters and yourself. Clearly, there were some lingering emotions that we did not previously notice. Now..." Kira watched as he turned his attention from her to the crowd and silently thanked him for that little bit of kindness. "You were brought to Sonnyville to learn about our society and to strengthen your abilities. Before we know how to train you, we must test you to find out what you already know. In two days' time, we will meet back here to have a formal examination of your skills. Until then, you will be staying with Mr. Bowrey and his family. Is that all right with you?"

Kira just nodded, not sure if the question was for her or Luke. She was still caught on that last bit, that "formal examination" thing he mentioned. Two days seemed like an awfully short amount of time for her to really learn anything new or get prepared for a test.

"I call this meeting to an end. Councilmen?" Mr. Andrews questioned. Kira watched as the six remaining council members stood.

"May the sun shine down upon you for all of your days," they said in unison.

"May it protect you until the end," the entire crowd responded. Kira even heard the rumble of Luke's voice as he murmured the words. Yet another thing she didn't understand, another thing that separated her from the others.

Kira started to walk off the platform, but Luke put his hand on her arm, gently stopping her.

"Wait," he said, letting the six remaining councilmen exit before them. The crowd parted like they had for her grandfather, but this time no one walked quite so far away. Instead, the council dispersed to find their families. Kira assumed they would want to enjoy the day, because despite everything, the weather was still beautiful. It was nearing late afternoon, but the temperature was warm, the perfect weather for a dip in the pool.

"So, where to now?" Kira spun to Luke, ready to follow him home.

"I'm going to find my family. I know they're here somewhere. But I don't think you'll be able to get very far." He smirked.

"What do you mean?" Kira asked. She followed his gaze to the stairwell where a circle of little kids had formed. They were staring her down. "Oh lord. Luke, you can't leave me here alone."

"Welcome to Sonnyville," he said with an even wider

grin. "Oh, and before I forget." He leaned in to whisper, "No healing, okay? It's the one thing I never told the council." Kira nodded in understanding, but Luke had already jumped off the stage to find his parents.

Warily, Kira turned back to the crowd of children. She had nothing against little kids, but she knew they had endless resources of energy and there was a lot of day left. She sighed and took a step forward. The kids took a step back. She kept walking until she reached the top of the steps. Each child looked on with wide eyes. Slowly, she dropped one foot down. They all put one foot back. She lowered again and they stepped back again.

"What? I'm not scary," she said, reaching her hand out to try and make contact. Her apprehension had been replaced with determination. These little kids would like her even if it killed her. She would never be okay with people fearing her. Vampires? Yes. Five-year-old conduits? No.

Kira sat down on the last step, waiting for one of them to approach her. The more time passed, the bigger the crowd became. Parents and older siblings had made their way over. She looked into their eyes and saw caution there as well.

"What to do, what to do..." Kira mumbled to herself. She thought back to the only memory she had of this life, the memory of her last moments with her parents. Before the attack, they had been playing with their powers. Kira had loved it. The colors and the warmth of the fire were exciting. And she realized that was it.

Kira reached her hand out before her with her palm facing up. Slowly, she let a tiny flame rise over her fingers. The moment the fire started, she knew she had their attention. Each child looked on in fascination. Their eyes were wide, and their bodies leaned toward her instinctively.

The flame was small enough that it demanded none of Kira's attention, so she searched the group until her eyes landed on a little girl that reminded her of Chloe, her sister. Not in looks of course, but in stature. Something about her, maybe the fact that she stood a few inches closer than the others or the adventurous glint in her eye, made Kira think of Chloe and her carefree nature. Her sister was down for anything. No jungle gym was too high, and no adult was too scary. Perhaps not even a mixed breed would frighten this little girl.

Before she could change her mind, Kira shot a little stream of light at the girl. The child smiled and, right as the flame was close enough to light up her features, clapped her hands together, squashing it. Then she giggled. *Success*, Kira thought.

"It feels funny." The girl laughed once more and moved closer to Kira. "Again! Again!"

Kira listened, grinning. She arched the next flame over, so it rained down on the girl like an exploding firework. More giggles followed and the girl came closer still.

"What's your name?" Kira asked.

"Kayla," she said, retreating into a slightly shy place now that she had to speak directly to Kira.

"Does it start with a *K* like my name?" Kayla nodded and let the sun rise on her own palm. Wanting to leave talking behind, Kayla released her powers. Kira caught the girl's stream in her palm. It felt pure and refreshing, like a cool drink on a hot day or a first kiss. There was something innocent about the light. Kira had only ever felt Luke's power, which was strong and comforting. Apparently, power had personality too.

"What does my fire feel like?" Kira asked.

Kayla shook her head. Kira wanted to ask again, but suddenly another flame shot at her face. It hinted of mischief and Kira scanned the faces before her. A little boy smirked from the other side of the circle, happy to catch her off guard. Kira playfully shot back, until a little sizzle hit her butt cheek and a squeal filled the air. She spun, letting a few flames rain down on the kids who had snuck up on her.

Before long, Kira was just shooting sparks into the air every which way. The little kids moved in closer to barrage her with fire, and all she heard were crackling flames and high-pitched giggles. She surrendered and fell to the ground, letting them climb all over her and tug at her hair. The little girls kept pulling on her ringlets, just to watch them bounce back into place.

"Enough," she finally heard a man's deep chuckle. "It's time to go home."

A different fire, one drenched in authority, rained down on the group. Immediately, all the children stood and walked to the side. Kira saw one man with his hand outstretched and knew it had been his power. Kayla ran over and hugged him around the knee. He picked her up and swung her onto his shoulders before turning to walk away.

Kira hadn't noticed the darkening sky until that moment. She was having too much fun. Before coming, freely using her power frightened Kira. But now, she had seen a glimpse of the life she had missed and was excited to maybe learn a thing or two from the inhabitants of this special town.

"Kira!" she heard Luke call from a distance. Kira stood and dusted herself off before turning to the sound.

Luke was walking briskly across the open field, waving at her. She looked over his left shoulder to the group of four people he had just left. A tall man with his same crooked nose smiled at Kira. He had the same build as Luke, slightly gangly but still strong and sturdy. His arm was wrapped around a woman's waist. She was much smaller and slightly rounder with full cheeks. Her smile was also warm.

Running behind Luke was a little boy. He was a mini-version of Luke, except for the wide-rimmed glasses that threatened to slip right off of his nose. His face was covered in freckles. He called after Luke to wait up. Luke rolled his eyes at Kira and stopped walking. Kira guessed that Luke's brother was eight, maybe nine, years old.

Not wanting to put it off any longer, Kira finally looked further to the side. Waiting with hips cocked to the side, arms crossed, and a special glare meant just for Kira, was Luke's sister. She was tall for a girl, all legs and super skinny like a model. Kira knew she was a year or two older than Luke, but she seemed more mature and far more adult than Luke. Maybe it was just the irritated look in her eyes, but Kira was wary. She'd figured Luke's sister would be the most difficult to meet, but she now realized she may have underestimated the situation.

"Kira, come on." Luke waved her over.

"Yeah, Kira. Come on," his little brother yelled, copying Luke's gesture.

Kira laughed and shook her head slightly. *Ready or not,* she thought and approached Luke.

Chapter Four

"Kira, meet my brother—" Luke started but got cut off.

"Hi, I'm Tyler Jacob, TJ for short. You can call me TJ, all my friends do. And you're Kira. I told everyone at school that you were staying in my house. Boy, are they jealous. And—"

Luke covered his brother's mouth to make him stop talking, but Kira heard him mumble through Luke's fingers. She smiled and reached out her hand. "Nice to meet you, TJ." He shook her hand up and down and up and down, until Kira looked at Luke with questioning eyes, and he pulled his brother away.

"TJ, go get Mom and Dad."

"But, Luke..." he whined.

"Go." Luke laughed.

"Fine, but when I get back, I want to show Kira what I can do. It's going to be so cool to have you around. My sister is so boring. She's always with her boyfriend or doing her hair or some stupid girl thing. But, you're going to be so much fun." And with that, he turned and ran over to his parents, leaving Kira slightly shell shocked.

"What did I tell you? He's your number one fan." Luke chuckled and ran a hand through his sun-kissed hair. "Well, come on, it's time to meet the rest of my family." He threw an arm over her shoulder and pulled her along.

"Are they all as energetic as TJ?" Kira questioned.

"Nope, he's one-of-a-kind."

"He's so much younger than you and your sister..." Kira let the thought linger, not wanting to pry.

"Yeah, well, my parents had a little too much fun on their anniversary one year. It's too gross for me to think about." Luke shivered with the idea of his parents...like that, and Kira definitely understood. For the longest time, she had thought her family had grown the same way, that Chloe had been a little surprise. Revulsion didn't come close to describing how she had felt when she discovered her parents were still...sexually active.

But, Kira shook her head, that was the absolute last thing she wanted to be thinking about when she met Luke's parents for the first time. She could already feel the blush rising on her cheeks.

"So, what have you told them about me?" Kira asked while they continued to walk across the field.

"A little about your powers, a bit about how we

became friends, and a very vague idea about what happened last December with Diana. I never mentioned anything about Tristan or you saving my life. Too complicated, you know?"

"Yeah." Kira shrugged. She did know. What would all of these people say if they found out she was dating a vampire? *A kind, caring, chivalrous vampire with a little bit of badass in him*, Kira thought with a smile. Considering the entire crowd had been shocked beyond belief when she talked back to the council, the idea of her dating one of the undead could easily be enough to give someone a heart attack.

"Well, here we are," Luke mumbled as they stopped a few feet from his parents and waited for them to close the gap. "Mom, Dad, this is Kira. Kira, my parents."

"So nice to meet you, Mr. and Mrs. Bowrey," Kira said and extended her hand, trying to be as kind and polite as possible. "Thank you so much for letting me stay with you for the next few weeks."

"Of course, Kira. We're delighted to meet you too," his dad said and shook Kira's hand. Up close he really did look just like Luke, with freckles spanning his face and the same friendly eyes. "And, please, call me Evan."

"And call me Sue," Luke's mother said and extended her hand. Kira couldn't see her resemblance to Luke quite as well, except for the wide happy smile that was similar to the one Luke almost always wore. "We're so happy to have you with us. Luke's barely been able to talk about anything else for the past few months. He—"

"Okay, Mom," Luke quickly interjected, and Kira thought she saw a blush rise on his cheeks. She almost laughed in surprise. Luke was her uber-confident and carefree best friend—he did not blush. "Come on, I'll introduce you to my sister." Kira followed his gaze to the now smiling girl behind his parents.

"Hi, Kira, so wonderful to meet you. Luke's been so excited for you to visit Sonnyville. I think I speak for everyone when I say welcome, and we hope you enjoy it here." The blonde girl came over and actually hugged Kira, pulling her out from under Luke's arm. Her smile seemed friendly, and her face appeared to be open. Kira breathed a sigh of relief. "Silly me, I'm Vanessa."

"Hi, so great to meet you. Luke's told me a little bit about you, mostly about the disco ball he stole from your room."

"Wow, he mentioned that?" Vanessa turned to Luke with surprise written all over her features. "Why don't you and TJ grab the picnic basket, so Kira and I can have a little girl time while we fold the blanket."

Luke grinned at his sister, and Kira read the love in his eyes. "Sure thing," he said and picked his brother up around the waist, tossing him over his shoulder before clutching the picnic basket with his other hand. Kira watched the two of them walk away with his parents. Maybe

Sonnyville wouldn't be so bad after all, she hoped. But when she turned around, the mirage was ruined.

"Okay, let's talk girl to girl." The crossed arms, cocked hip, and evil glare were back. Kira sighed quietly. *Here we go*, she thought.

"Sure," she said, waiting for the onslaught.

"My brother is totally gaga over you, okay? I see it. My parents see it. Heck, the whole town probably sees it. But I see something else too. You're toying with him, and I won't allow that. Got it?"

"Look, I don't want to fight with you. I know it would kill Luke if he thought we didn't get along, but I honestly don't know what you're talking about. He's my best friend. I would never want to hurt him."

"Oh, really?" Vanessa challenged.

"Yes, really," Kira responded, trying to reign in her frustration.

"Then what was that?" she asked, waving her hand toward the council's platform.

"What?" Kira looked over at the scene, wondering if it held some clue to this girl's anger.

"Luke saved my life," Vanessa mimicked Kira, using a high-pitched voice that Kira knew sounded nothing like her own. "He's the only one I trusted. I would be dead if it weren't for him...blah, blah, blah."

"That was the truth," Kira said, taken aback. How had defending Luke to the council made his sister so annoyed? She thought she would be happy.

"Oh my god, you really are blind. Didn't you see his face? He was practically glowing while you spoke."

"What?"

"Look, I really do want us to get along, but you've got to back off. Luke told us all that you have a boyfriend, and as long as that's the case, just leave him be." Vanessa shook her head and bent down to start folding the picnic blanket on the ground.

"I won't stop being his friend," Kira retorted.

"You will when you finally realize that it's breaking his heart," Vanessa said softly and finished her fold. She held the bundle in her arms and started walking toward the rest of her family. Kira watched her go.

The nerve, she thought, wanting to scream. *She doesn't know anything about our friendship.* Sure, Luke's feelings had seemed to veer from friendship in the past few months, but it wasn't that extreme. *He knows that I'm with Tristan.* Kira chewed her lip. *He knows that I'm in love with someone else.*

"Kira!" Luke yelled and waved her over. She saw his family waiting for her on the lawn outside of a modest two-story house, so she hurried to catch up.

"Luke," his mother said when Kira finally reached the house, "why don't you take Kira upstairs and help her get settled."

Luke nodded and motioned to Kira to follow. "Come on," he said, and Kira noticed that their luggage had miraculously appeared by the front door of the house. She had totally forgotten about her small suitcase. Luke grabbed both bags before she had a chance to help him. She was too distracted by her surroundings.

The house was so typically suburban that Kira almost wanted to laugh when she walked inside. Before arriving, she had thought Sonnyville would be so foreign, but so far the town looked like something out of a fifties television show. The family room had a cushiony sofa and a few chairs, all centered around the coffee table and a widescreen television. A few video games leaked out from the entertainment center, and books lined the shelves. To the other side there was a dining table, and Kira spotted the kitchen through an open door. More than anything, Kira noticed the personal touches. The family photos hanging on the walls and lining the shelves immediately caught her attention.

The wooden staircase directly in front of her was a gallery of sorts, and as she followed Luke up the steps, she gazed at the little flashes of the Bowrey family life. An embarrassing family Christmas card photo, complete with terrible sweaters, was the first to catch her eye. Then Luke and Vanessa as children playing in the backyard. The streaks of fire dancing between them looked more like Photoshop than real life. Another showed a more grown up Luke holding his baby brother who seemed barely a year old.

"I love that photograph," Mrs. Bowrey said from

behind Kira. She turned, not realizing that Luke's mom had started climbing the steps too.

"They look so much alike," Kira said. Even as a baby, TJ giggled with energy.

"My two boys." She smiled, creating two dimples in her slightly rounded cheeks.

"Not photos already, Mom," Luke said, bouncing down the steps to grab Kira's arm. "Don't believe anything she says," he whispered and started pulling her up with him.

"I heard that, Luke," his mother said in amusement. Luke rolled his eyes and Kira smiled. It was clear to her why Luke was so caring and open. He had grown up surrounded by love.

"Here we are," he said and pushed open the blue door at the end of the hallway. Kira walked inside and knew in an instant that it was his room. Superhero posters graced all the walls, and she saw a serious collection of comic books on the shelves. A wooden desk topped with notepads and a pile of old books sat in one corner. On the opposite wall, Kira's suitcase rested on a twin-sized bed covered in a blue comforter.

"Wow, Luke," she said while fingering one of the comic books, "you were such a loser in high school."

He laughed. "I had a bit of a superhero complex."

"Had?" Kira mocked and walked over to her suitcase to start unpacking. As she started to unzip the duffel bag, a wave of nerves hit her. She blinked in shock and rested her hands on top of the suitcase to take a breath. *What the heck?* She thought. Butterflies fluttered around, not in her stomach but in her head. *Strange.* She shrugged and turned to Luke to tell him.

He leaned against the wall, in a seemingly relaxed pose, but his eyes were intense as they watched her. The anxiety grew until it was all she could think about. Kira couldn't look away from him. Something strange was happening, but she had no idea what it was. The nerves quieted, replaced with resolve. But Kira's head spun as her own uncertainty pushed the other emotions back to the corner of her mind. Her heart felt only confusion, but her brain was racked with an overwhelming mix of different feelings.

Luke started to step forward, but they both jumped when they heard someone call his name.

"Luke!" Kira heard again and recognized TJ. Like a vacuum, the emotions were sucked from her head, leaving her alone with her confusion. She saw Luke's shoulders slump slightly as he yelled back to his brother.

"I'll give you some time to unpack," he said and walked out of the room. Kira closed the door behind him and leaned against the wood. Something odd was going on. That wasn't the first time she had been overcome by a strange flux of emotions, ones that felt foreign and not her own.

"I'm losing my mind," Kira mumbled and shook her

head, "literally." She walked over to the window and twisted the blinds open to let the dying light of the setting sun into the room. Feeling curious, she fingered some of the items on Luke's desk. A photo of his family, one of him surrounded by three other blond boys and one of him and a blonde girl were displayed in a three-fold frame. She picked it up, wondering what life he had had before she interrupted it. He was eighteen when he volunteered for the job. He moved to South Carolina to watch her family and prepare for her return. He waited there for a year before Kira finally arrived. He had left his family, friends, and maybe even a girlfriend behind. And Kira had never really appreciated that until now.

She put the picture down and leafed through the old books on his desk. Study material, she assumed. Kira opened one to read the table of contents and saw labels for conduit history, battles, and famous leaders. She would definitely look through it when she wasn't training.

The sound of a phone ringing made Kira turn—she recognized her cell. She ran to the bed and sifted through her purse to find the source of the muffled noise.

"Hello?" she questioned, seeing an unfamiliar number.

"Hey," the deep rumble of Tristan's voice sounded. Kira smiled involuntarily and sat down on the bed, curling up for a long conversation. It had seemed like far longer than one day since she had seen him.

"Where are you?" she asked and let her head fall back against the pillow. There were glow-in-the-dark stars stuck to the ceiling.

"Still in South Carolina," he sighed through the receiver. "Do you remember when I told you about Aldrich, my maker?"

"Yes," Kira responded, remembering that day by the Ashley River. It was the only time she could remember him mentioning the man and the painful memories he triggered.

"I think Diana is maybe trying to mess with me and not you. I followed her back to the mansion where we all lived almost a hundred years ago—she, Aldrich, and I. She knows exactly how painful it was for me to return to that place. The only reason she would go there is to screw with my head."

"I'm sorry," Kira said, wishing she could reach through the phone and comfort him. Just talking, Kira could hear the obvious strain to his voice. "Did you at least find anyone there?"

"No, Diana was gone by the time I arrived. But she's heading north. I'll find her eventually," he said, changing his tone to one of resolve and determination.

"Enough about that," Kira said, not wanting to harp on his journey farther and farther away from her. "I wanted to thank you for telling my parents that I'd gone. How'd they take it? My mom seemed upset on the phone."

"Please," Tristan scoffed, and Kira could almost

envision his grin as if he were lying next to her on the bed. "Your mom loves me. All I had to do was flash a smile and give her a hug. She invited me over for dinner later this week."

Kira smirked at the inside joke. "Too bad you don't eat food." Her parents always invited him to dinner, but he always managed to find some excuse. "And my dad?" she asked.

"I think he still doesn't like me." Tristan laughed.

"Yeah, well..." Kira trailed off. Tristan had told her the story many times. Months ago, after Kira had saved Luke but almost killed herself, Tristan was the one who rushed her to the hospital. He made sure the doctors called her family, but he never left her side. As Tristan described it, he had been caught off guard when her father was the first to arrive at the hospital after coming straight from work. Tristan had been leaning over her bed, giving her a quick kiss on the cheek, when the doors burst open. He had jumped up and reached out to say hello when her father promptly tried to punch him in the face. When he stepped out of reach, it finally dawned on him that he had forgotten to change into the scrubs the doctors had offered. Tristan was standing in her hospital room shirtless and covered in blood. Needless to say, their relationship had been strained ever since.

"I remembered to change this time." Tristan chuckled. Kira could only imagine what her father would do if Tristan had shown up in the bloody, ripped-up shirt she had last seen him in on that back road in Charleston. "So, did you see it?" he asked, and Kira could sense the excitement in his voice.

"What?" she asked, getting a little giddy herself.

"Have you opened your suitcase?"

Oh crap, Kira thought to herself. She had entirely forgotten that Tristan had packed everything for her. She almost didn't want to know which clothes he had thrown in. She just hoped he remembered the basics.

Kira sat up and unzipped the rest of her suitcase while Tristan urged her on. She peeked inside and resting on top of her clothes was the picture he had been drawing of the two of them. She reached inside and pulled it out.

"You finished it!" Kira was thrilled. She set the photo out on the nightstand and leaned it against a lamp. In the picture, he was smiling and crystal eyes stared not out of the page but across it at her.

"Not that. Keep looking," Tristan said, and Kira closed her eyes for a second to envision his face. When he was excited, his eyes widened and his smile stretched out to show all of his teeth. Usually, Tristan was more reserved and secretive, showing only a side smile with one upturned lip. But the more he opened up, the easier it was to make him happy. Kira could tell when he smiled like that it meant he had forgotten about what he was for just a moment. When he forgot to keep his teeth hidden, she considered it a personal victory, and she pictured him that way now.

"Did you find it?"

"Not yet," Kira said, enjoying his impatience. She shifted her arms until she felt something hard near the bottom of the bag. Pulling it out, she realized it was a frame. Tristan always gave her slips of paper, never finding his artwork worth the grandeur of a frame. She flipped it over and immediately felt a knot tighten her throat.

"You didn't," she said in shock.

"I did," he happily replied. "Consider it an early birthday present, since I won't be able to see you three weeks from now on the actual day."

Kira bit her lip to keep from smiling so widely that her cheeks hurt. She tried to blink away the slight pools of water welling in her eyes. Framed, in her hands, was a blown up version of the photo in her locket. Tristan had a skill for re-creating people's faces in his artwork, and she stared at the drawings, amazed because it looked exactly like the photograph. She was a baby with unruly curls in the middle of a fit of giggles while she stared at her mother. Her father, freckle faced and openly displaying his love, looked out toward her. And finally, Kira's mother, with the secret smile she had witnessed on her grandmother's face just that afternoon, watched on. In the bigger size, and especially with the muted color tones Tristan had added, Kira almost sensed that her parents were really gazing out of the picture. It almost seemed like they were watching over her.

Engraved at the bottom of the frame, Kira saw the words "Love Will Prevail" in cursive. She hugged the whole thing to her chest with her free hand. That phrase, which was engraved on the wedding ring hanging around her neck, had once belonged to her parents. Kira liked to think it belonged to her now.

"I met my grandparents today," she said softly, after realizing she hadn't said anything for a few minutes.

Kira heard him release a slow breath. He did that when he was thinking and trying to understand her feelings. "Are you all right? How'd it happen?"

Kira told him about the council and about her grandfather. She described the argument they had gotten into, the test she was issued, and finally playing with the children. She didn't want to mention Luke to him. The two of them always seemed to butt heads, and there was no reason for Tristan to worry about Luke trying something because Kira would never let it happen.

"I think it actually went well," Tristan said.

"What?" Kira laughed into the receiver. How could that meeting possibly be described as a good one?

"Look at it this way, the two of you fought, right?" Kira nodded. Somehow, Tristan sensed it and kept talking. "Well, you only really fight with the people you love. If he didn't care at all, he wouldn't have been emotional. The fight shows he was a little nervous about seeing you and that he lost control."

"I guess," Kira said dubiously.

"Come on, think of all the people you've fought with."

Kira took a moment—her mom, her dad, Tristan at times, and definitely Luke. "I see your point. I just...I want them to like me. I don't want to be the thing that got their daughter killed."

"Kira," Tristan sighed and spoke in a soft voice. "I promise you that they don't think that."

"You didn't see the look in his eyes or the way he said he didn't want to regret the decision." It was like he had the weight of the entire world on his shoulders, Kira thought, remembering the dark clouds she had seen in the old man's eyes.

"I didn't have to. You can weasel your way into anyone's heart, trust me. Besides, it sounds like your grandma is rooting for you."

Kira thought back to the tiny smile that had played on her grandmother's lips. "Yeah, you're right," she said in a slightly stronger voice.

"I know," Tristan said, playfully smug. "Haven't you realized by now that I'm always right?"

"How could I forget?" Kira mocked.

"Don't feel too badly," he continued, joking. "You're still young and naive. In twenty years, you might be able to start proving me wrong."

"That long, huh?" Kira rolled her eyes, wishing he

were lying beside her so she could punch his arm lightly.

"Eh, fifteen if you're lucky." He chuckled. She loved hearing the deep rumble of his laughter.

"Let's play a game," Kira said and rolled over in the bed, using her foot to push the duffle bag out of her way.

"Which one?" Tristan asked. They were used to this routine by now. When Kira had been in the hospital, there were very few activities she could actually do. They had become experts at turning daytime soap operas into mad-libbing games. They had spent hours playing board games. Tristan always beat her at Pictionary, but Kira thought she had the one-up in Charades. Of course, no one knew they were this cheesy and lame, Kira laughed silently to herself.

When she had finally left the hospital and started going to school again, they eased back into normal life. They went to the beach or did a little hiking or went to parties with her friends. But sometimes Kira liked slipping back into their secret double life, especially with one particular game they had invented.

"Hum-azing?" Kira asked. Yes...they made up the name together.

"Sure, you first." Tristan sighed happily, and Kira envisioned him lying down and settling in for the competition. She thought of a song, something current that he would never guess. Kira started humming Ke$ha.

"Oh, come on. That's not fair. I'm singing a song from the fifties when it's my turn," Tristan mumbled. Kira kept humming the beat. "Okay, that crazy girl. I heard this when you forced me to watch MTV." Kira smiled but kept going. "Um...Lady Gaga?"

"Nope," Kira said and waited for him to guess again.

They continued for a while, going back and forth with Kira using current songs and Tristan drudging up older ones she could almost never guess.

Eventually Luke called her down for dinner, and she regretfully said goodbye to Tristan, hoping they would be able to talk again soon. Now that she was here, she liked Sonnyville and wanted to stay as long as she could. She wanted to make conduit friends and learn about these people. She needed to stay to learn more about herself and her powers—how to control them and keep herself from going over the edge. Mostly, she needed to find out what had been in those missing pages. She wanted to know the secrets the old scholars had thought were too dangerous to share.

But as soon as Tristan found Diana, she would find a way to sneak out. Getting her mother back was Kira's top priority and nobody, not even the council, was going to stop her.

Chapter Five

"Really, Luke? Do we have to practice here?" Kira asked, surveying the town square and taking note of the council's platform. She had only just escaped being the center of attention yesterday afternoon. A repeat performance was not high on her to-do list. "Can't we just use your backyard?"

"I don't want it to seem like you're hiding. Besides," he continued, "conduits are going to stare at you no matter what. You might as well give them something to gawk at."

"And me practicing is something to gawk at?" Kira asked.

"Oh yes," Luke said and stretched his arms over his head.

Kira plopped down beside him on the grass to stretch out her hamstrings and continue stalling. She rolled up the sleeves of her T-shirt, slightly annoyed with Tristan. The one downside to having him pack for her was the noticeable lack of her semi-revealing clothing, something she was sure he did on purpose. All of her practice tank tops had been left at home. Sure, they were skin tight, but now all she had were bulky unisex tees that she could hardly move around in.

And they were hot, especially in the scorching heat resting over Sonnyville. The sun usually felt comforting, but in this town the heat seemed stronger than normal. She would have to ask Luke about that at some point.

"Let's go," he said and eased into a standing position. Kira reached her arm out for help, feeling too lazy to do it on her own. He grasped her palm and pulled her up, promptly ending the contact at that.

"What are we starting with?" Kira stepped back, putting enough space between them to make the practice difficult, but not above her level.

"Target practice," Luke voiced. He reached his hand out to the side, and Kira shot a small ball of light at his palm, more so a sudden burst of energy than her really strong powers.

When it touched Luke's hand, he moved to a new location. Kira fired again, trying to control herself and release the fire in small increments. They had done this drill many times before, but Kira still found it annoyingly difficult to focus her energy on the little target Luke's palm created. Even more difficult was reining in the river of fire that roared inside of her, the one that surged forward and tried to force its way out.

After a while, Luke motioned to stop and Kira noticed the fine layer of sweat on his brow. She reached her hand to her own face and felt liquid drops. *Odd*, Kira thought. She usually didn't sweat during their practices.

"Let's practice your off-switch," Luke yelled across the field. As they practiced, he continued to step back to make the target increasingly smaller and harder for her to focus on. But this next drill wasn't about control, not quite.

"Go!" Luke shouted and Kira let herself release. With her hands out, the flames burst forth and even slightly stung her palms with their intensity. Letting it drain always felt like a delicious release. But before Kira let herself have the satisfaction of letting everything go and giving into the power, she thought *off*.

Sometimes that was all it took and her fire would instantly cut off. This time, Kira felt the internal struggle and she willed her finger closed, shutting the light inside her hand and giving it nowhere to go.

The moment when Kira found herself on the verge of losing herself in her own flames was the moment she knew to cut it off. Luke and she had once tried to see how long she would last. Kira drained herself and tried to release it all, but she had gone into a semi-conscious state where she lost not only her control, but also her mind. Luke had needed to forcibly hit her over the head and knock her unconscious to get her to stop. They stopped trying to test her power after that.

Most conduits reached a point when they felt hollow inside, as if there was almost no fire left to fly, and that was their stopping point. For Kira, it was more of a breaking point, a moment when letting it all go could mean losing herself in the process.

Kira lowered her arms and looked at her teacher, wondering if he wanted to try it again. She could usually stop herself faster than she just had. Instead, he waved her toward him and tossed a water bottle in her direction when she got closer.

"What did I tell you?" Luke shrugged, a happy smile on his face. Kira followed his eyes and looked around to see a ring of conduits encasing the park. None of them ventured closer, but people stopped where they were and stared over at her and Luke. A woman with a stroller and a man walking his dog had forgotten their errands to focus on Kira. A few children who had gathered to play also stood at a slight distance.

"Why won't they come any closer?" she questioned and then gulped down her ice-cold water.

"I don't think they're afraid, per se. I think they're all just waiting for someone else to make the first move. And, you are sort of scary when you go all zombie-conduit like that."

Kira shoved him with her free hand.

"So, what's next, teacher?"

"Let's do some mental exercises for a while," Luke replied and tossed his water back on the ground. "Come on, let's practice on the platform so we have even ground."

Kira groaned inwardly. Mental exercises were her least favorite. Sure, calling her fire was tiring and exerted a lot of energy, but those drills were easy for the most part. She had almost no mental control, which was of course why Luke always made her practice this. And she had no desire to be even more visible to the town by doing this on a raised wooden structure.

Lining up next to each other, Luke and Kira stood with their feet together and arms by their sides. Then, on Luke's count, they moved into yoga-like poses, concentrating on their breathing and trying to find a Zen-like place of peace. Luke always seemed revived by these exercises, while Kira tried her best to keep her eyes closed in faux-concentration. It reminded her of when she used to pretend to be sick so she could stay home from school, a sort of "fake it till you make it" mentality.

"Mind if I step in?"

Kira eyes jutted open to look for the source of the deep voice—her grandfather. Stumbling out of her contorted pose, Kira moved to shake his hand or say hello, but Luke beat her to the punch.

"Of course, Councilman Peters," he said while stepping smoothly aside.

Now that the councilman had come forward, Kira couldn't help but notice the other conduits had also moved in closer, slowly creating a very defined circle around the podium. *This is not good*, she thought, as she gazed at the crowd, *I have no idea what I'm getting myself into*. In a moment of clarity, Kira realized this had probably been Luke's plan all along...the jerk. She had absolutely no desire to be the center of attention.

"Miss Dawson," her grandfather spoke, pulling her out of her reverie. "Shall we?"

"Uh, of course." Kira fumbled for words. Turning to walk a few paces away from the older man, she saw Luke position himself on the corner of the wooden platform, giving her plenty of space to get in the zone. She turned in time to see her grandfather drop his cane and slide it a few feet away from him. *Is this even a fair fight?* She questioned and studied the old man who was now slightly hunched over.

"On my go," he said in his deep, rumbling voice. "One...Two...Three..."

Kira waited for the *go*, knowing she would let him take the first punch, if you will. He was such a man of honor in this town; she didn't want to beat him. She would rather look mal-trained than embarrass the grandfather she was hoping could love her.

"Go!" he finally said, and Kira waited for the hit. In an instant, a ball of power slammed into her stomach. She had no time to dodge it, try to absorb it into her body, or hit it with her own shot. Instead, Kira was thrown back on her butt. She landed hard against the wooden floor of the platform with the wind completely knocked out of her.

"Whoa," she said in a daze while sitting up slowly. Her grandfather's power felt like steel and it oozed with authority. With a smile Kira thought, *I guess the old man still has it in him.*

She caught the smirk on his face before he replaced it with a focused frown. "Is that all you've got?" he challenged and an excited gleam rose in his eyes. He seemed younger with every passing second.

Shaking her head to clear her thoughts, Kira jumped up at the ready. "Let's try that again."

This time, when he uttered the word *go*, Kira was ready. She shot fire out of her left hand, hitting the ball of flames he flung at her. The two fiery globes slammed into each other and winked out of existence in midair. An instant later, another burst of her grandfather's power was flying toward her and she barely had time to meet it with her own flame. And another after that, and another, until Kira was sweating with exertion and panting from exhaustion.

Her grandfather was fast, and she was barely keeping up with him. Twice already she had had to skip throwing her power and instead absorbed his into her body. It was easier than meeting his power in midair, but it took more time. Soon enough, her grandfather was bulldozing her with his flames.

At the exact moment Kira knew that her strength had started to wane and had lost track of her grandfather's movements, Luke shouted to her.

"Left!" he screamed, and Kira shot left, deflecting a ball of flames she had not even noticed.

"Above you!" Luke shouted again, and Kira could not help but direct her next throw up into the sky, hitting another of her grandfather's globes.

"Left, Kira. Come on!"

"Right!"

"Low! Move faster."

"Center!"

Luke continued to yell out commands, and Kira couldn't stop herself from following them. She wanted to do this on her own. She wanted to lose to her grandfather on her own or win on her own, without Luke telling her what to do. But when someone was telling her the right moves, someone who had been instructing her for months, she couldn't help but obey—at least that's what Kira told herself, because he was the only thing keeping her alive in this fight.

"Your face! He's shooting for your face," Luke blurted out again and Kira deflected the shot. His screams were actually distracting her. Instead of watching her opponent to judge his moves on her own, she was listening and waiting for Luke's voice. Didn't he know it wasn't helping her? Wasn't her grandfather annoyed?

"Above!" Luke screamed, and Kira jumped out of the way, letting the flames crash into the wooden floor and disappear without leaving a scorch mark.

Kira sensed that Luke was about to shout again, but instead she turned to him and yelled, "Shut up, Luke! You're not helping me, okay? You are completely distracting me. I can't concentrate on anything except for your voice!" Taking a second to breathe, Kira looked into Luke's shocked face. Complete surprise and confusion covered his features. "I'm sorry for yelling," Kira apologized, "but I want to do this on my own. So can you please stop telling me what to do?"

"Kira, what in the world are you talking about?" he asked, concerned.

"What do you mean what am I talking about?" Kira said, annoyed.

"I haven't said a word since you started fighting."

"Luke, please. You've been screaming at me for the past ten minutes," Kira said, looking around for her grandfather to back her up. He was on his way over to the two of them.

"Kira, why would I do that? I swear, I haven't said anything." Luke stood his ground, and Kira was the one who was beginning to feel confused.

"But, I heard you," she said unsteadily.

"What's the matter?" Councilman Peters asked as he approached. Kira noticed that he too had a fine layer of sweat on his brow. It made her feel a little better, knowing that he was tired too.

"Um, nothing. I thought I heard Luke say something, but evidently he didn't," Kira said, not wanting to fight in front of her grandfather. If Luke wanted to deny helping her, he could go right ahead. But she knew what she had heard, and she knew Luke had to be lying.

"Good, then let's get back to work. Luke, I want you to fight Kira so I can observe both of your movements." And with that, he walked over toward his chair on the council and sat down to watch. Luke shrugged and moved to the other side of the platform while Kira tried to push her thoughts to the back of her mind.

"Ready?" Luke called. Kira nodded and waited for him to make a move.

After a few seconds of waiting for his move, Kira sensed that it would be a center shot. Some instinct in the back of her mind told her it was where he would go. So, almost at the same time as he released, Kira did too. The flames met exactly halfway between the two of them before vanishing.

Right, Kira thought and fired again. *Now above*, she heard the whisper in her brain, telling her it was the right move. She felt empowered, but exasperation was there too, gnawing at her.

The more they fought, the more in sync Kira and Luke's movements became, as though they were tethered together. They fired at almost exactly the same time, meeting evenly with neither gaining any upper hand.

Frustration was pushing even further into her thoughts, but Kira had no idea why. She had no reason to be annoyed—this was the best she had ever done against Luke. It was like she knew his movements before he did. If anything, Luke should be frustrated. He was throwing everything he had at her and nothing was making it past her defenses. If Kira were Luke, she would be confused, maybe slightly proud, but also ticked off that this was happening in front of a council member.

Kira glanced at Luke's face. Sheer determination was visible in his narrowly opened eyes, but the furrow of his eyebrows did read of slight anger. He was annoyed and frustrated. But why was she feeling that way too?

Kira traced the emotion back, searching for its source, but it seemed like some sort of cloud in her brain, something not connected to her body…almost like it belonged to someone else. And what if it did? Kira looked back at Luke, letting her instincts fight while her mind wandered. Could she possibly…was it possible? Was she actually reading his mind? Or were his thoughts somehow invading her head and forcing their way inside?

Utterly distracted, Kira forgot to fight back, and one of Luke's flames hit her smack in the middle of the face. Whiplash ensued as she stumbled backward, thrown completely off balance as the fire forced its way inside of her skin. Normally, she enjoyed taking in Luke's power. It was friendly and refreshing, but she had been completely unprepared for the blow. And, as it were, she was standing so close to the edge of the platform, that the stumble sent her flying over the side. With a thud, she landed on her back on a patch of not-so-soft grass.

Luke's face appeared above her as he leaned over the edge.

"You okay?" he asked with lips full of barely contained laughter.

"Yeah, yeah." Kira sighed and stood up, rubbing her bum free of grass. Of course, she had to careen over the edge of the platform with a massive crowd watching. She hadn't noticed until that moment that half of the town had arrived in the square to watch her practice. She looked around at smiling faces and muffled laughter. *Great*, she thought, and placed her hands on the platform to push herself back up.

"Up until a minute ago, you were performing admirably," her grandfather spoke when she was standing again. "I look forward to the trial tomorrow."

With a nod, he turned around and walked away. The clicking of his cane against the wood reminded Kira that he was an old man, but definitely one with spunk. She hoped he would someday let her into his heart, or at least over for dinner. Looking through old photographs of her mother would be more precious to her than he even understood.

"Ready to head home?" Luke asked. His voice called her realization back into prime focus.

"Luke!" she shouted practically into his ear.

Startled, he jerked backward. "Jeez, you need to learn some volume control. What's up?"

"Luke! I think something really crazy is going on, but you need to hear me out first, okay?"

He nodded and walked over to their bags. "Is this a 'let's go talk in private' conversation or an 'I'm so excited I need to spill my guts right now' sort of thing?"

"The latter, so just sit down," Kira said and placed a hand on his shoulder to force him into a seated position. She remained standing but took the water he offered. The thud of her sneakers against the wood as she paced was helping her think. *How to phrase this?* she wondered. Not one for finesse, Kira figured the blurting it all out approach would be simplest.

"So...I think I can read your mind."

"Ha! Very funny. Can we go home now? I'm beat." Luke started to stand.

"No, I'm serious. I think I've been hearing your thoughts inside my head."

"Kira, come on. That's ridiculous!" Luke laughed, but Kira thought he looked slightly worried behind his calm exterior. Something about the smile in his eyes wasn't quite like it normally was. The laugh lines weren't deep enough.

"No more ridiculous than being a human flame thrower." She shrugged and watched as he sat fully down, settling in to hear what she had to say. He shrugged back, signaling to Kira that he was prepared to listen, even if she sounded like a mental person. "I'm not sure when it started, but there have been times when I've felt overcome by foreign emotions, ones that suddenly seem to appear out of nowhere and take over my thoughts. Until five minutes ago, I never realized that it only happened when I was around you."

Kira thought back to the truth in those words. Yesterday in Luke's room something had happened, the day before during the fight, and when he had walked into her room before the party. *Even earlier*, Kira thought, *when I first woke from my coma, something was different, but I just didn't realize it.* When he came to visit, the few times Tristan wasn't there, Kira sensed his emotions. She knew exactly when he was upset or angry or hurting. Before, she'd thought it was just because they were such amazing friends, but it must have been this, some crazy psychic connection.

"Luke, you can speak to my brain—this is so bizarre," she said, still slightly in shock. After plopping down next to him, Kira finally met his eyes and waited for him to speak. Even though they were best friends, she would never want him to be able to know her thoughts, something so private and so intimate. Kira was perfectly happy being on the receiving end rather than having all her secrets spilled.

"Okay," Luke said slowly, twisting around so their bodies faced each other, knee-to-knee in an Indian style position. "Let's test it. I'll think of a number and you concentrate on trying to figure out what it is."

"I don't think it works like that," Kira said skeptically. Something so superficial wouldn't work.

"Just try it, okay?" Kira nodded and started to concentrate.

Focusing on Luke's forehead, she tried to see inside of it. All she ended up doing was noticing that his hair had gotten even blonder since they had come to Sonnyville and his tan was darker too. *Concentrate*, she told herself and switched her tactic. She looked into his eyes instead. *Number, what number are you thinking?* Kira questioned over and over again.

After a few minutes, both of them gave up at the same time, breaking their contact almost perfectly in sync.

"Nothing?"

"Nothing!" Kira sighed and blew a stray curl away from her forehead in exasperation.

"I was thinking of the number three, by the way. In case that helps." Luke shrugged.

"It's not exactly mind reading if you give me the answer," Kira joked and started thinking of another approach. "I think we need to try something with more meaning. I seem to only pick things up when there are strong emotional investments involved. Can you think of something you really want or a moment when you were really happy? Maybe I'll get something from that."

"Not completely sure that is something I want to test," Luke said and leaned back on his hands.

"Come on, Luke. We need to know if I'm having a moment of temporary insanity or if I can actually read your thoughts. Wouldn't you rather know?"

His brows came together as he squinted his eyes and worry lines appeared across his forehead. He closed his lids and brought his fingers to the spot on his nose right in between them, clearly in deep and difficult thought.

"Okay," he finally said, opening his eyes and looking at her again. "Okay, let's try it out. I'll think of something from when I was a kid and you concentrate on me. We'll see what happens."

After a deep breath, Luke's face turned very focused and Kira in turn concentrated on him, on looking behind his features and into his thoughts. She met his eyes again. After all, they were the gateway to the soul, right? That was how the saying went, and what better way to read Luke's mind than by peering into his heart?

In the back of her mind, a switch flicked on. Slowly, laughter tickled her senses, giving her goose bumps. It was pure joy. Kira wished she knew what past memory he was thinking of, what could have made him this happy. But she tried to stay focused and kept contact with his eyes.

The more the happiness spread, the more Kira could

tell it reflected in her own features. A smile gradually spread across her face and, though she didn't see it, her eyes began to sparkle, like twinkling stars almost too bright to look at. But Luke never shifted his gaze. His thoughts, however, were a different animal.

Kira sensed it, connected as she was to his mind in that moment. Pure joy was still there, but it was now rimmed with slight agony and something different, something Kira couldn't place. Not nerves, but some sort of excitement that still contained joy, just not one so pure and innocent. This emotion was strung through with complications. Still though, it lifted her up and made her feel light, like a floating bundle of happiness.

Kira began to feel almost drunk on the emotion. She was getting lost in Luke's mind. The distinction between what feelings were hers and which emotions belonged to him was slowly escaping her. Was that her fear or his? Her hesitation or his excitement? Slowly, like a whisper almost blown away in the wind, two words streaked across her mind.

Kiss me.

Her words or his?

Kira's eyes focused again on Luke as he sat in front of her. His pupils expanded. They were deeper, more thoughtful than she had ever seen them. He was leaning in now, his eyelids slowly shutting, cutting her off from his soul and trying to let her in a different way. Kira couldn't move, couldn't separate her thoughts enough to know what she wanted to do. Those two heartfelt words were still drifting in her head. He was coming closer. Her life was in slow motion. He was only a few centimeters away now. Her brain wasn't working. Did she want this? Did he want her to want this? Were his thoughts keeping her from pulling away or were her own?

Trumpets.

Trumpets? Kira thought, her mind completely freed now. Trumpets were playing.

Her eyes shot widely open and she jerked to the side, fleeing from Luke's encroaching lips and jumping for his phone. Trumpets were his ring tone. She forgot that he had changed it.

She dug through his bag, pulled out the vibrating phone and said, "Uh, do you want to answer this?" in a really lame attempt to change the subject.

Luke still leaned forward, completely immobile from the change of events. It took him a moment to even register what she had said.

"Sure, sure." He reached his hand out and sat back down. Kira wasn't sure where to look.

"Hello?" she heard Luke ask. "Tristan?"

Her eyes focused on the phone.

Chapter Six

"Tristan?" she mouthed at Luke, asking if she had heard correctly. He nodded and waved her away so he could concentrate on the phone conversation. Kira tried to pull at his thoughts, but they were suddenly ironclad and barred shut.

"He said he's called you like six times," Luke whispered while his hand covered the receiver. Kira dove for her phone—it was on silent. *Dang*, she thought when she saw half a dozen missed calls from an unknown number. *What happened to his cell phone?*

"Okay. Uh-huh. On their way here. Today. I'll notify the council. Yup. Okay, here's Kira." Luke passed her the phone. She raised her eyebrows, questioning the conversation.

"Good news or bad news first?" Tristan asked after they said hello.

"Um, bad." Kira sighed. *It's always better to have something good to look forward to than something bad to be afraid to hear*, she supposed. Although Kira didn't think she would ever understand why bad news always seemed to be lurking behind every good moment in her life.

"Vampires are gathering in Orlando. I'm not sure why, but it can't be good and it can't be coincidence that this is happening a few days after you arrived."

Kira fell back against the wooden platform. Some news was just better lying down.

"Do you think they're going to attack Sonnyville?"

Luke laughed behind her. "No, that would be idiotic. The town has defenses like you've never seen," he said, loudly enough that Tristan heard on the other end of the line.

"Agreed. I think they want to draw you out into the open."

"Simple then, I don't leave and they go away."

"Maybe, but I know you, and you don't let other people fight your battles for you. What would you do if they started killing people to force you to meet them?" Tristan said, already anticipating her answer.

"Yeah, I would destroy them, vigilante-style." Luke smiled in appreciation while Tristan sighed like he was hoping she would have said something else. "So, what was the good news? I'm sure Luke won't let me do anything without talking to the council first..." She looked over at

Luke, who nodded, and Kira rolled her eyes. He had completely lost his sense of adventure since they moved to Sonnyville. He was the rule abiding, town golden boy again.

"Well, if all the vampires are going to Florida..." Tristan said, letting the idea linger.

Kira jumped up in realization.

"You're coming to visit!" she practically shrieked. He was grinning on the other end of the phone, she just knew he was. "When will you get here?"

"Tomorrow afternoon, so I'll be eagerly waiting by the phone for your call. This is a new cell phone, by the way."

Luke reached out to grab the phone from her hands. She slapped him away. "Kira, we have to go get the council. This is serious. It's not some lover's rendezvous."

He's mean when he's jealous, Kira thought bitterly. But she understood his feelings, more now than ever before. Nothing would ever be the same between them, would it, now that she knew exactly how he felt?

"I'll see you soon." Tristan sighed through the phone, pulling Kira from thoughts about Luke. "I love you."

"Love you too," Kira responded happily. Tristan was coming, and right now that was all that mattered.

Kira couldn't help the silly smile that spread across her face. She missed him. She wanted Tristan around so all of this confusion with Luke would be over. She needed the distraction from Luke's thoughts.

Luke stretched out his hand, and Kira dropped his cell phone. He stood up, grabbed his bag, and walked off the platform. Kira had no other choice but to follow him or continue to sit there going crazy with curiosity. She ran after him.

"Where are we going?"

"I need to alert the council. And, the only way to do that is to talk with the head council member."

"Let me guess, Councilman Peters?"

"Bingo," he said and continued walking. Kira let herself drop slightly behind. She had wanted to wait for her grandparents to officially invite her to their home before barging in. As per usual, things were not working out as planned.

Kira followed Luke around the bend. They continued walking along the sidewalk until they reached a small, almost cottage-like home at the next corner. There were overflowing flower boxes and gray-blue shutters on all of the windows. The front door was painted to match, and the sidewalk was almost invisible due to the garden. Flowers, mostly bold reds and vivacious oranges, leaned over the worn brick, and drooping bushes covered the rest.

Taking a deep breath, Kira stepped past Luke. She wanted to be the one to knock on the door and say hello. Letting Luke do the work would feel like hiding.

With slight hesitation, Kira banged her knuckles against the door. One. Two. Three. Instantly, she heard feet shuffle on the other side. A fleeting sense of nerves hit her stomach when she saw the knob turn, but when the smiling face of her grandmother greeted her, Kira just felt relief.

"Kira! What a surprise. Please, come in."

She had a sweet voice, like a flute, both energetic and relaxing at the same time.

"Luke's here too," Kira said and pulled him into view. Her grandmother said hello and stepped aside to let both of them in.

The furniture seemed elderly somehow. The sofas were flowery with droopy cushions, clearly worse for their age. Surprisingly, there weren't many objects aside from furniture. A few books, a few photographs of her grandparents, and a few paintings on the walls—nothing very personal and nothing of her mother's.

Kira tried to hide her suddenly deflated mood. She had been hoping for a few answers and a few memories. Maybe a few pictures to stuff into her bag for later...

"Who's there, Lana?" Her grandfather walked, cane first, around the corner and then stopped in his tracks. Kira was still stuck on the name he had used—Lana. Her mother's name, and she guessed her grandmother's too. Instantly, a pang of sadness struck at not sharing the family name, but at least she had learned something about her history that she had not known before. It was something, even if a small something.

"Miss Dawson, Mr. Bowrey," he said, nodding. "What

brings you here?" He sat down on the sofa, pushing the flattened cushion deep into the springs. Luke stepped forward. It was his turn to do the talking.

"We got some news from a...trusted source that vampires are on their way to Orlando. They're congregating in a way we've never seen, and we think there is probably some plan to capture Kira."

The councilman held up his hand to signal Luke to stop talking. "How trusted?" he asked.

"Someone who has saved both of our lives more than once. Someone who cares a lot for Kira and would never let anyone hurt her." Kira nodded along, silently so thankful that Luke hadn't said Tristan's name. Or more importantly, let slip what he was. Being here made Kira acutely aware of one thing, no one in this town would have any tolerance for her relationship.

Luke continued describing what he and Tristan had spoken of, but there wasn't much to say. Vampires were on their way, the end of the world was imminent—*just another day in the life*, Kira ruefully mused.

"I will call an emergency council meeting to discuss this. Luke, take Kira home. Tomorrow morning at ten o'clock, we will announce our decision in the town square. Start spreading the word, please." He got up and walked away, just as quickly as he had appeared, leaving no time for Kira to bring up her mother or father. Lana, her grandmother, showed them out. Luke left first, but before

Kira could leave, a soft, wrinkled hand grabbed her forearm.

"Kira?" She turned around to look into the caring eyes that greeted her. "Please, give him some time. Just have patience."

"I will," Kira said softly. Her grandmother squeezed, putting an extra ounce of love into that touch and smiled that secretive smile Kira had seen before.

"You are just like my daughter—strong and willful. It scares him, because he cares so much. He always has."

Kira put her hand over her grandmother's and held it there for a moment. "I understand." She turned to leave, but stopped in the middle when she noticed the glistening in her grandmother's eyes. *This is killing her*, Kira thought, *maybe she needs me just as much as I need her.* They had no family, the Peters. They had had a daughter who died and a granddaughter who was taken from them. They had no one but each other. But now all three of them had the chance at family.

Reaching behind her neck, Kira unclasped the chain holding her father's wedding ring and the locket. Carefully, she pulled the locket free, then closed the fastener, and let the necklace drop under her shirt again.

"Until he's ready, why don't you take this?" Kira said, offering up the charm. Now that she had Tristan's drawing, she could bear to part with it for a little while. "I'll get it back from you someday soon. I'll stop by for dinner."

Her grandmother nodded and took the locket. Kira

walked away before the lump in her throat could grow any larger, but not before she saw how her grandmother's face glowed when she opened it.

Luke was waiting for her at the end of the path, forever patient. They started the journey back to his house.

"So..."

"Yeah..." Kira said, not liking the awkward silence starting to form. The air slowly closed in on her, stealing her breath and making it hard to think. The phrase "you could cut the tension with a knife" had never resonated so much. She couldn't help but ask, *is this me feeling so out of place or is it Luke?*

"So, that was weird before," he said softly.

"The fact that I can read your mind or the fact that we almost locked lips..."

Did I just say that? Kira asked herself silently. What in the world? That was the last thing she actually wanted to talk about. Kira couldn't meet his eyes.

He opened his mouth. No sound came out and Kira could almost see the gears turning in his head. Which approach would he take?

"Oh, was that you? You know, women are constantly throwing themselves at me. I can't keep it straight anymore."

Kira smiled and let out a little laugh. It was almost heartfelt. They wouldn't be bearing their souls tonight, thank god. But they would have to discuss it at some point. It was one of those inescapable things that only got more troublesome the longer one tried to ignore it. Instead of lingering on things Luke obviously didn't want to talk about, Kira slipped into her funny girl mode too.

"It must be tough to have everyone in this town love you. I mean, just today I saw dozens of beautiful blondes fighting over you. I, a lowly red head, clearly have no chance."

"A little hair dye and you'd fit right in with my adoring fans. Just a warning, I request that they follow me around holding 'I heart Luke Bowrey' signs at least once a week."

"Oh, shoot. I left mine at home."

"Unacceptable," he replied with a "tsk tsk".

"So, should we talk about this whole mind reading thing?" Kira asked after a moment.

"What, how you've gone all Professor X on me? No problem. I just need to buy a really sweet motorcycle helmet."

"Luke, I'm serious—"

"Me too. I can get flames down the side. Really badass." Kira shoved him. The move was becoming more and more common on her part, but it was the only way to get him to shut up sometimes.

"I just want to say, I'll never try to read what you're thinking. I would never actively invade your privacy like that."

"I know." Luke shrugged. "It's not your fault. You

saved my life and almost died in the process. We probably should have expected something like this to happen." Now it was Kira's turn to shrug. "Let's not tell anyone though, okay?"

"Agreed," Kira said as they turned down the pathway to Luke's house.

Would she tell Tristan? It would feel like lying to keep it a secret, but would any boy want to hear that his girlfriend had some psychic connection with her male best friend? Oh, the same one who happened to be crushing on her big time? Especially if that connection resulted in the two of them almost kissing?

Those questions plagued her for the rest of the night and through the following morning. Throw in obsessive thoughts about what Diana was planning and serious excitement at finally getting to see Tristan, and it was no wonder that the ten o'clock council meeting passed by in the blink of an eye.

All Kira remembered from the gathering was that they had decided to send out a scouting party to decide if the vampire situation was really a threat or if they had gotten faulty information. Luke was put in charge since he had received the information, and Kira had forced them to include her too, even though the whole town thought sending her would just make things more dangerous. Luke requested that his sister come, and since his sister just loved Kira so much, she requested the blonde girl from the photo in Luke's room come along too. The council approved the decision and here they were, getting ready to leave.

As she followed Luke, his sister, and his ex to the car, all Kira could think was this was probably going to be a pretty unforgettable car ride. Unfortunately, Kira feared, it would be burned in her mind for all the wrong reasons. But she wanted to start the drive in a positive mood. Especially since she had the feeling it would not stay that way for long.

"What, no car and driver this time? You guys are slacking," Kira joked when Luke walked to the driver's seat of the speedy sports car they would be using. Apparently conduits really liked traveling in style, because Kira knew this car was nice—black leather seats and a shiny black paint job. At least it had four doors, so they wouldn't be ridiculously squished inside.

"No. This car I like to drive," Luke said with eyes wide and mesmerized, like a little boy with a new toy. He ducked his head under the doorframe and slid behind the wheel. Kira started to walk to the passenger seat, but the back door flew open, stopping her.

"Come sit next to me," Vanessa chirped. Kira instantly knew the glee-filled voice was a complete sham, but the other blonde girl slipped by her and took the seat next to Luke.

"Sure." Kira sat down, ignoring the victorious smirk on Vanessa's face.

Luke revved the engine, letting it growl into the silent

morning air. Everyone else in town was already preparing for their return and thinking up plans for every possible worst-case scenario. But the four of them, for a short while, could try to have a little fun. At least, Kira knew Luke would definitely try to lighten the mood—something that was confirmed when he backed up and went from zero to sixty in the blink of an eye, shooting down the empty streets.

"Luke!" Kira said, grabbing onto the handhold. He just laughed and slowed down, but only a smidge. Last time they were in a car alone, Kira had been tethered to the bed of a pickup fighting a hoard of angry vampires. Somehow she felt less safe right now, especially with Vanessa's stare boring a hole into the side of her skull.

"So, Kira. Have you met Casey yet?" Kira shook her head.

"Hi," the girl said shyly from the front seat before turning around to wave. She had a sweet look. Her face was round and open and her hair was cut pixie short. She had on baby pink shorts that no evil immortal would find intimidating in the least. In fact, Kira felt almost like a biker chick compared to her, with her black leggings and cobalt blue blouse.

"Nice to meet you," Kira said. Quickly she checked her phone. No response from Tristan yet. She had texted him on the way to the car.

"You know," Vanessa said quietly, leaning in toward Kira as if to make small talk. "Luke and Casey were sort of a thing back in high school—"

"Vanessa, now is not really the time for that," Luke said shortly from the front seat.

"What?" she replied, wide-eyed and innocent.

"Actually," Kira interjected before Vanessa could open her mouth again, "I did know."

"What?" Luke and Casey both said from the front seat.

"Uh, yeah," Kira said, sinking into her seat and wishing for once that her somewhat big mouth would stay closed. "I wasn't snooping, exactly. But I saw a photo of the two of you on Luke's desk."

"You still have that photo...there?" Casey asked in a meek voice. Kira almost felt sorry for the girl. She knew Luke and the two of them never would have lasted. Luke's personality was too strong for her. He needed someone to keep him humble, not someone who would hang on his every word. At least, that was how Kira's mind was rationalizing the entire thing.

"Yeah, Luke. You still have that photo up?" Vanessa chimed in. Kira wanted to kick her.

"Actually," Luke said in a strained voice, giving his sister the evil eye through the rearview mirror, "I thought I put that away."

"Apparently not." She smirked back.

Kira realized what was going on. It was a show, probably for her benefit. Luke's sister must have put that photo back up in his room, anticipating that the four of them would be together at some point in Kira's few weeks with the conduits. *She's good*, Kira thought. It was a very well laid-out plan. Except that Kira could see Casey's reflection in the side mirror as they sped down the road, and she looked about to cry. She must have seen through Vanessa's idea too.

"What's your high school like?" Kira asked, hoping to change the subject.

"Same basic format," Luke answered for the group. "Hormonal teenagers, boring classes, and a mix of good and bad teachers. The only major difference is the classes we take. Instead of gym, we have training sessions. Instead of advanced math, we have conduit history lessons. In English, we study mythology rather than Shakespeare. We take religion classes, sort of like at a Catholic school. But conduits have their own interpretation of the Bible, and it varies from Protectors to Punishers. We study a lot of science, biology and chemistry to figure out how we operate and to try to understand how the vampiric virus works. You know, nothing crazy."

"Yeah," Kira said. Nothing crazy? That sounded like the strangest environment ever.

"You grow up a lot faster," Vanessa said, "knowing that you have a higher purpose and all. I mean, by the time I graduated, I knew how to, I don't know, treat my best friend with respect for example." She stared pointedly at Kira.

"No," Kira said under her breath, "I think you learned how to be a total bit—"

"Okay!" Luke interjected from the front seat. "Let's make peace, not war people."

Kira crossed her arms and looked out the window, letting an uncomfortable silence form in the car. The only sounds were the purring engine and the wind in the trees outside. There weren't even people or other cars to distract anyone.

"Where are we going?" Casey said. Her face was bright red from blushing.

At that exact moment, Kira's phone buzzed. She flipped it open and quickly read the text.

"It's Tristan. He said he would meet us on the road?" Kira said aloud, finally breaking her silence.

Luke just nodded.

"Who's Tristan?" Casey asked.

Kira and Luke answered at the exact same time.

"Our informant."

"My boyfriend."

Their eyes met in the rearview mirror, but Kira pulled hers away quickly.

"Wait, your boyfriend is involved in all of this? How? He's not a conduit, is he?" Vanessa questioned, sitting tall now that her curiosity was piqued.

"No." Kira laughed. *About as far from it as you can possibly get*, she thought, but instead replied, "He just knows a lot about this stuff."

"How?" Vanessa pressed the issue.

"Oh, you'll see," Luke said.

Kira couldn't tell if he was disgusted or laughing at the thought. But, she didn't mind. She did wonder why he wasn't telling the girls what Tristan was—why he wasn't preparing them. But, that was his call.

Kira looked out the window and tried to keep her legs from bouncing too much. She was excited, so much so that she couldn't contain it. The best she could do was look the other way at the trees flying by and hope she was covering her glee with an appearance of boredom.

Was it completely crazy to be so excited to see your boyfriend when it really had only been two and a half days? No, she decided. Not when the last time you had seen him, you had both been running for your lives.

"Hey, Kira?" She turned at Luke's voice. "When Tristan said he would meet us on the road, did he mean literally on the road?"

"I don't know," Kira said and followed Luke's pointed finger to a black blob in the distance. It definitely looked like someone standing on the side of the road. Kira dug her hands into the chair, hoping it was him.

Luke started to slow down and as they approached, Kira could clearly make out the swoopy black hair and pale skin she knew belonged to Tristan. His tall, muscular frame was hidden behind dark-washed jeans and a black T-shirt, but his eyes were on the car.

"Luke! Don't stop!" Vanessa jerked her brother's shoulder. "Do you know what that is?"

"Luke!" Casey yelled at the same time. She started rolling down her window, preparing to fire a shot. Luke stopped her when Kira didn't bother to interject. She was already unbuckling her seatbelt and grasping the handle. Pushing the door open, she ignored the shocked cries of the girls in the car and the darkening look on Luke's face.

Before Kira had time to fully stand up, Tristan's arms were around her. His hands pulled her firmly against his hard chest, and all she wanted to do was hold on tight and never let go.

Chapter Seven

Kira completely forgot about the three conduits in the car when Tristan cupped her face with his palms and kissed her. It was short, too short, but strong and full of passion, sending a lively bunch of butterflies right into the pit of her stomach and an electric jolt down her spine.

She wished she could say she had been the one to end it, for Luke's benefit or the sake of the two jaw-dropped conduit girls, but it was Tristan who cut the kiss short as per usual. He pulled off modern teenager very well, but he was still in a lot of ways a product of the nineteenth century. At school or at parties, all Kira got was a quick peck or maybe a kiss on the cheek paired with mild handholding. But the advantage of having a supernaturally speedy boyfriend was that he could sneak into her bedroom very, very quietly and very, very often.

"Hi," he said with a lopsided grin. Kira smiled back.

"Kira, what are you doing? Get away from him!" Vanessa's angry and fear-filled voice shouted from inside the car.

Tristan's face fell slightly. The movement was almost too subtle for Kira to notice, but she had expected it to happen. Who wouldn't be saddened by the fact that his girlfriend had not told anyone about them, or more specifically about him? *He probably thinks I'm ashamed*, Kira thought sadly. But it wasn't about what he was, it was just that no conduits would understand. She didn't want to go through everything all over again. It would be like reliving her first conversation about it with Luke, but tenfold with an entire community.

Before she could say anything, Tristan put his game face back on and adjusted Kira to the side so he could peer into the car.

"Judging by their utterly shocked faces, I'm guessing you failed to mention what I am?" he said quietly to Kira, letting sarcasm soak into the words.

"I told them we were meeting up with my boyfriend..." Kira smiled apologetically. "C'mon, I'll introduce you."

Grasping his hand, she turned around to face the car. Luke lazily relaxed in the front seat, Casey leaned as far away from the window as possible, and Vanessa stared at Kira in a deep rage.

"I know this is probably a bit of a shock, but Casey

and Vanessa, I would like you to meet my boyfriend Tristan. I swear he would never ever hurt either of you. You have absolutely no reason to be afraid."

"Hello," Tristan said and reached forward for a formal handshake, but both girls shirked away from his touch. Kira glared at Luke until he finally moved to speak.

"Kira's telling the truth," he said and got out of the car. He walked around to Tristan and shook his hand. "Hey, man. How've you been?"

"Good," Tristan responded a little stiffly. Nicety was not something Luke usually threw his way.

"Okay, now you, Vanessa," Luke said and reached into the car to pull on his sister's hand. She slid over to the window seat and slowly reached her hand out.

"Hello," she said. The words were so tense it sounded as though they had been forcibly pulled out of her body with a pair of pliers. Tristan quickly shook her hand up and down once before she jerked it out of his grasp and back into the car.

"And now, Casey," Luke turned toward her with an easy smile on his face. Kira wondered how hard it was for him to look so calm when he probably hated having Tristan there as much as those girls did, just maybe not for the same reasons.

"Hi," she said almost too quietly to hear. Tristan greeted her in return and motioned to shake her hand, but as soon as his fingertips touched hers, she pulled away.

"Well, now that we've dealt with this vampire problem, let's go deal with the second one," Luke said while hopping back into his car. Kira rolled her eyes and tugged Tristan into the car behind her with a sigh. She took the middle seat, loving that her right thigh was pressed up against Tristan, but not so much loving that her left one was smashed against Vanessa.

As Luke pulled away from the curb, a monotonous silence filled the car—no music, no other cars, and no trees rustling in the wind. All they heard were tires on asphalt and the rumbling engine.

But Kira didn't mind. Tristan's thumb gently rubbing the side of her hand provided more than enough distraction. With her head resting on his shoulder, Kira was completely at peace. At least she was until Vanessa spoke.

"Okay, sorry to disturb whatever weird pact the three of you have, but I just can't ignore it. He's a vampire. I'm sitting in the car watching a conduit cozy up to a vampire. It's unnatural. It's...it's...just gross, all right?"

"Oh, I'm sorry. Do you feel left out? I can hold your hand too," Tristan said, acting completely innocent with wide blue eyes. Kira elbowed him in the ribs, not like it did anything. Sweet Tristan was being replaced with defensive and slightly edgy Tristan.

But Vanessa was fully prepared for a verbal battle. "If you so much as try to hold my hand, prepare to fry... Or is that how you like it? Kinky."

Here we go, Kira thought. If Vanessa was anything like her brother, this could go on for a while. Settling in for a fight, Kira shifted her head from Tristan's shoulder to the seat behind her. She had already learned to stay out of the crossfire, and hey, fighting got people's feelings out. Better out than kept inside to fester, she always thought—well, mostly thought.

"You don't know anything about our relationship, so stay out of it," Tristan threw back.

"I know it's completely asinine and destined to fail. You know, that whole part where you guys are mortal enemies and all. Or, I don't know, the fact that you're immortal. Or maybe it's that whole blood drinking thing that freaks me out. Take your pick." Vanessa leaned back in her seat. *She might be even more vocally opinionated about this than Luke*, Kira thought with surprise. What she wasn't at all surprised with was the gleam in Luke's eyes. At least he was keeping a smirk off of his face.

"No one said being in love is easy." Tristan grinned at Kira. They had talked about all of those things for hours. The jabs were nothing new, and definitely nothing Luke hadn't tried to convince Kira of before.

Vanessa turned her attention from Tristan and aimed it at Kira instead. "This guy? Really? Over my brother? I just don't get it."

"Fortunately, you don't have to." Kira coated her words with sweetness.

"Actually, I kind of do. You see, I saw what happened in the town square yesterday. Ten more seconds and this would have been a completely different conversation."

Crap, Kira thought. Those words were as good as blackmail. "I don't know what you're talking about." Kira tried to play it cool, but she grabbed Tristan's hand again, squeezing it. His eyes were questioning and full of confusion. This wouldn't go away any time soon.

"I think you do," Vanessa threatened.

"Enough." Luke cut her off before she could continue. "We have more important things to talk about, like what we're going to do when we reach Orlando. We need to think of a plan."

Out of the corner of her eye, so Tristan wouldn't notice, Kira watched Luke. She didn't quite understand why he stopped his sister. Wasn't Tristan finding out about the almost-kiss exactly what Luke would want? A way to break them up? She couldn't decide if he was really just that focused on the mission or if other doubts made him stop Vanessa. For her part, Vanessa sat with arms crossed and a smug look on her face. Kira tried to ignore her.

"The plan," Tristan said, "is that Kira and I will scope out the head vampire's estate—it's right outside the city—and you three will do whatever conduits normally do to look into a vampire situation."

"Split up?" Luke asked Tristan. "I'm not sure about that."

"I agree with Tristan," Kira chimed in, "why not split up and cover more ground? We can all take care of ourselves."

Luke sighed. He had had enough fighting for one day. "Fine. Tristan, let me know where to drop you off when we get closer."

With that, Luke reached out to turn the radio on, and the silence in the car was drowned out with music, country of course. Tristan wrapped his arm around Kira's shoulder and she leaned against him, letting her head rest on his chest. Half of her listened to the twang-filled voices and the other half listened to the steady beat of his heart as it pumped foreign blood through his veins. After a while, Kira's eyelids began to shut and she let herself fall in and out of sleep for the next hour or so, until Tristan's body tensed with anticipation.

Sitting up was difficult in her relaxed state, but Kira peered with sleepy eyes out the window. She saw a few houses. Clearly, the group had finally reentered civilization.

"How much longer?" she asked, still feeling a little groggy.

"Maybe five minutes," Tristan said.

Kira nodded and stretched her hands high above her head, attempting to bring her body fully out of sleep mode. She looked around and saw Vanessa practically drooling and Casey with eyes closed in the front seat. Luke was still driving, but he glanced back when she woke up. He and

Tristan had been the only two people awake, Kira thought with sudden clarity. She didn't want to even think about what they may have talked about. She was stressed out enough as it was.

"Luke, you can pull up over by that bend on the right side of the road," Tristan said and slid his arm free of Kira's body. The car slowed down to a stop and Tristan quietly slid out.

"Kira?" Luke said before she could get out of the car. Kira turned back to her friend. "Be safe, okay?"

She nodded. "I'll call as soon as we find something out."

Tristan reached a hand out to help lift her from the car and she took it gladly. With a tug, he pulled her to her feet and they shut the door together. After a moment's hesitation, the black car slid off the curb and back onto the road, disappearing from sight.

Still holding her hand, Tristan led the two of them off the road and into the dense forest in front of them. *Why are we always in the woods?* Kira asked herself and wished she had worn boots instead of these sneakers, which already had a layer of mud on them.

"Where are we going? I thought we were going to some house?" Kira asked.

"We're stopping right here." Tristan halted in the middle of a slight clearing. Kira looked around but couldn't see any markers or anything really, except for trees.

"Here? Why?"

"Oh nothing, just this," Tristan said, and Kira caught the mischievous glint in his eye. With no warning, his hands were around her waist, pulling her close, and his lips were on hers.

Kira knew they should probably be concentrating on the mission, but she couldn't keep from tilting her head back to deepen the kiss. Bringing one hand around his neck while the other clutched at his arm, Kira let their bodies mold together. A perfect fit.

Dizzy with excitement, Kira let Tristan lead her back against a tree trunk. He put his arms on either side of her head, trapping her within his body, but Kira never felt anything but safe around him. Excited nerves danced around her stomach, sending shivers from her fingertips to her toes, and she started to smile against his lips. He felt it and widened his as well, as if the two of their mouths were strung together. Breathing heavily, Tristan pulled back. Their foreheads touched while the teasing distance of an inch separated their lips.

"I thought you deserved a proper hello," he said with a grin. Kira brushed her thumb over the dimple that appeared on his cheek.

"It's okay, I know that you find me completely irresistible," Kira joked.

"That I do," he said earnestly and searched her eyes. Kira wasn't sure what he was looking for, but a moment later he pulled back with a sigh and reached out his hand. "Come with me, we need to find the estate house." Kira latched onto his hand and let Tristan direct her through the forest.

He wasn't speaking. Kira knew by his slightly scrunched eyebrows that something was on his mind. He was acting distant. After that kiss, the last thing Kira wanted was distance, so why was he pulling away?

After a few minutes, he finally broke. "What was Vanessa talking about before?" Tristan asked, his voice soft and hesitant, almost as though he feared what the answer might be.

"Nothing, I promise," Kira replied, hoping it didn't sound like as much of a brush off to him as it did to her. *You have nothing to hide*, Kira reminded herself. Nothing happened. But somehow, it felt like she had cheated on him. Not physically, but for the first time, there was something she couldn't talk to him about.

"It doesn't sound like nothing. I want to believe you, but I know better. The strain in your muscles, the slightly higher octave of your voice, and the rapid jolt to your pulse—it all tells me you're hiding something."

Stupid hypersensitive vampire senses, Kira cursed silently.

Tugging against his hold, Kira forced Tristan to stop walking. Some things were more important than their mission. Kissing in the woods? Maybe not. Making sure the person she loved knew he could trust her? Definitely worth the time.

"Have I ever given you a reason not to trust me?" Kira asked, not liking the cloud of hurt that shaded his eyes.

"No."

"Then trust me when I tell you nothing happened, nothing that matters to me anyway. I promise I'll explain everything later, but right now we have bigger issues at hand."

"All right." He nodded, accepting that explanation for the time being. But lingering doubts were still etched into his features.

Sometimes, Kira found it too easy to forget that Tristan wasn't quite as strong as he pretended to be. Around other people, like with Vanessa in the car, he put on a tough act, one that was cocky and occasionally rude. But Kira had seen those walls come down. She had seen his insecurities, the self-loathing and the sweet nature that was too sentimental to show in a vampire's world. Even Tristan needed her reassurance sometimes, a promise that she wouldn't run away.

Kira cupped his cheek. "I love you," she said, placing extra emphasis on the "you" and urging him to understand she was in it for the long haul. He had never done anything to make her change her mind or doubt her decision to be with him. She wouldn't let anything, no mind reading and no best friend, change that.

He smiled, a wide teeth-revealing smile. "Let's go," he

said, walking forward and reaching an empty hand back behind him. Kira clasped it and moved with him toward the estate.

A few left turns and a ton of snapped twigs later, they stopped and looked through the leaves at a two-story house complete with oversized pillars and a wraparound porch that seemed right out of the Civil War era. Whitewashed with black shutters and a bright red door, the house seemed asleep. No movement stirred in the windows, most of which were opaque from curtains. No cars were parked in the driveway, no people could be heard moving in the gardens, and the place seemed completely deserted.

"Are you sure we're in the right spot?" Kira whispered. This seemed about as far from a head vampire's estate as you could get. Where was the staff? If vampires were congregating in Orlando, surely they would check with the city's leader first?

"Definitely the right place. I've been here before, just a few years ago, but things were far more active then."

He stretched an arm out in front of her to keep Kira from stepping any closer.

"Wait here. Something is wrong."

Tristan dashed through the open yard, a mere blur to Kira's human eyes. He reappeared against the outer wall of the house, crouching below a window. Slowly, he extended his body so his eyes were at the level of the window. With a leap, he latched his hands onto the second floor windowsill and pulled himself up to look through that glass as well. Kira didn't mind the view. Seeing her boyfriend as a human spider was a little strange to say the least, but the muscles bulging under his shirt were a lot more interesting than the creepy quiet of the grounds.

Dropping back down, Tristan disappeared around the backside of the home to continue the search. What was that saying, "sad to see him go but love to watch him leave"? Kira mused, letting her thoughts provide a distraction from the waiting.

Eventually, she would need to tell Tristan about the mind reading and the almost-kiss. The last thing she wanted to do was hurt him. But if Vanessa had seen, then Kira needed to make sure Tristan heard the full story from her and not a skewed version. Luke's thoughts had confused her and that was the only reason anything came close to happening. It had to be—

A hand grabbed Kira by the mouth, catching her scream and pulling her against a hard body. Another wrapped around her waist, holding her arms at her sides in an iron grip. A vampire. Kira knew it in an instant. That was the only thing that could attack her so silently and swiftly.

"Not a good place to get lost," the vampire whispered into her ear and then laughed in a shrill, hyena-like way. The cool touch of his breath and screech of his voice sent fearful shivers down her spine. Sharp teeth practically grazed her neck, just one small movement from piercing her skin. But before Kira let the fear take hold, she made fire explode from her hands and encircle the both of them. The arms released her and recoiled against her light, but she tried to hold on to the vampire's body to keep him from fleeing. He could have information. She used her Protector powers to trap him in place, surrounding him and holding him still without killing him.

"Tristan!" Kira screamed when she knew she was losing control. Boils sprouted all along the vampire's skin, turning once milky arms into pus-filled craters, and his brown hair started to singe. He would burn soon, but if she stopped, he would be gone before she could blink, just like when Diana had slipped her grasp so many months ago.

"I've got him," Tristan said from behind her, and Kira winked the fire out. Tristan caught the injured vampire before he had a chance to run and forced him to the ground.

"Where'd they all go?" Tristan asked. A wild cackle was all he got in response. The vampire wasn't paying any attention to his captor. Tristan may have had hold of his hands and a relentless grip on his throat, but the vampire's eyes stared only at Kira. The blue of his irises, almost neon in their intensity, bored into Kira.

"You're her," he said with wide eyes. He laughed loudly and carelessly, like a mental patient finally finding freedom. "You're her!"

"She's who?" Tristan said, trying to play dumb to get

more information. He clenched the vampire's throat until he gurgled with choking, but nothing made any difference. Not a punch to the gut or the slam of his face into the ground. The vampire went on shrieking, giving Kira goose bumps. Vampires didn't scare her anymore, but this thing was deranged. It had lost any last semblance of humanity long ago.

"They went to find her and here she is."

"They who? They went where?" Tristan continued questioning him, trying to make sense of his almost drunken ramblings.

"They left me behind. They said I couldn't come. And I found her!"

Kira looked away. She couldn't take the stare anymore. She had never seen eyes so empty of feeling. Even Diana's had held emotion—anger, hatred, and jealousy, but still emotion.

The vampire continued rambling about people leaving him behind. They had gone without him. They left. They disappeared. They'd be sorry.

Maybe they had gone to Orlando and left him behind, Kira thought, catching on to to what the vampire was getting at. Or maybe they...

Kira reached for her phone and called Luke immediately.

"Hello?" He picked up. By the honks in the background, Kira knew he was walking the city streets.

"Have you seen anything?" she asked with a sense of urgency. A thought was forming in the back of her mind—one she desperately hoped wasn't true.

"Nothing yet. It's weird. All the spots we usually search—the clubs, the blood banks, the abandoned buildings—all of them are empty."

Her heart sank. The wheels in her head were turning rapidly. Luke had said they would never even dream—that it wasn't possible.

"I found her. I found her!" The shrills continued to pierce her thoughts. Tristan looked at her in confusion. He couldn't comprehend what the lunatic was screaming about. But Kira knew. She understood.

"Luke, get back here immediately to pick us up."

"But, we haven't—"

"Just do it and fast. Tristan and I will be waiting."

Kira hung up and looked back into the wild eyes of the vampire in front of her. This beast was too crazy to let go, too dangerous to free.

"Tristan, on my count step out of the way. One, two...three!"

Tristan jumped to the side, and Kira encased the vampire in a blanket of her fire. Wave after wave rolled over his soon-to-be-corpse. The cysts that had started to recede in the past few minutes were bursting open like geysers. His skin cracked dry in between them. Deep ravines broke through the surface showing walls of cells and veins. But there was no blood. That had vaporized in the heat and boiled the vampire's body from the inside out.

Kira almost dropped her power. She had never seen what happened to her victims in such a slow motion way. The whole process was monstrous—both for the vampire and her. But Kira held on, thinking of the humans she might be saving, until finally, in a silent explosion, the entire vampire turned to ash.

"Kira, what is going on?" Tristan asked from a distance.

"The vampires," Kira said while turning and running over to grab his hand, "they're headed for Sonnyville."

Chapter Eight

The car ride back was tense. Tristan and Kira had waited for what seemed like hours for Luke to pick them up. When the jet-black car careened around the bend, they jumped in, and Kira blurted out her fear that the vampires were moving in on Sonnyville. Almost immediately, Luke pushed the pedal down to speed through the mostly deserted roads that led back home.

Luke tried to calm her. Vanessa and Casey did too. Sonnyville was prepared. The town had incredible defenses. All the inhabitants, even the children, knew how to fend for themselves. But then why was Luke driving so fast, and why was there a slight shake to his voice? No one, not even vampires, was stupid enough to attack an impenetrable town. They had to have something, some tool or idea that the conduits didn't know about.

Kira looked out the window, but all she saw was her

grandmother's soft and caring eyes, crinkled on the side from years of smiling. A blink and her grandfather appeared, hard as rock and stoic but still her family. Another blink and Kayla, the little girl who reminded her so much of her sister, was laughing and shooting sparks of fire with the other children.

They had to be okay.

Thoughts of vampires running through people's homes, stealing and killing children were hard to keep at bay. And these were Protectors; they couldn't kill the vampires with their powers. But maybe Kira was underestimating them. They had to have lethal defenses for this exact reason.

Without warning, Luke slammed on the brakes, which screeched in protest as the tires smoked against the pavement.

"Tristan, jump out now!" he screamed while the car swerved uncontrollably toward the front gate of Sonnyville. Knowing from the tone of Luke's voice not to question him, Tristan opened the door and leapt from the car in less than a second. Kira was about to yell at Luke for kicking him out when the car careened through the open gate.

An overwhelming sense of heat and calm passed through her body, making her nerves tingle in the same way as when she absorbed another conduit's power. She filled to the brim with sunlight, letting it warm her senses and heal any wounds she may have had. A brilliant smile lit up her features and she looked over at Vanessa to see the same reaction. Her hair stood on its tips, static from the sudden rush of energy.

As quick as it had come, the heat evaporated, and the car jolted to a halt, leaving Kira confused more than anything else.

"What was that?" she asked to no one in particular.

"That was what kills any vampires who try to enter Sonnyville. It wasn't on the last time you came through the front gate, but hopefully this means the town got wind of an attack," Luke told her. His hands gripped the wheel tightly, and Kira saw his eyes were wide and shell shocked, probably from the almost car crash.

"But, what is it?" Kira asked. It had felt like the sun but one hundred times closer and more wonderful.

"It's a UV wall," Casey said. Kira was happy to hear her speak up, even if it was only for business talk. "We've managed to trap sunlight and release it on command to create an invisible wall made of potent UV rays. It's one of the reasons our town is usually ten degrees warmer than everywhere else. But more importantly for us, any vampire who tries to walk through will get incinerated."

"Hence..." Luke shrugged in the general direction of where Tristan stood just beyond the open wrought iron doors. Kira raced out of the car and back to the gate. She reached out a hand, feeling for the heat. The instant her fingertips touched scorching air, she jumped forward, passing through the wall and again feeling the boost of energy fill her senses.

Tristan caught her when she landed and stumbled forward on the other side.

"As much as I love jumping from moving vehicles..." Tristan grinned, and Kira flashed back to the night on the pickup truck when he saved her by leaping off the truck and onto a vampire. "What just happened?"

"There's a wall made of UV radiation around the entire town."

"Ah, well that complicates things just a bit." Kira smiled at his smirk. "Any way I can jump over it with a running leap?"

Kira shook her head. "I don't think so."

"So you guys get to have all the fun battling it out inside, and I have to wait out here for you to come get me and tell me I can come inside. I feel like I'm in time out." Frustration clouded his features. Tristan wasn't used to being left out of her plans.

Kira sighed. "I'm sorry."

"It's okay," he said reaching for her cheek. "We've always known our relationship would be complicated. This is just one of those times. Besides," he said, and Kira finally saw a bright gleam enter his eye, "I might want to test this wall thing out. I'm sure there are still a ton of vampires in the woods I can fight and chuck against it."

"Is there absolutely no chance you'll just lay low and

stay out of sight until we can come get you?" Kira knew the answer as soon as the words left her mouth. If there was anything Tristan loved, it was making a little bit of trouble. Whether it was in the classroom last year, on the beach with their friends, or fighting a hoard of vampires, nothing quite got him excited like pissing other people off. Well, everyone besides Kira.

"Come on, would the man you love just chill on the sidelines?" Tristan grinned, circling her with his arms.

"No. Go on, have fun and I'll call you when everything is settled inside," Kira said and quickly kissed him. When they parted, he ran off with a mischievous grin, looking for some vampires to wreak havoc on.

Kira shook her head with a small smile, laughing silently to herself. How someone could be over a century old and still act like a little boy always amazed her. Letting her worries for his safety drop, she crossed through the threshold and sat back down in the car.

As soon as she shut the door, Luke took off toward the town square.

"What other defenses are there?" Kira asked while she looked out the window. "Is there anything else I need to be prepared for?"

"Unfortunately, no," Luke said. "That is our best defense. If that wall was turned on, then it means vampires are probably here and a few made it inside first. Everyone should be in the town square."

"Why would they all gather in one place?" Kira asked. In a terrible way it reminded her of a special she had seen on *Animal Planet*. Whenever dolphins tried to catch fish, they would surround a giant school and corral them into one center circle so they were easy pickings. She shuddered at the idea.

"We have drills," Vanessa chimed in, thankfully interrupting Kira's thoughts. "It's not like we've never planned for this sort of situation. Everyone gathers in the town square to form a protective circle around the children, and the parents take turns keeping vampires at bay with their powers."

But it couldn't last very long, Kira thought remembering her trainings with Luke. He was one of the best in the town, the youngest to ever get a solo mission, but still when they trained, he tired out before her. His power supply was nowhere near hers, and if he was one of the strongest, the Protectors couldn't last more than a few hours the way they were going. Vampires, however, had endless reserves.

"It's going to be fine," Luke said and grabbed Casey's hand in the front seat. Kira saw that the girl was silently crying through the rearview mirror. "There are ancient swords and things we're taught to use in case of emergency, so we can weaken a vampire with our powers and then behead them the old-fashioned way or at least drain them of blood so they can't move."

"Even though we're Protectors, there are sometimes no other options than to kill something," Vanessa added sadly. Despite her words in the car about Tristan and Kira, she believed what she had been taught. She believed vampires could be saved somehow, that there was something inside them worth saving.

Kira met Luke's eyes and wondered what he thought. After the past year, Kira knew without a doubt that he didn't believe vampires could be saved. Did he think being a Protector was a curse? To know this sort of evil exists and to only be able to temporarily protect humans from it and not to kill it. For the first time, Kira wondered if Luke ever looked at her powers with envy. Sure, every vampire along the Eastern Seaboard was out to get her, but she could fight them one by one. They feared her more than she feared them and that wasn't something a Protector could really say.

Before Kira could continue the thought, something banged into the side of the car, indenting the metal door and sending all four of them flying. Suspended in the air, Kira had the undeniable sense she was about to die. The seatbelt pulled taut across her shoulder as her butt lifted off the cushion and they flipped over. Her hair fell over her features, shrouding her in darkness. A scream caught in her throat. The scene was playing in slow motion. The sky window darkened as the image of clouds was replaced with that of grass, and Kira heard shrieks distantly in her ear.

Without registering her movement, Kira circled all

four of them in her powers. Her connection to Luke's body was instant, as if it were her own, but the other two girls took a moment longer to register.

Crunching metal thundered in her ears as they landed and continued flipping along the ground. Her neck whipped back and forth with the jerking movements, but her mind was somewhere else. Bones snapped and she rushed to fix them. Muscles tore, skin broke open from shards of glass, and blood flowed freely, but Kira used every ounce of energy she had to restore the lethal wounds. If it were her own body or someone else's, Kira didn't know. She acted on instinct alone.

Finally, the car came to a stand still, thankfully on its wheels. Kira opened her eyes to mangled steel, torn seats, and broken windows, but amazingly every conduit in the car was okay.

"What in the world?" Vanessa said as she arched her head up and twisted her neck around to find her muscles weren't even sore. But Kira peered past her at the charging vampire, the same one who had probably slammed into the car. Now energized, Kira easily sent a flame in its direction, turning the vampire to ash in a matter of seconds. When she was angry and warmed up, no vampire would stand a chance against her power.

"Get out of the car now!" Luke yelled and pulled himself through his window. Kira tested her door, which thankfully opened, and slid out. All four of them had run a

few yards away to regroup when the car burst into flames—
a fire none of them would have survived, not even with
Kira's help.

"How are we alive?" Casey asked into the wind. All
four of them stared at the burning car. It was only a matter
of time before more vampires would come, drawn in by the
smell of blood.

"We have to move," Kira said. They were on the
outskirts of the town, maybe a mile from the square.

Luke started walking with her, but Vanessa and Casey
stayed put.

"What aren't you telling us?" Vanessa asked, standing
her ground. Kira met Luke's eyes and even without being
able to read his mind, she saw the apprehension. As it was,
the emotion crept into her mind too. Fear for his sister's
safety and an overwhelming sense of guilt for keeping her in
the dark. She shook her head, forcing his thoughts out
before they confused her senses. Now was not the time to
be distracted, and they had the right to know why they were
still breathing.

"I can heal people," Kira said, and Luke grabbed her
wrist trying to make her stop talking. She pulled free. "In the
car, I healed you while we fell. But it's fine, we're all okay
and we have other things to worry about."

"You healed us?" Casey asked, looking at Kira in a
new way—almost in admiration.

"That's not possible," Vanessa said. "How could you

have healed all of us at the same time in a matter of seconds? No one has that sort of power."

"I do," Kira said and started to walk away, not liking the hint of fear that had crept into Luke's sister's eyes.

"Come on." Luke shrugged and caught up with Kira. "We need to stick together and we need to be careful."

They moved as one, sneaking through people's backyards and staying off the main road. They came across three more vampires but killed them easily with Vanessa, Luke, and Casey trapping each while Kira delivered a killing blow.

Twenty minutes later, they reached the town square. Hiding behind the hedges on the front lawn of a house right along the edge of the town's center, the four of them discussed a plan. Vanessa and Kira wanted to charge in to just take out any vampires in their sight, but Luke wanted to plan something more strategic. Without walking into the square and making themselves visible, they had no idea how many vampires were there and how the conduits were doing against them. They needed a vantage point.

"Into the house, let's go. We need to see how many there are," Luke said and nudged the girls toward the house. As expected in such a peaceful town, it was open and they slipped inside easily.

Kira followed Luke up the steps and to the attic while he explained to her that this was one of his best friend's homes. He had played there at least once a week while growing up and knew everything there was to know about it. The friend, who Kira had never heard him mention before, was on the West Coast with a group of other conduits in his grade, all of them working together to weed out a local vampire population.

When they reached the dusty attic, all four of them pushed their faces against a small circular window and looked over the hedges at the town square, which blazed with fire. Conduits stood in a circle that was four or five deep, taking turns throwing flames out toward the vampires. In the center, Kira could see the children. She envisioned tears drenching their faces and quickly looked away.

On the outskirts of the flames, Kira counted maybe twenty vampires circling the group. Through the light she saw dismembered bodies, reminding her of Jerome in the clearing so long ago when she had awoken from her daze and stumbled over his open chest, almost falling on the bloody heart that rested a few inches from his body. This time, heads spotted the ground.

Swords, Kira thought with slight amazement, *how medieval.*

But she saw something else that scared her more.

"Luke," she said while grabbing his shoulder and pointing toward the left side of the square. "Look!"

Somehow, they had captured a conduit. Three vampires knelt over one body, sucking the blood from someone's veins. From this distance, Kira couldn't tell who it was, but she knew exactly what it meant.

"Any moment they'll be immune," Kira said, flashing back to the image of her father as he died trying to free her mother. She knew exactly what happened when vampires became immune to a conduit's power. They would rip through the protective circle. They would go straight for the children in a mindless craze.

"We have to go, immediately," Vanessa said and jerked away from the window.

"No," Kira commanded and grabbed the girl's arm. "I have to go. You'll just get hurt. I'm the only thing they won't be immune to. Stay here until I've killed them and then join everyone else in the circle."

Luke understood and nodded, grabbing his sisters other arm to keep her in place. Without hesitation, Kira took off at a run, leaping down the steps two at a time and out the front door of the house, not caring who, or what, saw her.

"Stop!" she yelled when she reached the edge of the town square. Every single vampire, except for the three piled over the conduit, actually did pause to look at her. *Maybe not the best idea*, Kira thought and wanted to smack herself. Hungry eyes regarded her as she approached the feeding frenzy, but no vampires made a move to capture her yet. Maybe they had finally learned how powerful she was. Or maybe, she thought sickly, they knew they had all the time in the world to wait and watch what she did.

The conduit man on the ground barely struggled anymore. Limp limbs fell against the grass, and the sun-kissed skin turned gray like snowy ash. *Too late*, Kira thought wildly. Her emotions were starting to career out of control just like the car they had been in. And just like that car, Kira feared she was about to go down in flames.

Finally close enough, Kira let her power loose and plowed through the three vampires, who never once looked up at her approach. Now, through smoke and fire, they looked at Kira in shock as their skin burst into flames and they evaporated into ash.

Kira ran over to the conduit and knelt down beside him, searching his features for some familiarity. But Kira had no idea who it was. She leaned against his chest, listening for a heartbeat, but there was none. She reached into his body with her power, searching for wounds to heal, but unlike with Luke, there was nothing she could latch onto. He was gone and it was all because of her—all because she brought the vampires here.

Well, if they wanted her, all they had to do was catch her.

Kira stood and slowly let her eyelids rise to search around her. While she had been fighting, the vampires had surrounded her. Icy blue slits circled ebony pupils as the vampires stared with hunger in their eyes. Razor sharp fangs poked out of open mouths that grinned in anticipation of what they thought would be their next meal. Kira knew better. Silently, she dared them to approach.

One vampire stepped forward and Kira went straight for him, shooting her fire like a spear. It pierced his heart and the vampire fell to its knees before crumbling apart. Another charged and another fell. Kira was not messing around this time. In high school, she had let Diana go free. She felt sorry for hurting another person, but now Kira knew better. Tristan was different. He was an anomaly in his species—a vampire with a soul and a heart that was full of goodness. But Kira could read the bloodlust in these vampires' eyes and could hear the animalistic growls rumbling from their throats. Even if she wasn't thrilled with the idea, she didn't have time to hesitate.

Not waiting anymore, Kira flew little shots of fire at every vampire circling her. Each one took a step back as the flames hit their chests but remained standing. Annoyed expressions gathered on their features.

Come on, Kira thought, *come at me.*

For the first time, she found the fight thrilling. Blood pumped in her veins, probably making the vampires want her more. *Tristan must be rubbing off on me*, Kira thought with a laugh. She let the excitement build. Her power bubbled with it until Kira felt like she was a rubber band about to snap.

Then they came at her, fifteen vampires all at once, and Kira let go.

She circled her body in flames, making sure her neck was protected, and then shot the rest out. Finesse was not necessary, just raw power. She let herself drain, turning in circles, shooting instinctively in every direction. Luke would be angry at her for wasting so much energy, but Luke was beyond her thoughts now.

The more power Kira brought forth, the closer and closer she came to losing it. Her mind wasn't registering the town square or the conduits anymore. Even the vampires had been pushed from conscious thought. Her fight-or-flight instinct forced her arms to keep moving, arching in a circle, setting flames to anything that moved toward her.

Small black dots formed on her pupils, blinding her vision and expanding until she truly couldn't see anything. Kira had been to this place before—the place where she disappeared and everything became her power.

Had she been conscious, Kira would have realized that she had singed every vampire around her minutes ago. If any were still in the town, they would be running to face the UV wall rather than confront her.

If she had been conscious, she would have realized it was Luke who approached her and not an enemy.

"Luke, what are you doing?" Kira would have heard Vanessa shout. She would have seen the entire town watch her go up in flames with admiration and also hesitation clouding their features. They had never seen anyone with so much power and so little control.

As it were, Kira saw something approach through the haze of her delirium. Instantly, she focused everything she had on that spot, the only one moving around her. Still it came, so Kira focused more. *Why won't you die?* she thought. It had never taken this long to burn a vampire, not once she had harnessed her energy.

"Kira."

She heard the whisper along the back of her thoughts.

"Kira."

It was getting louder now. What was that?

"Kira!"

A scream now, ripping through her focus and her mind, shredding whatever ideas had been forming until all she heard was the screaming of her name over and over again. It sounded like Luke.

A sense of calmness blossomed in the back of her thoughts, pushing the anger and fury aside until there was almost no space for it. The spots blinding Kira began to recede. Her vision slowly returned in blobbed shapes.

Fire still roared from her hands, hands that seemed pressed up against something soft.

"Kira, come back. Control. Remember, you need to control it." Luke spoke into her thoughts. Kira pulled back trying to rein it in. Her palms screamed at her as she sucked the flames back in, making her blood boil in the effort.

Finally, Kira focused her thoughts. The first thing she saw were Luke's eyes, right in front of her face, pulling her back to reality. His thoughts in her mind and his eyes locked on hers were all that saved her from herself.

Stumbling back and fully awakened, Kira still felt confused. Luke reached his arms out to steady her. She looked around at the dusty wind around her. The vampires. The attack. The children.

Kira jerked around toward the center of the square. Everyone stared back at her, but she looked through the adults to see that even the kids were okay.

"Luke?" she asked, her voice raspy from exertion.

He nodded reassuringly, still holding her upright.

"I may have lost control." She smiled at him. Luke barked out a laugh and pulled her in for a big bear hug.

"Maybe just a little," he said into her hair.

"So, what now?" Kira pulled back and stepped out of his arms.

"Now, you sit down and rest, and let us do our job."

"Which is what?"

"Making sure all the vampires are gone," he said. Kira nodded with understanding. She shouldn't use her powers again for a while anyway, not when she was so close to the edge. Letting her feet drop out below her, Kira plopped down onto the ground.

Many of the conduits were still looking at her, throwing sidelong stares in her direction and waiting to see if she would explode again. After yesterday, Kira had thought she was finally starting to fit in. They had watched her battle her grandfather. She had gained his respect and theirs.

But she was still different, still an "other". And all she wanted was to find Tristan so that he could hold her close and tell her it would be all right. He understood feeling different, feeling like there was no place in the world where he fit in. Sometimes Kira thought the only place where she could feel perfectly at home and in control was in his arms. She wanted them wrapped around her right now.

But Tristan was still out past the wall. Locked out by the very thing that kept Kira alive—the sun.

Kira watched as Luke left with a bunch of other men. The further from the square they got, the more he blended into the crowd. Sonnyville was where he belonged. Kira thought that could be true for her eventually. She hoped she could find a place with her grandparents. But if there was ever a time to leave with Tristan, this was it. Staying in Sonnyville would be a danger to everyone, at least until every vampire understood that they couldn't mess around with her.

The only way Kira thought to do that was to help Tristan hunt Diana down. She would kill her and any other vampire that got in her way. It was the only way to show the world she meant business.

The only real question left in Kira's mind was, would she leave Luke behind or take him with them?

Chapter Nine

"Kira?"

She turned to the sound of his voice. In shock, Kira looked into the eyes of her grandfather. He reached out his hand and Kira took it as he pulled her to her feet.

"Hi," she said breathlessly, still exhausted from her fight.

"Would you follow me?" he asked. Kira nodded and walked next to him in silence as he led her back to his house.

Of course, Kira thought. The minute she decided to leave was the same minute her grandfather decided he finally wanted to talk to her.

He opened the door to his home and let Kira inside. Showing her to a seat in the dining room, he asked if she wanted tea and then disappeared into the kitchen. Kira waited on the hard wooden chair and looked around. Again, there were no personal photos really, just one of her grandparents at a much younger age playing in the waves at a beach somewhere. They were smiling and happy. For once, there was nothing mystical about anything. Just two people in love caught on camera.

"Here you go." Her grandfather eased into a chair and set a transparent brown liquid in front of her. Kira caught the smell. It hinted of chamomile, and she took a long soothing sip, letting the leaves do their work to calm her.

"So, Councilman, what can I help you with?" Kira asked, trying her hardest to stick to decorum.

"First..." He leaned forward and took hold of her hand. "You can call me Henry." Kira smiled back at him and let the name roll around in the back of her mind. It wasn't "grandpa" or "pop-pop" but it was a start. "Second, I want to talk about you. None of us knew you had such raw power. Luke mentioned something like it, but without seeing it for ourselves, no one on the council ever imagined. Taking on almost two-dozen vampires on your own is something to be proud of, but I sense that you are frightened too."

"A little," Kira responded, wondering how much she could open up. He was her grandfather, but he was also nearly a stranger. Although, it would be nice to talk to someone who wasn't Luke or Tristan, someone with more authority. Once, Kira had tried to talk to her mother about her powers. All she ended up getting was a strained conversation about nothing. And her father was still in the dark about her double life. Come to think of it, Kira realized, her relationship with her parents was almost back to normal, as long as she pretended that nothing had changed. It might be nice to have a family that she didn't have to hide her true self from.

Kira placed her attention back on Henry. "I used to be much more frightened. Now the only thing that really scares me is what happened today—when I lose control completely. It doesn't happen often, but when it does, I don't know if I'll make it back to myself."

"That's what I thought," he said and patted her wrist in a subconsciously affectionate gesture. "I don't know how to make you feel better. There hasn't been a mixed breed conduit in thousands of years, but I do have something that might help."

Reaching over to the chair next to him, he slipped a folder out from a bag Kira hadn't even noticed was there.

"I wasn't sure I would ever give these to you," he said while sliding the folder across the table. "I don't think anyone on the council knew what to make of you at first, least of all me. We have an entire world to protect, and to be honest, I'm still not sure where you fit into that plan."

Kira nodded. The words were hard to hear but she would rather have the truth. Taking the folder, she flipped it open.

"The missing pages," Kira said in surprise.

She recognized the chapter heading and writing instantly. They were from the book she had been reading so many months ago about the conduit history, the same one that had led her on a journey to Luke's home on the night before the eclipse. He had said all of those pages had been destroyed. "But how?"

"The council has always held onto this information in secret. But I have to warn you, after reading what is inside, you may not think I'm doing you a favor. Some of that will be hard for you to read and hear, but I think it's better you know what you are and what you may potentially cause, especially after what I saw today. People say that having too much power is a curse and that it brings the bearer to the brink of madness. I think some extra knowledge might help you control yourself."

"Thank you," Kira said and closed the folder with a gulp. She would save that for later.

Now, she had something else to fess up to. Her grandfather had presented her with the truth and it was her turn to do the same. He had a right to know. "Henry?" she said, noticing that he had been about to stand back up and show her out.

"Something else you want to discuss?" he asked and sat back down fully.

"My mother, Lana." His eyes darted up to hers instantly. "I think she might be alive, and I'm leaving tonight to go find her."

"Kira," he sighed, letting his forehead drop into his hands. "I used to think that all the time, but your mother is gone."

"A vampire told me she was still alive, held prisoner somewhere." He looked up now, eyes scrunched in confusion. "I have to try, and I don't want to lie to you and sneak out. I'm leaving and I want the council to know why. But I'll be back. Can't get rid of me that easily." She ended lightly, trying to ease the sense of dread emanating from Henry's face.

"A vampire told you?"

"It's a long story," Kira sighed, still not ready to talk to him about Tristan and what happened last year. "But I'll be traveling with a friend and I'll be perfectly safe."

"But—" he started and then stopped when he saw the tenacity written in her features. "Stubborn, just like your mother," he said quietly, almost like it slipped out without him noticing.

"Like my grandfather too, I think." Kira smirked. She squeezed his hand and then pulled her fingers free. She had a lot to do, and she sensed that he needed some time alone. Tonight was huge for their relationship, but they still had a long way to go, and it would happen one step at a time.

"Be careful," he said as she left. Kira looked back to see he hadn't moved from the table. He still sat sipping his tea and thinking silently to himself.

She clutched the folder tightly in her hands before

stepping out into the afternoon sun. The breeze had picked up a bit, but she enjoyed the cool touch. Kira imagined that all the conduits were still in the town square waiting for Luke and his search party to come back and tell them it was safe to go home. The UV wall, Kira knew, would be left on for a few days. Keeping the vampires out was the town's number one priority, so Kira knew she would never be able to sneak Tristan inside. The only way was to meet him past the wall. She sent him a text telling him to meet her by the gate in an hour and continued walking to Luke's home.

It was eerily silent when she stepped through the front door. Kira may have only been a resident for a handful of days, but the house, like Luke, seemed to always be alive and active. Whether it was TJ running around or Vanessa talking on the phone or Mrs. Bowrey cooking dinner, something was always going on. Now she walked up the creaking steps in silence, her feet like thunder on the floorboards.

When she got to Luke's room, Kira pulled her duffle from underneath the bed and started reloading her bag—the one she unfortunately had only unpacked the night before. *Typical*, Kira thought while stuffing her clothes back inside.

She didn't know how long she would be gone, so she gathered all of her things on the bed, placing them not so neatly in her bag. Tristan didn't know about her plan, but he had to see it coming. Kira had been anxious to find her mother ever since she had woken from the coma. A meeting with Diana was inevitable and there was no time like the present to go on a wild-goose chase. *But where do I find a vampire who is faster than the wind?* she wondered. Hopefully Tristan had some thoughts, because Kira, for one, was fresh out of ideas.

Once her clothes were packed, Kira turned to the two drawings by her nightstand—one of her with Tristan and one of her with her parents. She pushed the framed sketch deep into the middle of her duffle bag so it was surrounded by clothes and safe from breaking. Gently, she slid the one of her and Tristan into the folder her grandfather had given her. She wouldn't be losing either any time soon. But, Kira thought wistfully while reaching for the chain against her neck, part of her wished she hadn't given her grandmother the locket. She had the foreboding sense that she might need its small, yet calming influence in the future, but it was too late for that now.

All Kira had left to figure out was how she would get out of Sonnyville. She wasn't in love with the idea of theft, but stealing a car from someone was probably the only option. And hey, she had saved their butts this afternoon— a car wouldn't be a big deal, right?

Kira chewed on her lip, then slung her bag around her shoulder and left Luke's room. He hadn't come home and that made her decision easy. She would be leaving without him, which was probably for the best. Three's company didn't seem like such a great idea, especially when she would be smack dab in the middle of it all. She pushed any lingering doubts out of her mind when she reached the staircase and saw her exit so near at hand.

But halfway down the steps, the front door burst open.

"Yeah, that was so cool. I want to take fencing now! I want to chop a vampire's head off!" Kira heard TJ's excited voice and then saw the entire Bowrey family walk through the front door behind him.

She froze up, like a deer caught in headlights. Luke saw her as soon as he stepped through the door. His features lit up then fell into a mask of confusion. She dropped the duffle from her shoulder, letting it fall down the steps with a thud. He watched as it cascaded to the ground floor.

The rest of the family was oblivious to what had just passed between the two of them, but Kira could already feel Luke's anger in the back of her mind. She tried to push it out of her head, but it was like a festering wound that wouldn't go away.

"Kira! That was so cool the way you burned those vamps to a crisp! You were like, 'Die! Die! Die!'" TJ completed his thoughts with an all too real evil laugh, then ran over and pulled on her wrist so she would come downstairs. She tried to smile at him, but it was hard when someone else's thoughts were commandeering her brain.

"Kira." She turned to the sound of Luke's voice, not

sure if it was said aloud or in her head. "The porch?" He jerked his head to the side, and she grabbed her bag to follow him outside.

"Hey, Luke. What's up?" Kira said, trying to act casual now that they were alone outside. The warm air and stillness of the night only heightened her nerves. The porch light amplified the grooves etched in Luke's skin and his pupils seemed to glow in fury.

"Were you really going to leave without telling me?" he asked. The strain in his voice grated at Kira's heart.

So no small talk then, she thought with a grimace.

"You weren't home..."

Luke raised both eyebrows in astonishment. "Really? That's the story you're sticking with? At least be imaginative. Say a voice in your head told you that you had to go this instant or something."

"Well, technically you're the only voice in my head...so are you telling me to leave?" *Got him*, Kira thought happily when he cracked a smile. She almost never caught Luke in his own jokes.

"No, I'm just telling you that I'm coming."

"Do you really think that's a good idea? You, me, and Tristan—just the three of us—together on the hunt?" *Sounds like a complete disaster to me*, Kira ended her thought silently.

"What would the Flaming Tomato be without her trusty sidekick?" Luke asked and Kira laughed at the nickname he had given her a few days ago. She would definitely miss him if he didn't come.

"If you think you can handle it, then go get your stuff. I'll wait out here." He nodded in agreement and disappeared through the door.

Fifteen minutes later, Luke reappeared with a duffle in one hand and his entire family behind him. His mother looked notably depressed while TJ looked extremely jealous. His father's features were clouded with concern, and Vanessa just glared in Kira's general direction.

Luke shrugged, as if to say sorry, but Kira should have expected the prolonged goodbye. After another ten minutes of hugs and kisses, tears from his mom, and a final hushed speech about not messing with her brother from Vanessa, the two of them were off. And in a shiny new sports car no less.

Word got around quickly in this town, and Kira wasn't sure how, but almost every conduit family was outside of their house to wave goodbye to Kira and Luke as they drove away. She waved back. It wasn't goodbye forever, Kira reminded herself. As soon as things were figured out with her mother and Diana, she would be back. A little taste of Sonnyville wasn't enough. Just like Luke had predicted, the town and its inhabitants had gotten under her skin, and Kira knew she would be back for more.

When they reached the last house on the outskirts of the town, Luke sped up a bit and Kira sent another text to Tristan. He would be waiting for them by the gate. The minutes ticked by in silence, as both Kira and Luke were lost in their own thoughts, thankfully each in their own minds.

When they reached the front gate, Luke slowed to a stop just before the invisible wall. Tristan appeared almost instantly on the other side, materializing out of the trees. Yet again, his shirt was in shreds and his pale, almost marble skin was showing. The hard lines of muscle along his stomach were unmarred with cuts and Kira let out a sigh. She knew he could handle himself, but seeing Tristan whole and unhurt was still a relief.

She jumped out of the car.

"My, my—another shirt torn to pieces? What will the neighbors think?" Kira said while putting on fake airs and walking closer to him. She laughed when he looked down as if only realizing for the first time that his clothes were cut up. He recovered from his surprise quickly.

"The better to ravish you with," Tristan replied with a grin. "It's all part of the plan."

"Which plan is that?"

"The one to make you fall hopelessly in love with me, of course."

"Well, I'm sorry to break your heart but it's not working at all," Kira replied and passed through the threshold of the UV wall, letting the light warm her for a final time. Tristan waited for her right on the edge, as close as was safe for him. Kira put her hand on his chest and he breathed in as her hand singed his stomach. "See? I'm not attracted in the slightest."

Clearly not true, Kira thought. Her breath became slightly more labored when she took one final step closer to him. An icy blue flash passed through his irises.

"I guess I'll have to try harder," he said softly and took hold of her arms. Kira loved this part—the anticipation of waiting was almost as good as the kiss itself. The moment hung between them, excitement bouncing back and forth, building a sizzling electric current between their bodies.

Beep!

Kira jumped about ten feet in the air before realizing that it was just Luke honking from the car. Her pulse raced, but for a completely different reason, one that wasn't nearly as fun to think about.

"Luke," Tristan said tersely and waved in his general direction. Kira had a feeling he had been wishing he could have used a different gesture, one with four less fingers involved, but Luke just waved back cheerily from the front seat.

"Oh." Kira changed the subject, realizing that the playful moment between her and Tristan was over. "Luke wanted me to ask if it was safe here. Have the vampires all fled?"

He nodded and shouted for Luke to pull through the gate.

When the car shuddered to a halt, Luke shut it off and walked over to Kira and Tristan.

"Dude, your dry cleaning bills must be huge," he said to Tristan, taking note of the lack of clothing. "Luckily, I have a spare. Here you go," he said and tossed a blue cotton bundle in Tristan's direction.

"Thanks," Tristan said when he caught it, surprised at the gesture. After stripping off what was left of the black T-shirt he'd had on, Tristan pulled the new shirt over his head. It pulled tightly across his chest, which was slightly broader than Luke's and had more muscle tone. But that wasn't what made Kira bark out a laugh as soon as he put it on.

"What?" he asked. Kira shook her head with uncontrollable giggles, and Luke let out a chuckle too. Tristan looked down at what he had thought was a plain, blue crew neck. Boy, had he been wrong.

Ironed on to the front of the shirt was a puppy in a Darth Vader costume and the slogan, "Do I look evil to you?"

Immediately, Tristan started to tug it off. Kira reached out and grabbed his arm.

"Stop, I think it's adorable," she said with a smile, still not totally able to control her mirth. "Besides, we have more important things to discuss, like where we're going and how we're planning on finding Diana."

Hoping the boys would follow, Kira turned back to the car, but not so fast that she didn't catch the smirk Luke threw Tristan's way. It was going to be a very long drive. She sighed as she pulled the passenger side door back open and stepped inside.

"So, where to?" Luke asked and started the engine.

"The last place I tracked Diana to was Baltimore. She's been heading north, but I'm not sure what her final destination is."

"Baltimore it is then." Kira reclined her seat, trying to get comfortable. "That's what, a fifteen hour drive?"

"Probably sixteen." Luke put the car into drive. The sluggish engine mirrored his mood.

"Cool," Kira said, looking from boy to boy. *Well, this is going to be fun*, she thought into the complete silence of the car. *Sixteen hours and not a single thing to talk about...bring on the party.*

She looked over at Luke's tight grasp on the steering wheel, and then flicked her eyes back to Tristan's crossed arms. As always, it would be up to her to make peace.

"So, how was the fight out here?" Kira asked finally, trying to break the tension.

"Fun," Tristan said, the memory lighting up his features. "You guys really have something going with that UV wall. I was amazed it worked so well."

The image of Tristan catapulting vampires came to Kira's mind, and she couldn't help but smirk. The idea that Tristan didn't mind killing his own kind comforted Kira in a strange way. She knew he wasn't evil, and he would never be killing anything that had a shred of goodness in it. So, it must be all right for her to be doing the same thing. Truthfully, it had become all too easy to kill vampires at a moments notice. There was a numbness about it that she didn't like, an almost cruel lack of remorse or pain on her part.

The emptiness reminded her of the one fear she had when she found out what she was, the fear of being evil—of being destined to do terrible things. She had pushed those thoughts to the side since coming to Sonnyville, but her loss of control had reawakened those doubts, and they had slowly been invading her thoughts during the past few hours. Like her grandfather said, with the power came the moments where she lost not only the hold over her power but over her senses as well. What would she have done without Luke to break the spell? Would she still be in the center of the square throwing flames at nothing, or would she have passed out and maybe even died?

"Kira?" Luke asked.

"Hmm?" She looked over at him, distracted enough to force her questions away again.

"What's up? I just made an awesome joke, and I didn't even get a laugh out of you. You okay?"

"Maybe she just didn't think it was funny," Tristan said under his breath.

"Eh, not possible," Luke responded cavalierly.

"I didn't think it was funny." Tristan shrugged.

"Yes, but you're more than a hundred and fifty years old. You still think knock-knock jokes are funny. Kira and I, on the other hand, have a more modern sense of humor."

"Knock-knock jokes, huh?" Tristan questioned, egging Luke on.

He took the bait. "What, still too twenty-first century for you?"

"No, I just have a good one, come to think of it." Luke rolled his eyes in the rearview mirror, glancing sidelong at Kira in the process.

"What's your joke?" Kira asked, slightly nervous for what was about to happen. Her palms started to sweat a little.

"Knock-knock," Tristan said, a smirk starting to gather on his face. Kira caught the mischievous glint that always appeared in the corner of his eye when he was about to do something troublesome.

"Who's there?" Luke asked.

"My fist."

"My fist who?"

"Don't you get it?" Tristan asked, full-on grinning at this point, with dimples puckering on his cheeks. "I just metaphorically punched you in the face."

"Tristan!" Kira tried to reprimand him. But he caught the twitch of her lips. It was only there for an instant, but Kira knew any chance of lecturing him on treating Luke nicely was over for the time being. She couldn't help it though—the joke was funny!

"Yes, well," Luke retorted, "clearly we're just on totally different wavelengths because I didn't find that funny at all. That shirt, however, is hilarious." He looked pointedly at the adorable puppy on Tristan's chest.

Kira rolled her eyes and pushed the radio on with her toe, too lazy to sit up and do it.

"Hey, watch your feet. This is a nice car." Luke slapped her foot away and fussed with the radio until he found a station to stop on.

"Whatever, I'm going to sleep," Kira said and rolled over, turning her back on both boys and reclining her seat the rest of the way. If there was anything her new, slightly insane, life taught her, it was sleep whenever you got the chance because you never knew when a vampire was going to come along and try to flip your car over.

Tristan put his feet up and stretched them between the front seats. His hand appeared next to her face, and she reached hers up to clasp it. It was cool to the touch, but Kira had gotten used to the sensation. The freeze balanced out her normally scorching temperature.

Maybe this will be good for them, Kira thought hopefully. In Charleston, Tristan and Luke barely spent any time together. Luke could run off with Dave or Miles while Kira hung out with Tristan, and Tristan could easily disappear whenever he wanted to. Unless there were big school functions, like graduation or senior beach day, the two of them stayed pretty far apart. Come to think of it, even at those functions, they kept their talks down to grunted hellos and forced pleasantries. If they were both her best friends, then it only made sense that they were similar enough to like each other.

She squeezed Tristan's hand and he reciprocated. Too tired to turn around again, she pictured his relaxed face as it leaned against the back of the seat. He was always the first to wake up when he snuck in and spent the night. Tristan always blamed it on his heightened vampire senses—he always knew when her heart was speeding up to wakefulness. But Kira liked to think that he just enjoyed watching her sleep. Not in a creepy way, just for the few moments before she woke up—the few moments where her face was completely free of worried stress lines, and she was undeniably safe in his care. In all of his drawings, she looked so happy and at peace, and Kira guessed she only looked that calm asleep.

But that wouldn't happen this time because when she woke up tomorrow it would be all business. And well, she thought of the two men next to her, playing referee.

Chapter Ten

At the sound of loudening voices, Kira's eyes fluttered open. Bright light stung her pupils, so she instinctively closed her lids again. Upon hearing her name, Kira made sure to keep them shut. Conscious of her quickening breath, Kira counted to four and breathed out, held it, then counted to four while breathing in—a meditation exercise Luke had taught her. She wanted to hear what the boys were saying without Tristan picking up on her quickening pulse. It wasn't like eavesdropping was illegal or anything.

"Oh, come on, Luke!" Tristan said with frustration evident in his tone. His voice came from the front seat, and Kira realized he was driving now. She must have slept through the last rest stop.

"What?" Luke responded, feigning ignorance.

"Just admit it, will you?"

"I told you, I'm here to keep her safe. Nothing more."

"We both know Kira can hold her own in a fight."

"Maybe that's not what I'm keeping her safe from." Luke said in an accusatory voice.

Tristan laughed darkly under his breath. "From what, me? Do you honestly think Kira would still be with me if she was at all afraid of me? She's stronger than that. Just admit you're here to try and win her over."

"Why? Are you threatened?" Luke asked, and Kira could hear the slight strain of hope in his voice. He was trying to be tough, but it wasn't in him to be intimidating. He was too good-natured.

"Kira and I share something you'll never understand. We're both outcasts, and as much as I hate to admit it, we're both beings that sound bad on paper but strive to be good," Tristan said sadly.

"Are we talking about the same person here?" Luke asked incredulously.

"Come on, a vampire that needs blood to survive? Evil. But add a soul and the line isn't so clear—not good, but not evil either. Mixed-blood conduit that could mean the end of the world as we know it? Not good. But add Kira's will and heart and strength, and it becomes far more complicated." Tristan paused, trying to find the correct words. Kira hung on his breath like a lifeline, wondering whether the sentence that followed would push her off the edge or carry her to safety. "We both know what it's like to not fit in, to strive to change the destiny that's been set for us. Kira means everything to me because she gets it and she's the only one who ever has. You look at me and see a vampire, but she looks at me and sees a person."

Kira couldn't contain the smile that widened her lips, but thankfully, she was still turned away from them so neither boy noticed. *Conduits look at me and see something dangerous*, she wanted to say, *but you look at me and see something beautiful*. She couldn't help the sense of warmth blossoming in her chest, but Kira tried to still her emotions. She wasn't ready for the eavesdropping to be over. It was just getting interesting.

"Yeah, well, I happen to think Kira and I share something special too, something you'll never understand. Mortality, for one. And, how about a penchant for home-cooked meals? She does want to be a chef, you know. Pretty hard to test out new recipes with a boyfriend who can't eat food."

All the bitterness Luke never showed her was starting to seep out. He tried so hard to be the happy-go-lucky best friend who could always cheer her up, which she loved, but she wished he wouldn't keep so much inside. Sometimes, it was all right to be real and emotional.

And then the tone of his voice changed. Kira sensed that something inside of him was finally letting go.

"We'd be happy, Kira and me. I know you make her happy, but I would too. We're always laughing, and together we can make any situation a good one. I may not be alone in the world, but that's only part of what she is. The other part is all fire and that's something you'll never understand, Tristan."

But Kira understood. As much as she wanted to deny it, his words rang true. A sense of peace and pride leaked into her mind, bubbling over from Luke's head into her own. For the first time in a long time, Kira knew he was speaking from the heart. Part of her wished she could turn her ears off, but the strength of Luke's conviction kept her from blocking him out.

"She doesn't have to worry about being in control around me," he kept going, impassioned by Tristan's lack of retort, "because I'll always be there to ground her. You might be Kira's boyfriend, but I'm her other half. I'm her rock. When she goes into that dark place inside herself, you need to run in the other direction to save your own life, but I can run toward her to bring her back home. And that's what I meant by keeping her safe. Not from vampires and not from you, but from herself. Now you admit it, Tristan. Admit that I'm the only person who can do that."

The silence in the car was deafening, and it cut like a knife piercing Kira's heart. Tristan would never admit that he agreed with Luke, but his lack of response was all anyone needed to hear. She loved him, really loved him, but Luke's words were undeniable.

She wanted to reach out for his hand and tell him she didn't care, that she didn't need Tristan to save her. All she needed was more control, and she would get that and they could be together. It would all work out—Kira had to believe it. Tristan was too important to her, and their future together was too important to just drop without a fight.

She wanted to say all of those things, but instead Kira let her pulse race and turned over with a sleepy groan.

"She's waking up," Tristan said just to say something—just to keep Luke from having the last word.

Kira let her eyes open and played dumb. "Talking about anything interesting?" she asked, fooling herself with the scratchy, sleepy pitch.

"Just your obnoxiously loud snoring," Luke said, instantly carefree again. Kira could feel the change in her mind, the thoughts of his she had been trying to ignore just disappeared entirely. Sometimes, she wished she could flip the switch like that. Even now, her mind was running at a mile a minute because of what she had overheard.

"I do not snore," she said indignantly, playing the part as best she could.

"My bloodshot, sleep deprived eyes totally disagree with you. Look at them. I look like a creepy zombie or something." Kira looked back and choked on her own breath when she met his eyes. She did not snore, but something must have kept him up all night because he looked like crap.

Her eyes wandered to Tristan, who, she was happy to see, was still wearing the puppy shirt. He looked slightly defeated with hunched shoulders and a hollow straight-ahead stare. She reached over and entwined their fingers together, comforting him as best she could without giving anything away.

"So, what's the plan?" Kira asked as a sign that read "Baltimore — 30 miles" flashed by the window.

"Unfortunately," Tristan started, "I need to leave early to meet with the head vampire in this region. I need permission for a prolonged stay, and I want to question him. It's possible he may have seen Diana recently and could tell us where she is."

"And where is this guy?" Kira asked.

"An old plantation, of course. Vampires are nothing if not slightly old-fashioned, but it's only five or ten miles outside of the city."

"Okay," Kira said reluctantly. "And Luke, what's our plan?"

"Well," he said, and Kira knew instantly that he was about to say something she didn't want to hear. His voice always sounded slightly sweeter as if needing to sell her on an idea.

"Spit it out," Kira said with a sigh.

"I'm going to reach out to the local branch of Protectors to see if they've heard anything."

"Sounds fun!"

"Yes, but you can't come."

"What!" Kira turned around in her seat to stare at him

with an open-mouthed expression. "You can't be serious. Why can't I come?"

"It's full-blood Protectors only. That's just the way it is, I'm sorry."

"So what am I supposed to do then? Sit in the car and twiddle my thumbs?" Kira glanced from boy to boy, and she had the sneaking suspicion that Tristan was silently communicating with Luke through the rearview mirror.

"We were hoping you could figure out the hotel situation..." Luke said slowly, trying to gauge her anger as the words came out.

"Need me to iron your clothes and cook some dinner too?" Kira snapped.

"That would be awesome," Luke said, jumping out of the way of the punch he had anticipated.

"Seriously, I feel like I've been transported back to forties. The boys go fighting while the girl stays at home." She sat back and crossed her arms. "This sucks."

"But we'll both be back later tonight, and hopefully we'll have enough information to start working on a plan," Tristan told her.

"A plan that I'm part of." It wasn't a question.

Both boys nodded.

She placed her feet on the dashboard and settled in for the rest of the car ride. Tristan pulled off of the highway about seven miles outside of the city and swerved through country roads before pulling to a halt outside of a gated estate. He promised to call Kira with updates and then forced them to leave before he notified the vampires of his presence outside.

Twenty minutes later, Luke directed Kira toward a row house closer to the inner city. To her, it looked more like a movie-style frat house than a secret hideaway for conduits, but she trusted Luke and sent him on his way, only eighty percent jealous that she couldn't go.

Okay, completely and totally jealous that she couldn't go. But he had given her his credit card for the hotel room. And all that came to Kira's mind was the saying, "while the cat's away, the mice will play". Well, while her cats were off doing manly things, Kira would have a little fun, female-style.

She followed the signs toward the inner harbor and drove around trying to find the glitziest hotel in the city.

Brick after brick building greeted her, until she finally broke through to the harbor, which was lively and bright compared to the rest of the city. There were sculptures, a fountain, and crowds of people wandering around an outdoor shopping area directly next to the harbor's edge. The water glistened in the sun and made Kira feel like she wasn't in a city at all.

And right along the road was a humongous, glass-enclosed building that looked like the perfect hotel for her. She pulled in and let the valet take the car to the hotel parking lot.

"Welcome to the Hyatt Regency, may I take your bags for you?" A bellhop asked as she walked in and approached the concierge. *Very classy*, Kira thought and started to hand over her luggage.

She looked down at her and Luke's dirt-encrusted duffels, wondering what she herself must look like, and declined the bellhop's offer.

Kira walked past him toward the front desk. A hot shower was suddenly all she could think about.

"Hello, how may I—" a woman started cheerily, but stopped when she looked up from the desk and actually saw Kira. With a small cough, she continued. "Eh, how can I help you?"

"I'd like a room," Kira said and reached her hand up to her hair self-consciously. Was that mud hardened against her curls?

Another small cough. "Of course, of course. How many beds?"

"Two please. Doubles."

"Harbor view?" the girl asked dubiously.

"Yes," Kira responded. She wanted to splurge. And this woman was so prissy that Kira just wanted to slap her nose down to a normal angle.

"We do have one room available, but it will be four-hundred dollars a night." She looked at Kira with a tilted head and placed her hand under her chin, staring Kira down.

"I've got it, thanks," Kira said and slipped the credit card across the counter top. She tried to cover her gulp and silently hoped Luke would be okay with this. They had a private jet—a little hotel cost was probably nothing.

"Yes, well, I just need to check this card quickly—"

"Look," Kira paused, searching for a nametag, but she couldn't find one. "Look, lady, I've had a very long day, and I just want to take a shower and a nap and I don't need any attitude from you. If you have a room, great. If not, I'll take my loaded credit card somewhere else."

"Just following protocol, miss," she said and continued checking the card. Kira sighed and rolled her eyes. So much for a stab at bravado. "And will there be anyone else staying with you?"

Ah, crap, Kira thought, *there goes my last hope of maintaining any shred of dignity against this woman.*

"Um, yes. Two other people."

"Names please, just so we know when they arrive."

"Tristan Kent and Luke Bowrey," Kira mumbled. The woman's eyebrows shot up to the sky.

"Two men?" she said with a smirk. "I just need to confirm their gender for when they come in."

"Yes, that's right. Two boys, each about twenty years old." Kira said with a dismissive wave. *Think what you want*, she hoped the gesture said, *I don't care.*

"Room 12B." She slid a room key across the desk. "Have a nice stay."

Kira took it with an overly sweet smile and caught the glass elevator up.

As soon as she opened the door to her room, the view took her breath away. She could see the entire harbor, out past the city even, to where the horizon faded and it was too hard to tell what was ground and what was cloud. When she looked down at the harbor below, Kira noticed a giant wooden ship floating in the water, like something out of a pirate movie, and an awesome triangular shaped building, the famous aquarium from a brochure downstairs. Her gaze followed the water to a raised hillside park, and she itched to look at that view too. Being so close to the water reminded her of Charleston. It almost felt like she was home.

While the view was mesmerizing, Kira dropped her bags and retreated to the bathroom. In the fluorescent-lighted mirror, she looked even more terrible than she hoped she had looked downstairs. But hey, what could she expect when she had fought a deranged vampire, got in a car crash, and went on a slightly insane killing spree? Kira was amazed that all she had was a little dirt in her hair. Okay, clumps of mud in her hair and swipes of it across her face. All right, she would admit it. It was downright nasty. She bolted to the shower to wash off before taking a long, steaming bath.

Maybe staying behind wasn't the worst thing ever.

It was only a few hours later, after she had cleaned up, gazed at the sunset, watched oodles of television and ordered room service that she realized waiting sort of stunk. She wasn't worried per se, mostly just impatient, but it was a relief when the knob turned fifteen minutes before midnight and Tristan walked through the door.

"Hey!" She sat up from her spot on one of the beds to give him a hug.

"You look comfy," he said with a laugh. Kira looked at her outfit—plush robe, hotel slippers, and her favorite pair of fuzzy socks. *Sexy lingerie*, Kira thought wistfully, *why don't I own any sexy lingerie?*

"Oh, yeah. Well, you know," she said with a shrug. "Anyway, how was your day?"

He ran a hand through his silky black hair. "You know what?" he said, meeting her eyes quickly. "Let's get out of here. Let's do something fun and let all of this go for a night. Luke will want to hear about everything I learned anyway. Let's just leave that for tomorrow."

He grabbed Kira's hands, and she felt giddy from his energy. His blue eyes flashed with excitement.

"Let's do it!" she said and retreated into the room to change into jeans and a blouse. Tristan, she had noticed when he walked in, wore a crisp white button-down, something she was sure he had borrowed from the head vampire.

When they walked out of the hotel, Kira secretly wished the annoying concierge woman was there to drool over Tristan and feel immensely jealous of Kira. But she unfortunately wasn't.

Instead, Kira walked hand in hand with Tristan toward the harbor, which was still perfectly amazing to her.

The night sky was full of stars that twinkled in the soft waves lapping against the harbor walls. The sound lulled Kira to a peaceful place, and her heart beat slowed to the soothing pace.

Tristan watched her as she stared out at the water, as far down the harbor as she could.

"Come on," he said, pulling her hand, "follow me."

Kira walked with him around the bend, ignoring a sleeping homeless man who was sort of ruining the mood. Instead, she looked at the moonlight on Tristan's face, how it glistened in the dark circles of his pupils, all the while casting an incandescent glow on his pearly skin.

They stopped outside of a latched gate that led down a short dock toward bicycle boats. Tristan dropped Kira's hand to grasp the lock.

"Tristan!" she whispered harshly, looking around for anyone who might see them. "What are you doing?"

"We're just going to borrow a boat. No one will even notice," he said sneakily while crushing the lock open.

She followed him down the pontoon dock, her adrenaline pumping with a mix of nerves and excitement.

"Your chariot, my lady," he said while arching his arm over to one of the paddleboats. Kira laughed at the grand gesture but took the hand he offered to help her into the boat. She sat down, placing her feet on the two pedals and waited while he untied it.

"Are you sure we should be doing this?"

"We'll be fine. Have I ever been caught?" He didn't wait for her answer. "Nope. Not when I snuck you into the church or to the Angel Oak that one night this past spring. Or what about when I took you to the aquarium after hours—how much creepier was the shark tank at night when no one else was around?"

"Yeah, okay." Kira eased back into the seat, relaxing. He was right. No matter how many crazy things they did, he never got in trouble.

Tristan jumped into his seat and pushed off the dock with his foot, grabbing Kira's hand in the process.

They pedaled out toward the center of the water, enjoying the silence. After a while, Kira stopped moving and leaned over to put her head on Tristan's shoulder. He stopped too, releasing her hand to put his arm around her.

She looked up at the scene above her. No tall buildings or glaring streetlights blocked her view of the endless glowing specks spattered across the sky—some larger, some brighter, and some nothing but dusty glitter.

Normally, people looked up at the vast space and felt small, nearly insignificant. With so many endless possibilities, how could one person's life be so important? But Kira saw something else.

"What are you thinking?" Tristan asked softly.

"I'm thinking of the stars and how much they scare me sometimes."

"Scare you?" he asked with a hint of surprise in his words.

"So many planets are just floating around in space with no purpose, completely devoid of life. It scares me. The earth is one in a billion, one in a trillion, and I don't want to screw it up." She shook her head. "But that's so stupid, isn't it?"

"Not at all," he said, hugging her a little closer. "But you have nothing to be afraid of."

"Don't I?" she asked, staring up at him and then down at her palms, so small and dainty yet powerful at the same time.

"You know, I tried to draw the night sky once," he said and hugged her closer to his body. "It was a long time ago, right after I'd seen Van Gogh's *Starry Night* for the first time. But I found that it was too difficult. Something about that endless darkness, sprinkled with light but still the blackest black you'll ever know, is too emotional. You have to look inside yourself to paint something that raw, and I've always been too afraid to actually do it."

"You, afraid?" Kira laughed at that. He was always the first one to step into a fight.

"It's easy to draw other people and look inside of their heads to come up with a secretive expression or an open smile, but it's another thing entirely to look at the truths in your own heart." He kissed her on the forehead. "And that's okay, Kira. I promise."

"Eventually, I'll have to face it though."

"Yeah," he said, "but eventually is not tonight."

Kira reached up and pulled him into a long kiss. One that only ended when a beam of light landed on their faces and a voice shouted. "Hey, you!"

Kira jerked back and covered her eyes from the unbearably bright whiteness.

"What do we do?" She punched Tristan on the shoulder. "You said we wouldn't get caught!"

He grinned down at her. "I've been known to be wrong on occasion. Rare, but it happens."

"Pedal!" She wanted to scream but whispered as if it would keep them hidden for a moment longer.

"Relax, do you see that guy? He's not even a real cop, just harbor police. And, I think he's had one too many donuts if you know what I mean."

Kira rolled her eyes and kept pedaling. They skipped the dock since the cop was standing right there and pedaled toward their hotel instead.

"Stop!" the man yelled at them.

They slowed when the harbor wall neared, and Tristan jumped three feet high to land solidly on the brick path. Kira reached her hands up, and he easily pulled her free of the boat, which was carried away from them by the waves.

She put her arms around his shoulders and let Tristan carry her piggyback-style toward their hotel. They made it through the lobby doors, into the elevator, and into their room before Kira erupted into giggles.

"Did you see his face when you lifted me out of the water?" she asked Tristan, who imitated the wide-eyed shocked look of the cop, causing another fit of laughs.

They stumbled together back into the room, and Kira noticed Luke on one of the beds. He was sprawled out and belly-down with his face planted firmly against the pillow.

Quieting down, Kira pulled off her jeans and slipped back into the shorts she had been wearing earlier. Tristan beckoned her to the bed where he was already stretched out and she crawled in next to him, curving her body to fit against his.

Kira grabbed his hand and drew his arm across her stomach, letting him cradle her. She fell asleep peacefully, listening to the sound of his breath in her ear.

Chapter Eleven

Kira wanted to puke. *Wait,* her sleepy mind asked, *do I want to puke or do I need to puke?*

Her eyes weren't even open yet. All she knew was that Tristan still held her in his arms, she was still in bed, she could feel his breath a tantalizing millimeter from the back of her neck, and she wanted to vomit.

Kira stirred, moving her muscles and waking Tristan in the process. He kissed the soft spot under her ear and whispered, "Good morning," just loud enough for her to hear. Instinctively, Kira smiled and rolled over to look into his clear blue eyes.

"Morning," she said, still half-asleep.

Her gag reflex grew stronger. She wanted to smile and continue dozing in the peaceful confusion of waking up, but her stomach recoiled. Kira sat up and held her head. What was going on?

Tristan looked at her, concerned. She slipped her feet over the edge of the bed to put her head between her knees, but halfway bent over, she caught Luke's eyes—Luke's fuming eyes—and everything became clear.

"Luke!" She wanted to scream but it came out as more of a painful groan as the vomit feeling started anew—at the exact moment Tristan's arm rested on her shoulders.

"Do you know what's wrong with her?" Tristan asked Luke, confused.

"Not a clue," Luke replied, but Kira heard the overly cheerful tone in his voice. She glared at him and tried to separate the gagging sensations in her mind from her bodily responses. Reading his mind could affect her physically now? This was so not cool. And judging by the almost smirk gathering on Luke's face, he knew just what his thoughts were doing.

Kira tried to focus but she was still so tired that separating his thoughts from hers wasn't easy. Forcing herself to think happy thoughts, she slowly pushed the sick feeling to the back of her brain. But not fast enough, she realized, still clutching her stomach.

How dare Luke work mental sabotage on her! Okay, yes, she had sort of forgotten that he was sleeping in the bed next to her and Tristan. And yes, that probably frustrated him. But, it's not like they had been making out or anything. She had been asleep!

It was time for him to pay, Kira thought, as the need

to vomit slowly got replaced by the need to slap Luke across the cheek.

"I'm going to kill you!" she shouted and bolted upright, charging him. Luke slid over to the other side of his bed and stood. Kira jumped on the bed and lunged for him, ready to wipe the grin off of his face. Luke easily evaded her and ran toward the foot of the bed.

Not caring how ridiculous she looked, Kira raced after him. Luke dodged again and before Kira could make another attempt at a lunge, strong arms held her from behind.

"Let me go, Tristan," she said, struggling against his iron grip.

"As much as I would love to see you beat Luke up, I have to ask, what is going on?"

"Your girlfriend has officially gone insane," Luke said. His features were still alive with laughter at the game of cat and mouse he and Kira had just played.

Kira stopped struggling against Tristan, suddenly realizing what she had done. She would have to confess now and tell Tristan she could read Luke's mind. But it would hurt him so much to know they had a connection like that. *Maybe*, Kira began to think of an idea...

"Luke gave me food poisoning."

"I did not," he said indignantly.

"Really? You're ready to bite his head off over food poisoning?" Tristan was highly doubtful.

"When it makes me want to throw up, I do! It must have been the snacks in the car," she added, trying to think on her feet, but it sounded lame even to her.

"This is all in your head, Kira," Luke said, trying to come off as serious. His attempt was undermined by barely contained laughter.

"All in my head? I don't think so." She jerked her arm again, hoping to surprise Tristan but he held her steady. "None of that was in my head." She stared pointedly into Luke's eyes. To think, when she had first realized she could read his mind, she was worried he would think she would invade his privacy. Who was the one being completely ridiculous and unfair now?

Luke shrugged. "Then I'm sticking with my initial diagnosis—temporary insanity."

"Gah!" Kira breathed in frustration. "I'm going to the bathroom. Let me go," she said, and Tristan's grip instantly fell.

"Women," she heard Luke say to Tristan as she walked off.

"Tell me about it," he responded.

Great, Kira thought, *they both think I'm PMSing*. She slammed the door behind her and splashed water on her face. Should she have told Tristan? It would have been the perfect moment to come clean about the mind reading. Now, if he found out, it would seem like Kira had been hiding it from him, like she had been keeping a secret. And what if Luke ever mentioned it? Kira didn't think he would ever go behind her back like that, but things had a way of coming out in the heat of the moment.

Trying to let it go, Kira brushed her teeth and mindlessly continued with her morning routine.

A few minutes later, she emerged from the bathroom, much calmer but still giving Luke the evil eye. Both boys sat in armchairs bent over a piece of paper resting on the low coffee table. Tristan eyed her with caution.

"I'm okay," she told them. She held her hands up. "I promise. No secret weapons or anything."

"Don't believe her," Luke said and leaned in toward Tristan. "I think I saw one of those poison dart guns in there earlier."

Kira rolled her eyes and ignored him.

"We were just talking strategy," Tristan said, steering the conversation away from any more bickering.

Kira tugged one leg underneath her bum and sat on the couch to look at the piece of paper. It was blank.

"I see you've been very successful," she said sarcastically.

"Well, it turns out neither of us found any useful information." Tristan sighed and dropped his forehead into his hands. "I know Diana was on her way here two days ago. She may have stopped in somewhere else first, but I know she was looking for someone or something in Baltimore. But no one's seen her here yet. No vampires at least."

"Same here," Luke chimed in. "No conduits have seen her around."

"So where does that leave us?" Kira asked. Both boys remained silent but shared a telling look. "No!" She looked at them with wide eyes.

"Just one more day," Tristan pleaded.

"No, you can't leave me behind again. That is totally unfair!"

"It's not because we don't want you to come," Tristan said while taking her hand, "it's because we can't afford to be under attack again. We got pushed out of Charleston and pushed out of Sonnyville. If the local vampire population gets wind that you're here, we might be pushed out before we can find Diana or any clues to her whereabouts."

"It will keep all of us safer," Luke added.

"Fine," Kira said while collapsing against the back of the couch, "but only for one more day. Deal?"

"Deal," they both agreed in unison.

"So where will you be going? So I can at least live vicariously," she said while grabbing one of the complimentary apples to munch on for breakfast.

"Tea," Tristan said looking sheepish. Kira stared at him under raised brows. "What? The head vampire here is five hundred years old. He couldn't give up his English ways if he tried."

"Can vampires even have tea?" Luke asked. Tristan glared at him.

"It's not tea, exactly…"

"Oh, right," Luke said while looking uncomfortably toward the floor.

Maybe that wasn't on purpose, Kira thought.

"Anyway, he said we had things to discuss in a wonderfully profound way. After I hear what he has to say, I'll do some digging around the city."

Kira nodded and turned to Luke.

"Ditto. The local conduits are going to show me their usual hotspots." He leaned back in his seat and put his feet on the table. Stretching his arms over his head with a yawn, he said, "The real question is what will you be doing? What I wouldn't give for a day off right now."

"I don't even know. Maybe take a bath?" Kira said, knowing she would really look at the papers her grandfather had given her. But they were private, and she didn't want to tell Luke or Tristan. If she was about to uncover some deep, dark secret about what she was, she wanted it to stay that way—a secret.

"In our four-hundred-dollar-a-night bathroom?" Luke asked with a smirk. Kira choked on an apple chunk.

"About that…"

Luke waved her off.

"Don't worry about it. I'm only kidding. I'll find a way to pay for food somehow."

"Luke," Kira said sternly, trying to see if the price actually mattered or not.

"No, really. I've heard that Baltimore has a thriving strip scene," he said, pretending to consider it. Kira tried to contain herself, but the image was too much to handle.

"I don't think you could pull off a thong."

Tristan covered his face so his grimace didn't show.

"Hey, I'll have you know," Luke started saying, but then he shook his head and burst out laughing. "Okay, okay, you got me. I do not even want to joke about that."

Kira smiled with success. She barely ever beat him at his own game.

"Are we done with that...forever?" Tristan asked from behind his hands.

Still chuckling, Kira said yes and got up to get dressed. Within twenty minutes, she had said goodbye to both of the boys and was alone in the hotel room deciding between reading those pages or some healthy procrastination. She opted for the latter and picked up her cell phone.

Her mom answered on the second ring. She sounded happy and, Kira thought, blissfully ignorant of what was going on in her daughter's life. She didn't want to talk about conduits or vampires or Kira's powers—that was all part of the life she had given up a long time ago. And though she told Kira she would always be there to talk, it was hardly true. If Kira needed to discuss boys or school or college or cooking, her mother was there in a heartbeat. But about anything Kira actually needed to talk to someone about?

No, she looked the other way.

They had found a happy peace since Kira had woken up from her coma. But it wasn't real, not the way it used to be, before Kira had found out she was adopted. And maybe that was why she wanted to find her real mom so badly. She wanted a family who could accept her unconditionally. Her current mom refused to accept her powers, her father was ignorant of it all, and Kira knew if she mentioned Tristan to her grandparents, they would never understand.

Her real mother was someone who had given so much up for love. She just might understand what Kira needed to hear.

And that was why Kira finally picked up the papers after hanging up the phone. At first, she was going to call Emma, her boy guru, to talk about Luke. But she needed to face what she was. In the end, Kira hoped it would help her gain control.

Sighing, Kira walked over to her duffle and pulled out the wrinkled folder. She made a cup of chamomile tea from the hotel coffee pot and nestled into the armchair by the window to read. With one wistful glance at the harbor and sunny afternoon, Kira pulled the pages free and started reading, thankful that, like the book she had stolen from Luke, the text was written in modern English. Well, at least as modern as eighteenth century English, which for an ancient and secret civilization, was pretty well updated.

Months ago, Luke had explained to her that merely a

year or two after printing in the early 1700s, the same conduit scholars, both Protector and Punisher, who had gathered under the anonymous title to write the histories down, decided the knowledge was too dangerous for every conduit to have. Definitely a pre-freedom of speech move, Kira thought, but they had removed the final chapters and all the copies printed since—made as textbooks for young conduits to learn from—had simply never even mentioned the two missing chapters. Most people had forgotten about them, but Luke's copy, which she did eventually return, was one of the original texts—a family heirloom passed down through countless generations.

In Kira's hands were photocopies of the original missing pages. Something that, up until now, had remained only in the hands of the council members.

"Chapter Four," she said, reading the title out loud. "A Mixed Breed."

"*The story of how we began is perhaps the most controversial topic in our society's long and prolific history: the mixed breed. How did they act? What did they look like? Were they dangerous? What powers did they possess? What weaknesses? And most importantly, what would happen should they return?*

"*Answers, however, are the one thing we do not have. They are what we seek and what we need to find to secure the future of our people, but they are also the hardest things to come by. How do you search for information about a species that died out more than ten millennia ago—a time that predates written language itself?*"

Kira could not help but gulp. She knew she was the first mixed-blood conduit to come by in a long time, but ten thousand years? It was almost an impossibly long time to imagine.

"We can only look to myths, legends, and of course, history. What we've told you thus far are our theories about the evolution of our separate species. Almost ten thousand years ago, a time when pastoral civilization was only just beginning to arise, the species began to evolve apart. We of course believe that as families began to settle and discard the hunter-gatherer lifestyle, colonies of like-minded conduits formed. Because of this, the species stopped intermixing and new powers evolved, ones that reflected their like-minded souls. In our modern words, Protectors to protect what they believed were the lost souls inside of vampires, and Punishers to destroy what they believed was an inherent evil. Was our God involved? Perhaps. But in this text, we will discuss only science.

"Like vampires, conduits evolved beside humans, to look like humans, but we are not humans. We are genetically different: from mystical sources or from natural ones, we will probably never be certain, but what we can do is hard to describe without introducing divine magic into the equation. And that is more relative to ancient conduits than any of us could ever believe, for their powers, according to legend, were limitless. Myths of many ancient civilizations discuss fire bringers—modern tales have turned us into ludicrous creations like fire-breathing dragons—but ancient texts do mention myths of human-like beings capable of spinning fire. For a long time, we believed these words were about our current species, but now we must fearfully turn to these myths

for answers. Fearfully, because in the times these ancient legends look back on both conduits and vampires were the evils in the stories. In a word, they were mad."

Maybe this wasn't such a great idea, Kira thought while looking away from the pages and down at the active harbor outside of her window. If the species had spent ten thousand years evolving apart, how had her parents managed to have a child anyway? And what was to say she wasn't just a new breed entirely, something completely different than the ancients were? The whole idea that a book written two hundred and fifty years ago held all of her secrets was ridiculous. No one had answers. The only thing she saw here that called out to her was the word magic, because that was the only way to explain her life.

Even knowing it could all be false, Kira's eyes fell back onto the text. Ever curious, she needed to know more. She needed to be prepared to face whatever she really was.

"Unlike us, the ancient ones were ruled by their powers. Though hard to believe, it is said that they lacked control, that sometimes a conduit would go blind in rage, spouting flames for days on end with no stop until death finally took them. In these legends, they did not burn vampires alone. Myth says when an ancient one lost control, entire villages would be burnt to ash. Entire families killed. Animals charred beyond recognition. It is because of these legends that we now strive for control.

"Vampires are evil because they give in to carnal instincts. When the hunger strikes, they go on a killing rampage, brought

completely out of humanity's grip in blood lust.

"What are conduits if not controlled? If we killed everything we touched, we would be just as evil as the very things we were born to fight. We believe that at first, this unconscious need for control helped split the two species. Now, we consciously strive to keep it that way. Because we are always asking, what if a half-breed returned? Would humans be more at risk from it or from the vampires?

"And, even though Protectors will kill a vampire when they must, if the time came could any of us, Protector or Punisher, murder one of our own?"

Kira let her head fall against the back of the seat. She stared up at the rippled white ceiling seeing only flames and screaming people, running not from vampires but from her.

But she had never lost control like that—never so badly that anything but vampires were affected.

Suddenly, Kira thought of Luke. Had he been right? Was he the only reason she had never fallen so deep and had never lost so much control? If he hadn't been there in Sonnyville to bring her out of her delirium, would she have turned the entire village and every conduit to dust, just like the vampires?

For the past few months, Kira had only ever thought that conduits had her capture to fear—that if vampires caught her they would be immune and they could go on a killing spree. But that wasn't really why conduits weren't allowed to interbreed. Every council for the past three hundred years had been keeping their entire society's biggest fear a secret—the fear that one of their own might be the greatest danger in the world, that one of their own might be a monster.

The only thing Kira didn't understand was why would they hide this? If every conduit knew this, they would never risk mixing blood. Her parents would have probably stayed away from each other.

The healing, Kira thought. The scholars must have written about her powers of healing. It was the one thing that made her existence good, the one thing conduits might risk madness for. After all, Kira had risked it to save Luke not so long ago.

Kira skimmed through the following pages, skipping past the countless myths all describing the same thing—the ancient ones' insatiable power and fall into madness.

She was almost about to stop reading, haunted enough by what she had learned, when she came across a change in tone.

"While we would love to remain with these ancient myths of horror, we feel honor bound as men of academics to produce the other side of the story. Fearful as they were through the stories we have just now told, all conduits throughout history have been things of light. Our powers are that of God and goodness, and while madness might be our undoing, our powers give us strength.

"With this in mind, we must admit that all of our findings have not been full of blood and horror. We believe with every ounce of our combined beings that bringing a new mixed breed into the world

would mean the end of life as we know it, but stories do tell of ancient fire bringers capable of restoring life. They could, we believe, heal humans and conduits alike as long as they kept the madness at bay.

"*And while we were not sure if we would write these words, we almost believe that a mixed-blood conduit today might be able to hone this power. When we think back to the lives of the ancient ones, we must remember that the world was a different place. There were no rules, no governments, and no notion of civility. There was food, killing for food, and staying alive no matter the cost.*

"*If a mixed breed were born today, in a society governed by control and regulation, there is no telling what may occur—no telling if the conduit would be a mad man or a savior. But knowing what we do, we wholeheartedly agree that finding out is not worth the risk.*"

Kira looked at the name of the next and final chapter—*The Prophecies*—and realized she didn't really want to hear any more about how her life meant the end of the world. A prophecy was a rigid proclamation, an unchangeable destiny, and she didn't want to feel like her life story had already been written for her.

Instead, Kira slipped into a jean skirt and flip-flops to wander around in the busy harbor below. She tied her hair in a ponytail, put on her oversized sunglasses, and donned a baseball cap—if that wasn't camouflage, she didn't know what was. Her hair and eyes were covered, and no vampire would have any idea who or what she was, or at least Kira hoped not because she had to get out of that hotel room.

Of course, sitting on a bench and basking in the sun

still didn't do very much to appease her thoughts. Without Tristan or Luke around to distract her, Kira was pulled right back into dark territory the minute she sat down. The beautiful weather helped a little, but the sun didn't have its usual effect of calming her. Rather, as Kira let it soak into her skin, she couldn't help but feel dangerous with the power.

The mind reading or whatever crazy psychic connection she shared with Luke was still a mystery, however. It was the one thing Kira held onto because it was the one concrete thing she had that made her different from the ancient ones with their uncontrollable powers.

She had felt dangerous at times, almost insane. She had also felt unstoppable at times, especially when she healed someone or something. But according to myth, so had all the other conduits thousands of years ago. But the connection she and Luke shared was an unknown, the one thing that might just help her hold on to her humanity.

Kira shifted on the otherwise empty bench and stretched out. As she turned to the side to lift her feet onto the wooden planks, a mass of long, straight, glistening black hair caught her attention.

Kira sat taller in the seat, stretching to see the woman who looked almost familiar. Her skin gleamed white in the sunlight. Her frame was long and lean, almost absent of fat, and she wore a loosely flowing dress in a deep plum color. Tendrils of fabric blew in the breeze, creating a fluid train down the back of the dress. It was low-cut to show the pale curve of a skinny back.

Slowly, as if searching for someone, the woman turned around. The pointed curve of her nose and taut lips came into view, but all Kira could see were her icy blue, piercing eyes.

Diana.

Chapter Twelve

Immediately, a rush of hatred coiled in her stomach, winding its way through her senses, but Kira suppressed it and tried to push those feelings all the way down to the tips of her toes. She needed to stay focused on finding out what Diana was doing here. Eventually, Kira would be able to interrogate her. Eventually, she would find out everything she needed to know, but that time was not in the middle of a huge and bustling tourist spot.

Kira ducked behind the bench, using the backrest as a shield to keep her face completely hidden from view. She poked her head up, hoping the visor of her cap and her sunglasses kept her masked enough, and watched Diana. There was no doubt in Kira's mind that she was waiting for someone or something. She scanned the crowd, her blue eyes darting back and forth, reading each face carefully.

Well, Kira thought, *I'm just going to have to be the one to find out what Diana is up to.*

While Tristan and Luke had been out there searching for her, Diana had fallen right into Kira's lap. Not that Kira was complaining, but she knew the boys would be really annoyed that she had not only left the hotel room but also did what she was doing now, which was follow Diana as she walked away from the harbor.

Sneakily, Kira stood up and walked over to a storefront, peering not through the glass at the clothes but on the glass at the reflection. Diana continued walking, thankfully at a human pace, and Kira watched until she was almost out of view before chasing after her. Kira had never been so grateful for her time spent in New York City as she was then. Walking around on crowded city streets had taught her the all too precious weave—how to duck and jump and swivel her hips to keep from getting bowled over by the crowds. Without her years' worth of knowledge, Kira had no doubt she would have lost Diana in the crowd.

As it was, she tracked Diana around the harbor to a giant grass hill, some sort of park overlooking the water. Taking each stone step slowly, Kira followed her up, hoping it wasn't a trap. When she reached the top, Kira scanned the area and saw Diana's burgundy dress as it billowed before a gleaming white marble monument. The contrast luckily made her easy to spot, which may have been Diana's intention. Kira was certain Diana had no clue she was being followed.

To keep it that way, Kira quickly dashed behind a tree, and then peered around the trunk to observe. When she was sure Diana was looking the other way, Kira sprinted behind a different tree that was much closer, so she was only ten or fifteen feet from her prey—because that was how she always wanted to think of Diana, as prey and not as predator.

After ten minutes of peeking at Diana as she did nothing but stare down at the harbor, Kira was getting a tad impatient. Yes, it was a plus that she had found Diana, but sitting out in the heat and leaning against scratchy bark to hide from a blood-sucking vampire was not really ideal.

Finally, just as Kira's annoyance was reaching an all-time high, Diana stood a fraction taller. Kira instantly became alert. Diana focused on something toward the bottom of the hill, arching her neck for a better view, before straightening out her dress and quickly feeling her hair for stray strands.

She's nervous, Kira thought.

A second later, a man appeared by Diana's side. He materialized out of thin air in a crisp tuxedo, his pearly skin immediately letting Kira know that he was a vampire. Even at a distance, she saw the crooked bend to his nose and silently felt a little sorry that he was stuck with that for all eternity. Diana smiled widely, in a subservient way that Kira didn't recognize from her, and the man extended a gloved hand. Placing her fingers in his palm, Diana let him lift her hand for a kiss.

Kira was seriously confused. Was this business or pleasure? Had Diana given up on ruining her life for some strange vampire lover? The more the two vampires interacted, the more Kira felt like she had been transported to a period film, some sort of Jane Austen fantasy filled with curtsying and overly polite manners.

Diana produced a fan from the folds of her long dress and started flicking it around like some secretive language. The man held out his arm and she grasped it at the crook of his elbow so he could lead her on a stroll around the park. They looked more like sweethearts during a secret rendezvous than evil plotting villains, but Kira knew something else had to be going on. Diana was not the sort to give up on revenge, especially when she had been plotting for months.

Kira circled around her tree, wishing the meandering couple would just stay put so she didn't have to keep jumping around the trunk like a crazy tree-hugger to keep out of sight. Her poor hands were scratched red from the wood, but Kira knew there was no choice but to wait. She needed to see what was going on. This might be the only clue to Diana's plan that any of them ever got.

Eventually, after circling the entire park once, Diana dropped her hand and turned to face the man, who had reached into his pocket to pull out a gleaming white envelope. From that distance, Kira couldn't read the words scribbled across paper, but she saw the image of a blood-red rose drawn on the front and watched as crimson petals cascaded to the ground when Diana pulled out a note.

Diana politely inclined her head. Kira assumed it was some sort of an acceptance. He slid a small vile into her hand and kissed her fingers one more time. Then, as quickly as he had come, the man disappeared. Diana pressed the note against her chest, smiling widely, but Kira didn't miss the calculating focus of her eyes. This was not schoolgirl glee at a crush finally returning her emotions—it was the giddiness of a plan falling into place. Surely that meant Diana had no idea she, Tristan, and Luke were there...hopefully.

For a moment, Kira had the incredible urge to just blast Diana with a ball of fire right there in the middle of the park. She didn't care what passersby would see, how they would run in fear at her power or how someone would snap a photograph making the conduits seem like horrible monsters.

For a moment, all Kira wanted to do was catch Diana and make her pay. She hadn't been this close to her since that day in the woods, and just like the evil witch had planned, her words were never far from Kira's mind. This vampire was the only way Kira would find out any information about her mother. Diana was the only tie and Kira was close.

Without realizing it, Kira outstretched her arm in

Diana's direction, preparing to blast her with flames.

But as quickly as the thoughts had come, Diana was gone, and Kira had missed her opportunity once again. The girl was crazy fast. Kira sighed and leaned against the tree. She would need Tristan's help when the time came.

Letting her hand fall back to her side, Kira walked over to where Diana had been standing. Kneeling down, she picked a few of the silky rose petals from the grass, wondering if Tristan would know what the peculiar invite had been about.

As late afternoon approached, Kira knew it was time to head home and slip back into the hotel room before either of the boys showed up. She picked up a snack and happily walked through the lobby. Once inside, Kira ran back over to the chair and quickly stuffed all of the papers she had been reading back into her folder. Carefully, she slipped the folder inside a T-shirt in her duffle, keeping it completely hidden from view. She placed the rose petals in a pile on the table and hunkered down to wait.

And wait.

And wait a little more until Kira just about thought she would go crazy. Patience was so not a virtue. It was torture, especially when she had two boys with hero complexes chasing after evil vampires.

When the doorknob finally clicked, Kira zeroed in on the entryway, shocked to see Luke and Tristan enter at the same time, chuckling with one another.

"What the heck?" Kira said and stood, staring at them angrily. It was one thing to leave her at home and go their separate ways, but it was a whole different thing to leave her behind and go adventuring together. They didn't even like each other! Though Kira supposed she should take it as a good sign that they were laughing and not at each other's throats as per usual.

Tristan walked over to pull her into a tight one-armed hug and said, "Oh, nothing. Luke's friends tried to kill me," which caused another burst of guffaws from Luke.

Kira shirked out of the hold to turn and look at him. It took all of her will power not to angrily point in his face. "What?"

"Dude, they weren't trying to kill you. They were just trying to throw you off the roof."

"What!" Kira spun to face Luke now.

"*Trying* being the operative word."

Kira spun to Tristan again. Being the third wheel was utterly dizzying. She couldn't stop from spinning around to try to edge her way into the conversation.

"They sort of succeeded." Luke grinned.

Enough, Kira thought.

"Stop!" she yelled to finally make the boys pay attention to her. "What is going on?" Each boy stopped smiling as if noticing Kira's frustration for the first time. Was steam coming out of her ears yet?

"It's not a big deal," Tristan said while lightly rubbing

her arm. "Luke texted me to meet him on some roof because he'd found information, so I went. But by the time I had gotten there, a few other conduits had joined in and thought I was trying to attack them, so they fought back—"

"Ah," Luke took over, "don't skip over the best part! When Tristan landed on the roof, my friends tried to blast him off of it with their power, but they just sent him flying right into a water pipe that burst like a geyser. It was just like one of those cartoons. Tristan was butt-smacked off the roof by the blow!" Luke could barely finish the story before he doubled over in another fit of laughter.

"Are you okay?" Kira turned back to Tristan, finally taking in the slightly damp quality to his clothing.

"Yeah, it was awesome. I haven't been surprised like that in a while. One minute I'm standing on the roof, the next I'm flying." He grinned boyishly.

"Getting catapulted off of a roof was fun?" Kira asked, deadpanning. Tristan shrugged and she rolled her eyes. Some things she would just never understand.

"Kira, you would have died if you were there. I can't stop playing the picture of him somersaulting through midair," Luke voiced while he collapsed into an armchair.

"I'm glad you two had...fun..." Kira said and sat down on the couch, shaking her head. "I had a good day too," Kira started, not sure how to tell them she had sort of broken their rules and gone outside.

"What did you do?" Tristan asked and settled on the

couch next to her, dropping an arm around her shoulder.

"A little of this, a little of that—you know, some reading and well, some spying on Diana—"

"What?" Tristan sat up and turned to face her.

"I swear, I didn't mean for anything to happen. I really didn't go out looking for Diana. But, you didn't really expect me to stay inside all day, did you? I was bored out of my mind."

Both boys shrugged to say, "Yeah we sort of did think you would stay inside." But in Kira's mind, they should've known better.

She continued, "Anyway, I was sitting on a bench out by the water when I saw her." Both boys sat up straight, about to ask the same question, but Kira cut them off. "No, she didn't see me. Relax, I was completely incognito."

Kira told them about the meeting on the hill and how Diana had been acting strangely, like some sort of love stricken puppy. Finally, Kira ended with the invitation and pointed to the roses on the table.

"You saw Baltimore's head vampire. His name is Bronson," Tristan said with a sigh. "His nose is the unfortunate monstrosity you described, but it's said that he can smell anything a mile away—even the sun on a conduits skin. It's a miracle you weren't seen."

"How can we be sure?" Luke asked.

"The fact that she is sitting in this room completely unharmed means she wasn't seen," Tristan whispered, and

Kira couldn't suppress the gulp that slid down her throat. "Bronson is not one for leniency, and out in the open like that, he would have taken her for sure. Or at least tried."

"And this is the same guy you had tea with?" Luke asked in disbelief.

Tristan nodded.

"But what was with the invitation and the strange back and forth between them?" Kira asked.

Tristan leaned forward in his seat to pick up a stray rose petal. He rolled the red strip between his fingers, lost in thought.

"Unfortunately, I know exactly what this is—the Red Rose Ball." Kira and Luke looked at each other, both scared by Tristan's ominous tone.

"Why is this ball so important?" Kira asked, not a hundred percent sure she wanted an answer.

"Not important, but elite—very elite. I've never been invited, but I know what it is. Once every generation, the head vampire of a region will take his or her turn hosting the ball. They invite every vampire who meets one single requirement—immunity."

Kira squinted, not liking where this was going. "Immunity...to conduits?"

Tristan nodded. "There are two balls—the Red Rose Ball and the White Rose Ball. In order to be invited to the Red Rose Ball, a vampire must own a captive Punisher. For the White Rose Ball, a Protector." Tristan ended quietly.

Kira and Luke looked at each other like they were going to be sick.

"How have we not known about this?" Luke asked Tristan.

"It's kept very private and it's a very rare event. I can't believe that this is what Diana is here for. I don't even know if more than three have been held in my lifetime."

"And is it true? How can you guys be certain all of the vampires invited actually have enslaved conduits?" Luke leaned forward, his brow furrowed in concern. Trapped conduits were the exact thing he had been taught to fear for his entire life—the one thing every conduit was told could mean the end of the world.

"There's a test. The host will welcome each guest with his own enslaved conduit, in the case of the Red Rose Ball, a Punisher. If the guest can walk through the conduit's flames, they live and enter. If not, they die. It's not a gamble most vampires would be willing to risk."

"Which means Diana found herself a conduit?" Kira asked.

"I don't think so," Tristan said, "but there's no other explanation is there?"

Kira thought back to the way Diana had been acting. Before Bronson showed up, she had been nervous. When he got there, she acted sort of like a lovesick girl and as soon as he left, Diana had become calculating again. And what was it he had slipped into her hand at the last moment?

"What if she doesn't have a conduit? What if she's just made friends with the right people?" Both boys looked at her, waiting for her to continue. "I think Bronson gave her a vial of Punisher blood to cheat the system, so she could come to the ball. I think maybe they've been dating."

"Isn't she, you know, a little too evil to date?" Luke asked while pretending to act like the killer in a slasher movie.

"It makes sense in a way," Tristan said. "She must have gotten wind of the ball and come up here after everything happened that day last year. We stopped John and Jerome, so she had no one left to run to. Why not cozy up to a head vampire with connections and means of protecting her?"

"And means of sneaking her into the ball," Kira added.

"But why? I mean, I get that this ball is some huge macho vampire event," Luke chimed in. "But why go to so much trouble for a party?"

Kira and Tristan shrugged.

"That's exactly what we need to find out," Tristan said.

"How?" Kira asked.

"I need to go to that ball," Tristan said while looking over at Kira sadly. At first she didn't understand why he looked so distraught, but after a moment Kira got it.

"My blood," Kira said softly. "My blood will get you inside."

This is not a big deal, Kira thought quietly to herself, *Tristan's a vampire and I'm his girlfriend and it's just a little blood.* But sometimes Kira found herself forgetting Tristan was a vampire. Well, not forgetting, but pushing it from her mind. The super strength and reflexes, even his age and immortality never bothered her. In fact, she found it sort of cool and definitely sexy.

But the blood thing was a little too much to think about, a little too disgusting sometimes. She would make excuses, like he never ate around her because he wasn't hungry. They had even turned the fact that he couldn't come over for a meal with her parents into an inside joke. But now, with the thought of him sucking her blood staring her in the face, Kira couldn't help but feel a little queasy. Or maybe, she thought hopefully, it was just Luke invading her brain again.

Realizing she had been quiet for a little while, Kira nodded an affirmation in Tristan's direction to let him know he could of course have her blood. It was no big deal. Everything would be completely fine, but she couldn't keep another thought from creeping into her mind, a lingering doubt from months before.

"Can I ask you one question first?" Kira said hesitantly. Tristan nodded, telling her to continue. "Well, I thought conduit blood was supposed to affect vampires and make them lose control, you know go a little crazy, but you seem to be fine with it..." She trailed off, not sure what question she was even asking. All she could picture was the sight of him chained up, swallowing her blood as Diana looked on with glee. Kira never understood why he hadn't been affected that day, why he didn't go crazy, and there had never seemed to be a good time to ask until now.

"Oh that," Tristan said quietly, unable to meet her eyes. "Conduit blood only affects vampires if they aren't used to it. But, I've had it before."

"What?" Kira said in disbelief. She fought the urge to jerk away from him.

"Not like that," he said quickly. "Aldrich forced me to when I was newly turned—he wanted me to be strong enough to help him capture new conduits when the time came. I left before he could use me like that, but I've been exposed to enough conduit blood that it will never affect me like that again."

Kira understood, she really did, but she couldn't quite fight the sense of betrayal in the back of her mind. He had drunk the blood of other conduits and enough of it to last a lifetime? It just seemed wrong. But could she really be angry with him for something that happened more than a century ago?

No, it wasn't fair to be mad at him, Kira realized. The only reason any of them survived the eclipse was because her blood hadn't turned him. *I won't let it affect our relationship,* she promised silently, *I won't think of him differently.* But still, Kira found herself purposefully looking across the room to avoid meeting Luke's eyes—to avoid facing the disgust she knew they held.

"Just one problem," Luke said from his chair, speaking into the silence and smoothly changing the subject. "We have no idea when the ball is."

"I think I do," Tristan spoke up. "Bronson has been lying to me for the past two days, not really unheard of in my world, but he mentioned he would be gone this weekend. I think it was to keep me from unexpectedly dropping in. Saturday at sundown—that'll be when it starts."

"I need to go," Luke blurted out while jumping up from his seat, like a slingshot finally being released. "I'm calling an emergency convention. If Tristan's crashing the party, we can too."

"What do you mean?" Kira asked.

"Protectors, we need to go in. We need to find out where all of these trapped Punishers are and rescue them."

"You'll need every conduit in the area to trap these guys, Luke," Tristan warned. "They're some of the most powerful vampires in the world. I'm not sure you know what you're up against."

"Don't worry about me," Luke said while grabbing his cell phone. "I'll be back later." He disappeared out the door with a determined expression. Kira could almost see the wheels spinning in his head. Luke had three days to amass an army and it definitely wouldn't be easy.

Kira leaned into Tristan's chest. He responded by hugging her closer and absently rubbing her arm with his fingers. Kira held his free hand, letting her fingers dance along his palm, but her mind was elsewhere.

At best, her mother was being held captive by some vampire, and at worst, she was dead. Or maybe it was the other way around. Should she be hoping to find out her mother was really dead—that she had been spared that sort of slavery? Kira couldn't help but wonder if her own mother had been the ticket to get someone in to a white rose ball, some sort of meal and display of power.

But she didn't want to go down that path of thought. The endless wondering would get her nowhere.

Instead, Kira focused on Diana—the vampire completely determined to destroy her life. From the moment Diana had laid eyes on Kira, she hated her. The feeling was definitely mutual, but Kira would've never acted on it had Diana not made the first move so long ago, all the way back in their high school auditorium.

In the time she had known her, Diana had attacked Kira, almost killed Luke, nearly turned Tristan bad, and risked the lives of all of her friends. Like it or not, Kira knew there was no other option than to kill her at the ball. This time, Kira couldn't hesitate.

But it all came down to one thing—what did Diana want? They had to figure that out first, because if Kira was right, Diana was concocting a plan that would haunt Kira long after Diana herself had died.

"Tristan?" Kira asked. He murmured in her ear to let her know he was listening. "What do you think she's up to? Is this really just about telling powerful vampires who and what I am?"

"I was thinking that too," he said, "but I can't imagine that is the only reason she went to so much trouble. If that were the case, all she would need to do is visit the homes of head vampires and spread the word."

"There's something we're not seeing, like with the eclipse last year. I'm worried we won't realize what it is until it's too late."

"Whatever it is, we'll make it through together. I'm sure of it."

Tristan gripped her hand and she smiled up at him. They would make it through, they always did, but at what cost?

Kira still vividly remembered the first time Diana had attacked her. The feel of Diana's teeth grazing her neck still sent shivers down her spine. She could still remember the moment her powers burst forth for the first time. She would never forget how her blood boiled, how her powers felt like lava melting her skin apart when it rained from her palms. That moment was also when Kira first found out what Tristan was. The sight of his eyes flashing in pleasure at the slight taste of her blood still haunted her thoughts. Now she understood it was involuntary, but back then it had almost torn them apart.

And what about the eclipse? Before that day, Kira had never killed anything. She had never known what it felt like to drain a vampire of its very life force, burning it to ash. Before that day, she had also never really seen the darker side of Tristan, the past he tried to keep hidden from her. She loved the man he was now, loved how he understood her and how he saw her. She loved the way they laughed and the way they could tell each other anything. She loved that he never judged her and always let her make her own decisions. But for a minute on that afternoon so long ago, Kira had seen something else, something only Diana could bring out in him, and she never wanted to see that side of Tristan again.

Which was why Kira couldn't help but feel dread as she thought of the coming Saturday. A face-off with Diana had been a long time coming and it was inevitable, but what would she, Luke, and Tristan walk away with? What scars would they carry this time?

Chapter Thirteen

Seriously, Kira thought, *why are we always in the woods?*

In the movies, spies were always in glamorous dresses attending society affairs while sipping cocktails and scoping out the scene. They had professionally applied makeup, super high-tech gadgets, and of course airbrushing. In reality, Kira was ankle deep in the mud for what felt like the millionth time in her life. The head vampire of course lived in another old plantation estate on the outskirts of Baltimore. And the ball was of course happening in his home rather than some glitzy downtown bar. Kira was beginning to wonder how the North even won the Civil War when so many vampires seemed stuck in the plantation era.

As a waft of skunk, or maybe animal feces, filled Kira's nose, she couldn't help but sigh in frustration. It was safe to say the wonderful smell of twenty-dollar-a-bar soap had worn off. She just hoped she had time to shower before life threw her another curve ball.

"Kira, come on," Luke whispered and waved her over to his tree. Kira walked over, trying not to let her sneakers squelch in the mud. Yesterday, as she gazed out of the hotel window to watch the rain fall into the harbor, Kira had thought it looked beautiful. Rain, she reminded herself now, was never beautiful—at least not the next day when you were, for all intents and purposes, off-trail hiking.

"Do you remember the plan?" Luke asked when she got closer. Kira rolled her eyes—they had only gone over it one hundred times.

In the woods all around them, but nowhere Kira could spot, were Protectors. Somehow Luke had done it. He pulled together an army, well more like a gang of loyal followers, but enough conduits to trap some of these vampires and make them talk.

Now Kira and Luke were scouting ahead and waiting to give notice for the conduits to charge. But that wouldn't be for a while. First, the two of them had to watch the guests enter and count how many there were. They had to wait for Tristan to go into the party and give them the signal. They had to find a way to jump through the window into the first floor study where Tristan was planning to lure Diana. They had to get the information about Kira's mother out of Diana. Then they had to find a way to kill her even though she was immune to Kira's Punisher powers. Oh, then finally the conduits could charge in, save the day, and get the rest of the vampires. Simple, right? Kira almost wanted to laugh. Simple just wasn't in her vocabulary anymore.

Luke motioned to her again and she followed him to another tree a few feet closer to the house. Tristan had assured them both that these vampires were too full of themselves to set out patrols. *Absolute power often comes with absolute arrogance and absolute idiocy*, Kira thought.

When a liquid-black Rolls Royce pulled up in front of the house, Kira stilled her inner monologue. A pale white leg with hot pink five-inch heels appeared first, followed by a long black sequined dress that must have cost a fortune. Finally, the bright blonde head of a vampire appeared. From this distance, Kira couldn't make out any of the vampire's features, only enough to know that it wasn't Diana, and she was slightly jealous of those shoes.

The woman strolled forward and the car pulled away, disappearing around the bend. She mounted the steps, halting right before she reached the wraparound porch, and Bronson greeted her. He gently cupped her fingers and lifted them to his lips. They exchanged pleasantries and Bronson stepped aside to let her continue. Finally, the vampire let her foot crest the top step.

Immediately a wave of flames shot out of the door, encircling her. But rather than fly backward with the force, the vampire stepped slowly across the porch and through the door, smiling the entire time. When she disappeared from sight, so did the flames.

They may not have been able to see the captive Punisher, but Luke and Kira knew what the source of that fire had been. Next to her, Luke let out a frustrated sigh. Kira was sure that until that moment Luke had been hoping that Tristan was wrong and that there were no captives. It was hard to have such a hope when the reality was staring them in the face.

Before the two of them could talk, another car—now a Lamborghini—stopped in front of the house. A male and female vampire stepped out, he in a tuxedo and she in a chiffon ball gown that seemed to float over the sidewalk. Even from the woods, Kira was almost blinded by the gleaming diamond jewels draped on the female vampire's body. Apparently, when Tristan had said it was an elite party, he wasn't lying. These people not only had conduits, they had money—lots and lots of money.

Twenty-seven more vampires made it past the front door before Kira clenched Luke's shoulder hard enough to make him wince.

"Hey, Incredible Hulk, lay-off," he said while grabbing her fingers to make her let go.

"Sorry," Kira muttered, not taking her eyes from the car now approaching the mansion. "It's Tristan," she said and nudged her head in his direction, forcing Luke to focus on the mission again.

Panther-like in his smoothness, Tristan emerged from the car. Kira's breath caught in her throat. He looked pretty darn good in a tuxedo, even if they had found it at the last second and couldn't get it tailored. The diamond cufflinks Tristan had bought—yes bought not stolen—were like stars twinkling on his wrists. Unlike the other male vampires that had arrived, he hadn't gelled his hair back. Instead, it fell naturally over his forehead, casting shadows over his eyes.

Thinking of his eyes, Kira flashed back to a memory two hours earlier, all the way back in the hotel room. Luke had already gone to gather the conduits, leaving Kira and Tristan with a few private moments, just enough time for him to take her blood and prepare for the ball.

Kneeling down in front of her, Tristan gently cupped her wrists and looked up into her face.

"You're nervous. I can feel your pulse racing." Kira shrugged in response and tried to calm her furiously beating heart. "You trust me, don't you?" He asked, suddenly losing the confident bravado.

"I do," she said, smiling at him warmly. "It's just...it's a little weird."

"Don't I know it." He smirked, letting two pointed teeth press into his lower lip.

"It's fine though. Go ahead," Kira said, pulling one of her hands free from his hold. Tristan took the hand she left him and lifted it to his lips, placing a gentle kiss on her vein.

Kira became instantly alert. Her entire body buzzed, making her feel even more nervous, but for what she didn't know. Maybe because it was the first time he was doing this, but it was so intimate—far more intimate than the kissing they had done and she had nothing else to compare it to. It wasn't fear because Kira knew without a doubt that she could trust Tristan. But handing over the controls and putting her life in his hands was still a little nerve-racking. It was one thing for him to swoop in and save her life, but quite another for her to offer it to him willingly.

Kira's heart about dropped to her stomach when he flicked his cool tongue across her skin. And then in one drawn out second, with her breath caught in her throat, he bit down.

At first, all Kira felt was the screaming of her body as it jumped into protection mode. The sunlight gathered inside of her and she forced it away, trying to convince her instincts that Tristan was not an enemy.

She caught his blue eyes, the fire started raging inside of her, and held on to them. She had seen vampires aggressive and hungry before, but this was different. The blues of his irises were warm and not the icy cool she was used to seeing in a hungry vampire. His pupils had gotten smaller rather than aggressively dilated. And when she stared into their depths, she felt perfectly safe. The power inside her calmed.

And before she realized it, Tristan was finished. He slipped his teeth from her skin and kissed her wrist one more time. Subtly, so Tristan wouldn't notice, Kira used her power to heal the puncture wounds.

"Not so bad?" he asked quietly.

"No." She smiled and gently held his cheek with her hand, running her thumb along the bone. She held his gaze for a minute,

letting him understand that she was fine and they were perfect. "It wasn't what I was expecting though," she said, changing her tone to playful and standing up. She had to get him ready for the ball.

"Oh yeah? What were you expecting?" Tristan asked while following her into a standing position.

"I don't know. In all of the books, a vampire's bite turns the heroine into a raging sack of hormones. But you know, it didn't do anything for me." She grinned and walked over to the bed to get his tuxedo jacket.

He raised his eyebrows, accepting the challenge. "That's because I wasn't trying. If I turned it on, you would be like putty in my hands." He turned around so she could slip the black coat over his shoulders.

Turning him to face her, Kira adjusted his bow tie before responding, "Oh really?"

"Hey, I've got moves you've never seen," he said with a smirk.

"Really? You're going with that line?"

"How about this one?" he said and took a step closer, gripping her hips. "When I hear your heart flutter or skip a beat or speed up like it is right now, I want to know it's because of me. Not because of what I am, but because of who I am." Kira opened her lips to speak, but the words caught in her mouth when he leaned his forehead against hers. "When I feel your skin heat up or hear your breath shorten," he said while moving his lips closer and closer to hers, "I love to know that I made it happen." He kissed her, making Kira feel all of those things, before pulling away with a lopsided grin. "Better?"

"Much better," Kira breathlessly told him.

"Kira," Luke said, jolting her out of her memories and back into the stink of the woods. *Dang*, Kira thought, *talk about a one-eighty.*

She waved Luke off to focus back on Tristan. *Bad Kira*, she chastised herself. She was not allowed to think of kissing when her boyfriend was about to face a test that could kill him.

She watched Tristan walk toward Bronson, holding her breath the entire time. When Bronson reached his hand out in greeting, Kira let the air out. The plan was going to work. Tristan shook Bronson's hand and walked onto the porch, letting the conduit's flames engulf him. Halfway to the door, he looked out into the woods, searching for her in the darkness. But before Kira had the chance to do anything or even smile at the gesture, he was through the entry and inside the ball. Tristan had passed the test.

"Come on," Luke said, motioning away from the house.

"Shouldn't we wait for Diana?" Kira asked, still eying the mansion.

"Something tells me she's already inside," Luke said. The two of them watched Bronson sliver through the front door and close it shut behind him. But, something felt wrong. If Bronson had given Diana the blood, then why hadn't she used it to get into the party the correct way? Why would he just let her rest inside?

Luke grabbed her hand and pulled her deeper into the

forest. Time for phase two—Kira tried to quell the surge of impatience already rising in her chest—time to wait.

They circled around to the backside of the house. Kira looked at the third window on the left, the one Tristan had said was the study. Now, she and Luke just had to hunker down and wait for the sign. When he had Diana, Tristan was supposed to flip on the light, open the window and make his presence known.

When they reached the far side of the house, a spot in direct sight of the study, Kira stopped walking next to an uprooted tree. She could see the house from here, well enough to know if it was time to move in, so why not sit down for the wait? Diana had been evading Tristan for weeks, and Kira didn't think she would give in so easily. No, it would take a while for him to convince her that they needed to talk privately.

Looking down at her shoes, sunk half an inch in the ground, Kira plopped down on the trunk. Her feet were already a disaster; she might as well let her butt get covered in mud too. The wet bark dampened her shorts almost immediately. Luke turned to the sound of crunching leaves and sat down next to her.

"What do you think is going on in there?" Kira asked. From the seat she could also glimpse into the ballroom. Gorgeous chandeliers twinkled against the windows. Sweeping curtains kept most of the room from view, but Kira could just tell it was extravagant.

"The usual I'm sure—sipping on cocktails and," he leaned closer while deepening his voice, "plotting to take over the world."

"I'm serious." She nudged him.

"Hey, me too. It's like an evil mastermind convention in there."

"I bet they're dancing." Kira smiled wistfully, imagining some sort of orchestra playing a waltz while couples twirled along the dance floor. The vampires inside might be evil, but something told her the ball was all about fun, about remembering an older time all of the ancient vampires missed. Kira, at least, would not have been able to plot anything in those outfits. Ball gowns were for spinning around, not complacently sitting and talking.

"We could be dancing," Luke said after a moment.

Kira rolled her eyes. "Yeah, the sound of insects buzzing in the air really sets the mood."

"It's like music to my ears, especially that obnoxiously loud croaking noise behind us," he said while turning around. "What is that? It sounds like something is dying."

Kira listened for the sound, cringing at the wail when she finally heard it.

"So what now?" Luke asked. Kira shrugged. There wasn't really anything for them to do except wait for Tristan's sign, which could take who knew how long. "Well, if we're stuck here anyway," Luke continued, "there's sort of something I've been meaning to talk to you about."

Kira heard the quiver in his voice—the one that told her this was something heartfelt and not another joke. Kira shifted on the trunk, looking at him but putting more space between the two of them in the process.

He took a deep breath before he started talking, and the tingling sensation of nerves crept into Kira's mind. She forced it out, putting extra effort into blocking his thoughts and making sure he stayed out of her head. "First, I want to say sorry for the whole vomiting situation the other day."

"The one where you totally abused our friendship and made me feel physically ill with your thoughts?" Kira asked, knowing she was being a little petty in not accepting the apology outright. But he hadn't been acting very Luke-like recently. She wanted her carefree friend back.

"The one where I was insanely jealous and didn't handle it very well," he told her quietly, not taking his eyes off the ground. Kira forced herself to shut up so he could let whatever he was holding inside, out. "The truth is, I know I've been a little mean sometimes, but I told myself it was justified. You and Tristan were wrong for each other, and it was only a matter of time before you broke up. I was just doing my part to move the process along."

"But?" Kira said, making him continue.

"But, I realize now that it's something you need to see on your own."

"And why do you care so much?" Kira asked. They had avoided this conversation for so long, it was inevitable they would need to talk about it. Maybe in the woods, alone, waiting to charge a house full of powerful vampires wasn't the ideal time, but it was all the two of them had. There was no going back now.

"Because you're my best friend." He shrugged, still not looking at her. Kira watched him, watched as he finally met her gaze. His fiery eyes were so like her own, but she didn't recognize them now, not when they were so filled with hope and pain. "Because I'm in love with you," he finally said, letting the words float up and fill the empty space of the forest, making it feel both cramped and vast at the same time.

There it was. The six words that Kira had been dreading since graduation. The six words that could never be taken back. The six words that would change their friendship forever.

"I love you too," Kira said, hating the pity in her voice.

"But you're not in love with me," Luke finished the sentence for her, visibly deflated.

For some reason, she couldn't get the words *no, I'm not in love with you* out of her mouth. She tried, she wanted to give him the closure he needed, but her throat closed on the sounds, trapping them inside her body. Instead, Kira just quietly responded, "I don't know what you want me to say."

"Like I do?" Luke said with a snort. "I know you're with Tristan. I mean, hello, road trip third wheel talking."

He pointed at himself, and widening his eyes. "But I just thought you would see reason and you would break things off. I kept telling myself to just wait until graduation and then we'd be in Sonnyville together and everything would right itself."

"Luke," Kira said, shocked by the crack in her voice at seeing him so vulnerable. "I'm in love with Tristan. I mean, I'm only seventeen so I can't say it's forever, but it feels that way to me now. And I don't want you to waste your life waiting. I wouldn't wish that on anyone, let alone my best friend." She stretched out her hand, wanting to place it around his shoulder or across his back or even in his own hand, but she stilled herself in midair then let it drop. The inches between them on the damp fallen tree were too long to cross right now.

"But I will be waiting," he said and dropped his head into his hands, letting out a long ragged breath. He ran his fingers over his blond hair, flattening it to his head. "I," he started to say but then needed to swallow the breath that caught in his throat. "I have this feeling deep in my gut that even if I tell myself I've moved on and I start dating other people, a small part of me will still be waiting."

Screw it, Kira thought. She scooted over next to him and wrapped him in her arms. "You can't think like that."

"But you don't know, Kira," he whispered. "You don't know what it was like to wake up covered in blood with no memory of what happened and to see your best friend lying dead on the ground next to you. You don't know what it was like for me to see you so pale, to see you asleep and attached to machines for three months, to see what life would be like without you. That's when I realized I loved you, that we were so much more than best friends. Even if you were still in that hospital bed I would be there holding your hand, just waiting for you to open your eyes and wake up."

Kira really didn't know what to say, but she guessed sometimes that was the point. Sometimes people moved beyond words. She kept her mind closed, not wanting to read his tumultuous thoughts, but hugged him closer. It was strange to feel heat drain into her skin. Tristan's was normally cool, but when she pulled Luke close he was hot to the touch, just like Kira—always a few degrees warmer than everybody else.

What was she going to do? Now that everything had been said and let out into the open, she wouldn't be able to pretend. She wouldn't be able to ignore the moments when his desire leaked into her own mind. If she caught him looking at her and Tristan, she would know it was jealousy and not annoyance. When they were alone together, joking and laughing, it would always mean something else to him.

Kira knew she was being selfish, but she wouldn't be able to let him go. He was her rock, just like he had said before, and she needed him. But was it possible to need two people—to have two people she couldn't live without?

"Kira?" He moved away from her and sat up, but Kira didn't drop her arms. Instead, they moved with him, changing places from around his waist to over his shoulders. Luke looked at her arms around his neck and followed the trail back to her face. Shifting his gaze left and right, he tried to read her expression. Kira suddenly found herself not just looking but gazing into his heavily lidded eyes.

Realizing how close they were, Kira unlatched her hands and slowly pulled them away, but the more she retreated, the more her heart began to hurt. At first, it felt like a dull twinge, but as she rested her hands in her lap, it felt as though someone had taken a hammer to her chest.

Looking into his eyes, Kira couldn't deny that the pain she was feeling was purely her own. Was it the pain of knowing their friendship would never be the same? Or the pain of knowing that eventually she would lose him, that eventually he wouldn't be okay with second place? Or was it something deeper, an idea she had buried so far down in her heart that it needed to forcefully dig itself out?

Ever since she had met Tristan, she had thought of no one else and hadn't allowed her mind to even stray in that direction. And maybe it was only because Luke had finally admitted his feelings, but Kira couldn't lie to herself anymore. Here she was, staring deep into the fiery depths of Luke's soul, finally admitting that she couldn't survive without him. Finally admitting that when she saw him lying dead on the ground and risked her life to save his, there was far more than just friendship in her heart.

Inside the house, a light turned on, sending bright rays deep into the forest where Kira and Luke sat. The sudden spotlight filled the darkness, blinding them. Kira dropped her gaze, the spell broken, and rubbed her eyes.

"Ow," she said nervously.

"I think that's our signal," Luke said. He stared into her face for a moment, burning Kira with his gaze, before standing up. "We had better go."

Kira stood too, looking toward the house just in time to see a shadow pass through the light in the open window—Tristan, her boyfriend, the love of her life.

I need to stop spending so much time in the woods, Kira thought while shaking her head. The insects were getting to her brain.

She focused back on the mission. Tonight was not about deep conversations or professions of love, it was about payback. To Tristan and Luke, it was maybe about keeping her safe and keeping the people around her safe. But to Kira, this was sweet revenge. She wanted that battle with Diana, the one that should have happened months ago. And nothing, not even Luke, would distract her. Which was why Kira stopped paying attention to the dirt and the muck and the bugs and started paying attention to the house. What was going on inside of those walls was the only thing that mattered.

When Kira and Luke reached the edge of the forest,

they stopped to think of the best approach. Would a mad dash across the open field work best? Would going slowly make them less noticeable? The vampires in the ballroom could still see out of a few windows, might have even been able to spot Kira and Luke where they stood. But the two of them needed to get to the study, and the sooner the better.

"What are you thinking?" Luke asked. Kira eyed the distance. It couldn't be more than twenty yards.

"I say we make a run for it. And hey, it's not like that approach hasn't worked for us before," she said, thinking back to the airport. The run from the parking lot worked out perfectly fine and this one would too.

"Okay, you ready?"

Kira nodded. With his fingers, Luke counted down from three. As soon as his hand balled into a fist, Kira sprinted for the house, beelining to the open window. While she ran, her sneakers sank into the grass, creating divots with her toes.

Sliding in the mud to a halt, Kira slammed against the side of the house, smacking the wood, and Luke banged beside her a moment later. *Not my finest*, Kira thought and touched her temple to feel a slight bruise. That was when she realized that the first floor of the mansion was raised. Arching up, she saw that the window was two feet above her head and completely out of reach.

Luke scanned the tree line, making sure nothing had come out after them. Then, he knelt down and cupped his hands together. Understanding the move, Kira stepped one foot into the pocket he created and Luke lifted her up. She reached for the windowsill, clutching the opening with both hands and pulled herself in with a little help from Luke.

Grace had never really been one of her strong suits, and Kira rolled head first into the study. After a somersault and slight crash on the floor, she stood up and dusted herself off to make room for Luke, who easily slid through the window a minute later.

Nicely done, Kira thought, impressed by Luke's stealth. She was about to point it out to him, but before she could, someone else spoke.

"Well, well. Bronson really will let anything inside these days," a high-pitched voice laced with iron spoke from the other side of the room. Kira immediately flipped around.

On the far end of the study, sprawled out lengthwise along a mahogany desk and draped in pearly necklaces, was Diana.

Chapter Fourteen

Kira tried to still her beating heart, not wanting the vampires in the room to feel her nerves. She had been waiting for this moment for a long time. Tonight she would find out the truth about her mother, and tonight she would end Diana once and for all.

"What's a party without some crashers?" Luke said smoothly. He walked past Kira to stand next to Tristan. Both boys leaned casually against a tall bookshelf, but Kira saw the aggression in their eyes. They were alert as ever and ready to nab Diana if she tried to run.

For her part, Diana looked completely at ease. She wore a long, midnight blue shift dress that fit snugly against her body, leaving very little to anyone's imagination. Strings and strings of pearls dangled from her neck and a feathered headpiece decorated her hair, clipped to keep the long black strands from falling over her face. Mostly, Kira took in her attitude. Diana exuded arrogance and smugness, like everything was going her way rather than the other way around. Even the manner in which she reclined over the desk suggested she was in control. And all Kira wanted to do was wipe the smirk from her face.

So she got right down to business—no witty comments and no games. Kira stretched out her hand, sending a wave of Protector flames at Diana. Immediately the vampire catapulted off the desk and slammed against the wall, cracking the painting that had been hanging there. Kira walked slowly across the room, not letting up until her thighs hit the curved edge of the desk.

Finally, she dropped her powers and let Diana crash to the floor. "Where is my mother?"

Diana stood slowly, smiling as if nothing had happened. But Kira saw the angry flash in her eyes, how the blue of her irises lit up for a moment.

"Oh, Kira." Diana sighed. "You got a little bit of training and now you think you're my worst nightmare. Well, don't get too full of yourself, sweetie, because tonight I am untouchable."

"If I were you, I would listen to my own advice. You have no idea what I'm capable of, Diana." *No one does*, Kira thought, remembering the pages she had read. No one in the world, not even Kira herself, knew what she was capable of. Diana may have Punisher blood running through her veins, but that was not the same as being invincible.

233

"Yes, well, whatever you say," Diana smiled sweetly at Kira, looking down on her like a child before turning her gaze to Luke. "You look wonderful for a corpse, Luke. Didn't I kill you months ago?"

"People just can't seem to stay dead anymore, can they? It's an epidemic," Luke replied with a nonchalant shrug.

"I have always liked a challenge," Diana said while twirling her beads around her pointer fingers.

"Drop the attitude, Diana, and tell us what we want to know," Tristan said. "It is three against one if you can't see that already."

"And what? We can do this the easy way or the hard way?" Diana said, laughing. Tristan crossed his arms and raised his eyebrows, responding to the challenge. It was Diana's choice how all of this went down.

"Do I need to throw you against another wall?" Kira asked while placing her palms on the desk and leaning over in an attempt at intimidation. "Tell us what we want to know—where is my mother?"

"I'd rather not say."

In the blink of an eye, Tristan had grabbed Diana by the throat and lifted her against the wall.

"Spit it out, Diana," he yelled. He squeezed her throat tighter. At first, Diana pulled against his hands and kicked at him, struggling against his grip. But the tighter he squeezed, the stiller she went, until his fingers dug deep into her body, ready to rip her head off. Just as Kira was about to speak out and tell him to stop, tell him that they needed Diana alive, Tristan dropped her.

From the floor, Diana breathed heavily and looked up at Tristan. She stood, still looking him in the eye, and ran her hand up the length of his arm. "I love it when you play rough," she whispered, loud enough for everyone to hear and soft enough to come off as sensual.

Tristan shirked her hold and stepped back, blinking away the lethal look in his eyes. Kira clearly wasn't the only one who wanted Diana to pay.

"What is it going to take for you to tell me more about my mother," Kira asked and ignored the lusty look Diana was throwing in Tristan's direction. They didn't have time for all of this. A group of immensely powerful vampires was in the room next door and they could bust in at any moment. All it would take was for one of them to notice that Diana and Tristan had disappeared, for one of them to go searching, and then the jig would be up. She needed answers now, and all three of them needed to move fast if the conduits in the woods were going to have any shot at a surprise attack.

"The only thing I want is to ruin your life," Diana said. Kira rolled her eyes.

"Yes, I got that from all of the vampires you've been sending my way and by the fact that you tried to kill me. Is there anything else you want?" Kira hated this, she wanted to burn the answers out of Diana, but Diana was immune to those flames. Her Protector powers wouldn't be enough. Tristan had told her one time about how different the two flames felt. Punisher fire, he had said, burned him to his very core, lighting his body up like a bomb about to explode. Protector powers felt different though, less painful and more solid. Rather than burning a vampire, they acted like a wall pushing the vampire away—weakening but not lethal.

If her flames weren't burning Diana from the inside out, they wouldn't be effective in getting answers. All three of them had been naive to think that Diana would just give everything up without a fight. And a physical battle wouldn't accomplish anything right now. Well, Kira thought, throwing Diana against a wall again would make her laugh...but no. Kira stilled her hand in midair. She just had to play whatever game Diana wanted to for the time being.

Diana sat down in the desk chair, lifting one leg over the other and folding her hands in her lap. Kira's stance over the desk hadn't affected Diana at all. She was the picture of ease. "I want to play a game."

"Darn," Luke said with a smile. "I knew I should have brought Monopoly with me."

"A game?" Kira asked, ignoring Luke. She did not like where this was headed. Why wasn't Diana a little more afraid? Sure, she knew they wouldn't kill her right away, not until she told them what Kira wanted to hear, but the girl didn't even look frightened at all. It was like she knew they couldn't touch her.

"How about a game of truth or dare? Girl to girl? I'm sure the boys wouldn't mind."

Kira looked across the room at Luke and Tristan where they stood next to each other, backed by the wall of old books. Each boy was just as confused as Kira was. What was Diana's angle? Tristan nodded at her, telling her to go with it for now.

"Fine," Kira said, sitting down across from Diana in an armchair next to the desk.

"Excellent," Diana said. "I'll go first. Truth or dare?"

"Truth," Kira said. No reason to let Diana dare her to bust into the other room or something. And it wasn't like she had anything to hide.

Diana let her gaze rest on the two boys, each one staring intently at Kira. With a smirk and a cocked brow, Diana asked, "Have you ever lied to Tristan?"

"No, of course not," she said immediately. But her body betrayed her. A rush of blood filled Kira's cheeks, warming them to a slight blush. A jolt in her heart brought a hammering sound to her ears. And, from the corner of her eye, she watched Tristan shift his weight from one foot to the other. He knew she had lied.

"Spare me, Kira, I know you're lying right now," Diana said lightly. She lifted her hands, wove her fingers together, and rested her elbows on the desk. "If you're not going to play by the rules..."

"Fine." Kira shifted in her seat, totally uncomfortable by the change of events. "Yes, I have lied to Tristan. Well, not so much lied as hidden parts of the truth."

"I've been alive for hundreds of years, Kira, and that distinction still feels old to me. Care to share with us all?" She rested her head on her hand, staring at Kira with an innocent yet almost cunning expression. Her eyes were open like a child's, but her smile was razor thin. "I mean we're all friends here, aren't we?"

Kira really wanted to slap Diana in the face—no, not slap, punch her so hard she doubled over. But instead, she looked at Tristan and played along with Diana's game. He looked so handsome in his tuxedo, but so sad. This wasn't how it was supposed to happen. This wasn't how he should find out about Luke's connection with her or their almost-kiss. And, Kira suddenly realized, there was no reason he had to find out now. She had another lie, something she had hidden from both boys and had been meaning to spill. She took a deep breath and fixed her eyes on them

"There's something I haven't told either of you, something that I found out about myself." She paused to meet their eyes. Tristan's held concern and confusion. Luke's confusion and a hint of anger, letting Kira know he had been hoping she would spill the other secret. "I found the missing pages. Well, actually my grandfather gave me a copy, but I found out that the immunity isn't really the reason mixed breed conduits have been forbidden." Kira gulped when Diana leaned forward in her chair, listening intently to this secret piece of otherwise lost information. "Ancient conduits used to be uncontrollable and dangerous. They used to kill more than just vampires. In moments of madness, they burned human beings too. And that's the real reason the species separated, to keep from ever having to sentence one of their own to death."

She gulped and raised her eyes back up, meeting Luke's first. It would hit him harder because he understood better than anyone else what she meant. All of those times he had pulled her back from insanity had much stronger implications now. And he knew it too. Kira saw the realization pass over his features—curious tilted head, to furrowed confused brows, to wide shocked eyes, to a hard and knowing frown.

Tristan on the other hand looked relieved in a way, which Kira found darkly humorous. If anything, this realization only brought them closer together and made them more similar. The worse her fate got, the more he could be there for her in a way Luke couldn't. Or maybe he was relieved because he, like Diana, judging by her shocked face, was expecting a different confession. And Diana was clearly disappointed. She had obviously been hoping to create a rift between Kira and Tristan, but the fact that her plan had backfired only made Kira feel better.

Kira did make a quick mental note to be more

truthful. Not that she ever thought she would find herself playing truth or dare with a vampire ever again, but being a pathological liar wasn't exactly on the to-do list.

"My turn," Kira said, this time crossing her legs and looking snidely at Diana. "Truth or truth? I don't do dares."

"Truth then, Kira."

"Where is my mother?"

"I don't know," Diana said with a shrug. Kira stood, struggling to keep the power gathering in her body at bay.

"What do you mean you don't know?" she fumed.

"I don't know where she is." Diana smiled. "I only know who has her. But, those are two very different questions, and it's not my fault you wasted your turn."

"Tell me," Kira yelled, not caring anymore. She was done with this, done playing games and done with Diana.

Diana leaned back in the leather chair, chuckling quietly to herself and smiling at how visibly angry Kira was. Her teeth had elongated during her mirth, making her look more evil and more deranged.

"I'll tell you something, Kira. You are a fool. All three of you are fools," Diana said, twirling her black hair absently through her fingers as if bored. "Do you really think we didn't know you were coming?" Diana's gazed traveled sidelong to Tristan. "As soon as you showed up on Bronson's doorstep, I knew Kira was with you. I knew you wouldn't be able to resist dropping in uninvited. And I knew you would be idiotic enough to think you had gotten the best of me. But," she said while rising, letting the long train of her gown cover the floor behind her, "one scream is all it takes for me to have the entire party in this room. And you know how fast vampires can be."

Diana raced forward, reaching for Kira's throat before she could register the movement, but Tristan got there first. He caught Diana's hand in midair, easily keeping her at bay.

"Who else knows we're here?" he asked in a menacing deep voice.

"I told Bronson my suspicions," Diana said, finally a little afraid. Even if Kira couldn't kill her, Tristan could and the look in his eye was deadly.

"And why here? Why this ball?" he questioned.

"There was someone I've been meaning to find and I thought I'd find him here. An old friend I've lost touch with." Diana smirked.

"Who?" Kira asked, not liking the dark look slowly gathering in Tristan's eyes.

"Oh, Tristan, you finally understand," Diana said and patted his cheek with her free hand while slipping out of his now loose hold.

"Is he here?" Tristan asked. He still had not moved.

"Of course, Tristan. He's been here for hours, enough time for us to catch up and chat. You must have missed him outside." She pouted for effect.

Tristan finally moved. He grabbed Kira's arm, lifting

her easily into his arms as he flew toward the open window. Diana blocked the exit, and for a second, Kira thought he was going to bowl her over, but Kira still had questions and she didn't intend to leave without answers, no matter what Tristan wanted.

"Tristan!" she said while struggling to break free of his hold. "I'm not leaving without answers."

"But," Tristan started and she cut him off.

"No!" she shouted, tired of all of this. The two boys might have been doing this whole mortal enemies thing longer than her, but they weren't the only ones who could make plans. They weren't the only ones who had a say in what happened. She forced herself out of Tristan's hold and stepped closer to Diana. "Tell me who is here and what you know and who has my mother."

"Or what?" Diana challenged back while looking down her nose at Kira with an obviously superior expression.

And with that, Kira broke. All of the stress she had been carrying for the past few weeks released like a floodgate—Luke for trying to kiss her and awakening those feelings inside of her, her grandfather for not welcoming her with open arms, Tristan for picking the wrong time to be macho, Diana for being Diana, and the historians for writing down truths about herself she didn't want to hear.

Her rage flew out in the form of flames, blasting Diana's skin. Diana laughed at the slight pain.

"I told you before, I'm immune." She smiled, but she couldn't move from the corner that Kira's Protector powers had pressed her into.

And Kira? She ignored Diana. Her powers pushed her beyond words. But Kira sensed a difference this time. She was focused and controlled, she wasn't mad. She knew exactly what she was doing and for the first time, she was perfectly content with her desire to kill. Diana had to die and if it took all of her strength, Kira would find a way to make it happen.

She pushed out her Punisher fire, feeling for the walls around Diana that kept her protected. Every vein in Diana's body was covered in an invisible shell, some sort of magic Kira couldn't break through. She felt along Diana's body with her powers, searching for a weakness, but there wasn't one. She encased her heart in flames, trying to dry it out, but nothing would stick. The fire rolled around Diana. It slipped past her, unable to find anything to hold on to.

Diana still sat crumbled in the corner, grinning at Kira's failed attempts.

But she didn't realize that Kira was reaching that point, that place where she started to shut her powers off out of fear that she would never return to herself. Kira wasn't afraid this time.

Two images flashed through her mind, one of Tristan bloodied and broken being forced to swallow her blood and a second of Luke ashen and lying immobile on the ground.

Like a broken film reel, the two images flashed in her mind, one to the other, back and forth until Kira couldn't tell what she was seeing. She could only remember the excruciating pain of her heart ripping from her chest in each moment.

She funneled the pain into her flames and rode on her emotions, no longer searching for a weakness and instead throwing everything she had into her power. She was too focused on killing Diana to feel the walls around her powers come down. All she felt was the extra burst of energy, the new scars burning into her palms as power forced its way out.

Distantly in her mind, Kira heard Luke call her name, but she shut him out. He wasn't going to stop her this time. She didn't need saving. She wasn't falling into madness—she was walking there willingly.

And that's when Diana stopped laughing.

They both felt it—the immunity waned. The invisible wall wobbled against Kira's flames. The heat warped whatever magic was there and melted it away. And then, as if Kira were watching a movie in her head, a crack formed in the shell encasing Diana's heart.

"Stop! I'll tell you everything," Diana cried, trying to stand, but unable to move even a muscle. "Kira! It's Aldrich. He has your mother. He's here. You can go find him." She screamed with tears forming in her eyes. "He's had her for years. I saw her with him ten years ago. She's alive!"

But it was too late. Kira was beyond stopping and her

flames unrelentingly continued.

"She's with Aldrich! Aldrich!" Diana yelled and those were her last words, because the wall shattered like glass and Kira's fire greedily swallowed Diana whole.

When it was done, Kira's mind snapped back into focus. She had accomplished her goal, and it was time stop. Forcefully, she shut her powers off and pulled all of the flames back into her body.

When the black spots receded and she regained her vision, Kira noticed that scorch marks traveled up the walls and across the ceiling. The curtains were burned apart. Giant holes, black around the edges, spotted the fabric. A pile of dust sat in the corner, a mix of Diana's ashes and burnt paper.

Kira swallowed. She had done it. She had broken through. She had killed Diana, but at what price? Her fire had touched more than the vampire; it had burned more than Diana's skin. Kira had willingly stepped right into the destiny she never wanted.

She stumbled back, off balance by the realization that the ancient conduits had been right. She was dangerous. The thought pierced her like an arrow sinking deep into her chest and she spun around, needing Tristan or Luke to say something, to make her feel like this darkness suddenly sprouting inside her, wrapping around her like a vine and suffocating her, would go away.

But there was no solace in the scene behind her.

When she looked up for comfort, both boys instead jumped away in fear.

Fear of me? Kira thought, confused. She looked down at her hands, expecting to see starbursts on her palms, but instead there were burns up to her wrists. And not just redness, but raised boils like a mountain range on her hand. Strange that it didn't hurt, she thought. Still, Kira lightly touched her healing powers and watched as the burns faded to a dull pink and then disappeared altogether. She twisted her hands, stretching sore muscles.

Again, she looked up at Luke and Tristan. They cringed with wide eyes.

"What?" Kira tried to say. It came out as less than a whisper. Her throat ached from the effort. "What?" she said more forcefully, slowly pulling her body back together. She used her own strength to force the black doubts clouding her mind away.

"Your eyes, Kira," Luke said, walking toward her.

"They're blue," Tristan finished the thought.

"What?" she asked, still groggy and confused, not yet fully recovered from using her powers. Had she heard them wrong?

Tristan reached her first and put his hands on her cheeks.

"Your eyes are blue," he said while staring into them, searching for something. *Searching for me*, Kira realized. But he recovered from the shock, and he still gazed at her with love sparkling in his eyes. It helped ground her, helped pull her mind back to reality.

"How is that possible?" she said, feeling more like herself with each passing second.

"I don't know." Tristan dropped her face, letting Kira look behind him at her best friend.

But Luke wouldn't come any closer. Tears welled in Kira's eyes, and she reached her hand out to him. She couldn't stand the look on his face, the one that regarded her as a stranger.

"Luke?" she asked, her voice cracking. They looked at one another in a standoff—Luke finally realizing Kira was sometimes beyond his saving, and Kira finally realizing what it felt like to lose his love even if only for an instant.

Like they always do, the moment passed. Luke stepped over, offering her a hug, stiff but still a hug. Kira returned it, holding him tight against her body.

"Just don't turn into a smurf on me, okay?" he whispered into her hair. Kira laughed into his shoulder. Everything was going to be fine.

And then the door behind them burst open.

Kira, Tristan, and Luke turned around instantly.

Two vampires stood in the massive wooden doorway. Kira recognized Bronson from the other day in the park. His crooked nose gave him away, but the man next to him was a mystery. His light-brown hair was slicked back. His eyes were such a dark blue that they seemed all together black. He was tall and thin, making the shorter Bronson look stocky, and each man had on elegant tuxedos. But while Bronson searched the room, his eyes darting in circles, the other man looked only at Kira.

Tristan jumped in front of her, blocking her view of everything but the curve of his back, and he held her there with his arm.

"Aldrich," he sneered.

"My dear Tristan," Aldrich said warmly, "it's been far too long."

"Where's Diana?" Bronson interrupted in a deep voice.

"If you mean the pile of ash formerly known as Diana, she's in the corner," Luke said, moving to stand next to Tristan, effectively blocking Kira completely.

"Pity," Aldrich said, but Kira heard no remorse in the words.

"How is that possible?" Bronson asked with a quiver in his voice. "I gave her the blood myself."

Kira put a hand on either boy. She pushed Luke and Tristan to the side as if they were curtains. Feeding off of the dramatic effect, Kira said, "I killed her. And I will kill you both if you don't tell me where my mother is."

Aldrich stepped forward and walked up to Kira, who held Tristan and Luke at bay. He cupped her chin, tilting her head back so he could look at her eyes.

"Marvelous," he said with a grin, as if he had been

expecting them to be blue.

"My mother?" Kira asked.

"Safe and sound," he said.

"I seriously doubt that." Kira slapped his hand from her chin.

"I'm not keeping her prisoner, Kira."

"You're lying," Kira said. She couldn't help it, the obstinate words popped out unwittingly. She wouldn't believe his lies, even if something in his voice sounded strangely sincere.

"Spoken like the child you aren't," he chided her.

Before Kira could think up a snappy retort, another vampire suddenly appeared next to Aldrich, jerking him away from Kira. She recognized the blonde in the pink high heels, the first vampire she saw enter the party.

"We have to leave," the woman said urgently while yanking him away. Aldrich pushed her aside, throwing her against the books on the wall. Bronson just watched it happen, uncaring.

"You step above yourself, Clarissa. You may have finally landed an invitation to the Red Rose Ball, but you do not order me around."

"I'm sorry," she murmured. "It's just that—"

And then the windows shattered, throwing glass everywhere. Flames rolled past Kira and Luke, smacking into all four vampires and sending them flying.

Chapter Fifteen

Kira spun just in time to see three Protectors soar through the windows to land neatly on their feet, never once waning in their powers. Like a swat team, they had come sailing in from the roof, using rope to catapult themselves through the old and easily breakable windows. Kira wanted to look at Luke and roll her eyes—he watched far too many movies. It was so obviously his genius plan for them to come storming inside rather than take a stealth approach.

Unfortunately, there was no time to make fun of Luke because one of those vampires stuck like a bug against the wall was Tristan. And Aldrich, closest to the hallway, was slowly inching past the conduit flames to slip away.

Kira grabbed Luke's hand.

"You need to stop them!" she shouted.

"What? We need to nail these guys," Luke said, bewildered.

Kira looked around. All three of the blond men who had come flying inside were determined. Sweat dropped down their faces, but none of them moved or let their powers weaken.

"What are they going to do?" Kira had never seen a conduit mission in action before. It was a lot more intense than she realized. One man reached into his belt to pull out a long curved knife. "Luke!"

"It's fine," he tried to calm her, but it wasn't easy when her boyfriend was easy prey and flames were still roaring all around them. "We have to drain their blood. It'll weaken them enough for us to interrogate them. We need to find out where they're keeping their Punishers."

"But Tristan!" Kira pointed at the wall. All of the vampires were slowly slinking away, as if the flames were causing them to move in slow motion. Aldrich, Kira realized, already had half of his body out the door. The conduits went to work. The Protector with the knife moved to the woman first and cut her wrist open, sending splatters of blood down the wall and to the floor. The other two conduits controlled their powers, each with one hand focused on a single vampire.

"Luke, you have to help him," Kira said, pushing him toward Tristan. He wasn't supposed to be caught up in this. Typical Tristan, she thought, he hadn't wanted to take too much of her blood so he had lost the immunity before he was supposed to. She thought the feeding had gone by rather quickly. He had only taken enough to be immune to the Punisher at the door, but not enough to stay that way. Quickly, she eyed Aldrich, her gaze torn between both vampires. "I have to go, but please, promise me you'll keep him safe."

Luke followed her gaze, seeing Aldrich about to sneak away, and nodded. He knew exactly what she was up to. "Just be careful, okay, Kira?"

She smiled and instinctively kissed his cheek before looking through the flames one more time. Both of the female vampire's wrists were sliced open and the conduit was moving to other areas as well. She was getting visibly paler, and she couldn't even move through the flames anymore. Tristan was next.

Kira met Tristan's gaze, smiling, and mouthed, "I love you" before chasing after Aldrich, who was, at that very moment, on the outskirts of the flames and disappearing through the door.

Kira pushed her way into the ballroom just in time to see Aldrich sneak around another set of conduits. There were maybe forty people in the gigantic room, but Kira tried to ignore the flames haphazardly dancing around her and vampires moaning in pain as the blood was drained from their veins. Broken shards of glass and trampled red roses covered the floor, mixing with the blood. Aldrich was already past the conduits, all too concentrated on their prey to notice him, and he pushed another set of wooden doors wide open. Kira dashed after him, trying not to slip on the blood.

She threw herself through the doors, only to have them shut loudly behind her.

Quickly, Kira stood up to face Aldrich as he bolted her one escape closed. She put her hands in front of her in warning.

"I don't want to hurt you, just tell me what you know about my mother."

"My, my, you are a determined little thing, aren't you?" he said while taking a seat. Looking around, Kira realized they had made their way into the formal dining room. A huge wooden table surrounded by wooden chairs with green silk cushions filled the space. A sweeping chandelier cast a soft glow around the room, lightly illuminating paintings of hunting scenes on the walls. "Please, join me." He motioned to the chair next to him.

"I would rather stand, thanks. Now, what did you mean when you said my mother wasn't trapped?"

"I see being with Tristan has given you a false sense of security around us," he said, ignoring Kira's question. "But when I tell you to sit, it is not a polite request." Suddenly, the chair shot out from the table behind Kira, slamming hard into her legs. Her knees buckled beneath her and she landed heavily on the padded cushion.

"What the?"

"Tristan," Aldrich said, cutting her off, "has the

perfect physical composition, which was why I chose him so long ago. But he lacks the mental authority one needs to become truly powerful. You, however," he said, grabbing Kira's chin again, "are different. I can feel the power churning inside of you. I have plans for you, very big plans."

Kira let a flame rise on her palm as she grabbed his hand from her chin. "Do not touch me," she said, feeling the burn seep into his skin.

He laughed, the excited mirth of a boy with a new toy. "Oh, I understand now why Tristan has been following you around like a little puppy. You're so exciting," he said while slipping free of her hold. "Nothing like the girls I used to bring him. They were weak and terrified. I should have known he would want a challenge."

"Stop talking about Tristan like you know him," Kira said while crossing her arms and trying not to picture these kidnapped girls. "It's not like that."

"Oh, but it is, with a vampire it always is. You'll see."

Frustrated, Kira released her power on him, trying to break through his shield like she did with Diana. She needed to intimidate him.

Instead, a bowl knocked against her hands, banging them to the side so her power went harmlessly flying toward an empty wall. Shocked, Kira stopped.

"Yes, before you ask, my vampiric abilities came not in the way of force like your Tristan, but in mental power. Try burning me again and I will send something larger at your head." There was no anger or frustration or remorse in his tone. His voice was like steel, cold and unemotional, and it sent a shiver down Kira's back. For the first time in a long time, she felt very afraid to be facing a vampire, especially on her own.

"Now, where were we?" Aldrich ran a hand over the top of his head, smoothing his hair back while he took a moment to think. "Oh yes, your mother. I'm sure she would love to see you. I—"

"Where are you keeping her?" Kira interrupted, trying to find the strength to stand up to him. He flashed annoyed eyes in her direction, and the chandelier above her head began to wobble, chiming as the pieces of glass clinked together.

"This conversation grows tiring. She lives with me—"

A loud bang on the door stopped him mid-sentence.

"Aldrich!"

Kira heard a pained scream from the other side of the door. It took a second to realize the mangled voice belonged to Tristan.

Another boom reverberated along the walls as Tristan slammed into the door again, making the entire room shake with his strength. Kira looked at Aldrich. He sat calmly in his chair, not bothered by Tristan in the slightest.

"He tried to leave me once, maybe a year after I turned him," Aldrich said, turning to Kira conversationally and ignoring the yells beyond the door. "He banged and banged on the door until even his vampiric skin was breaking open and bloody, not an easy feat I assure you. But he always forgets that physical strength is the weakest kind. With my mind holding the door shut, he will never break through."

"Why'd you let him go then?" Kira asked, intrigued despite her fear.

"A moment of weakness I regretted for a long time," he said. Kira almost believed the honesty in his words.

A loud crack caught her attention, and she eyed the door in time to see a huge fissure splinter the wood. Another bang and scraps flew off, landing against the floor and leaving a hole in the door.

Through it, Kira could see Tristan back up and prepare for another charge. He looked beyond coherent thought, with tears streaming down his face and his muscles bulging.

"Well, it seems he has gained a little more mental control in the hundred years since I've seen him." Aldrich's voice was one of happy surprise. Kira thought he even sounded proud for a moment. "It seems I must bid you farewell."

He picked up Kira's hand and lifted it to his lips. Though she was afraid, Kira kept her powers inside. She didn't want to test Aldrich, and she had the oddest sensation that he really didn't want to hurt her, that if he wanted to hurt her she would already be dead. He had other plans in mind—big plans like he said before, something far worse than killing her. Kira forced herself not to pull her hand from his grip as fear crept further into her mind.

In the same instant that his mouth brushed against her skin, the door behind Kira flew off of its hinges.

"Aldrich!" Tristan bellowed, but Aldrich was gone. He disappeared out the window and into the night.

Tristan ran to Kira and embraced her, pulling her hard against his body. Kira hugged him back, throwing her arms over his shoulders. It was only after her hands met at the base of his neck that she realized there was a small paper stuck to her palm.

"Are you okay? Are you hurt?" He pulled her back and examined her face.

"No. I'm fine. I promise. We were just talking," Kira said. Quickly, she stuck her hand in her back pocket, dropping the little paper there for later. Curiosity was almost killing her. She needed to know what Aldrich had written.

"Come on." Tristan tugged on her hand. "Luke is meeting us outside. They're going to blow the house apart, we need to leave now." Kira let him pull her along until they reached the window.

The note would have to wait until she had time alone. No matter what it was, neither Luke nor Tristan could be involved, at least not yet. Kira knew exactly how powerful Aldrich was and if she couldn't handle him, then neither could they. She still wanted to find her mother, but if this night had taught her anything, it was that sometimes patience was a virtue. Not one Kira currently possessed, but one she needed to work on.

Tristan slid through the window first, preparing to catch her. But right when Kira lifted her foot to step over the windowsill, her eyes caught a strip of metal that reflected her image back at her.

Stunned, Kira tripped over her own foot and fell against the wooden floor. She looked around for a mirror and saw a large metal plate hanging on the wall. She ran over, ripping it from the wall and holding it before her face.

The boys had said her eyes were blue, but Kira still wasn't prepared for what she saw. Whereas before her eyes had been a rusty orange in the center, leaking into a deep olive green with flecks of yellow, they were now bright blue. Not a turquoise or aqua or navy, but a bright cobalt blue that alarmed her.

The perfect royal blue started at her pupils, extending to almost the edge of her iris where a small ring of red-yellow waves pushed their way in. Those looked like her flames, fighting and struggling to stay with her, reminding her of her fight and her power. But now she didn't recognize anything else or any part of her when she looked in the mirror. Her new eyes changed the entire look of her face, and she didn't like it.

Blue was for vampires. It was a color without heat and without spark. Despite the saturated hue, there was no life. Blue was the color of death. It was the pale gray that crept along the body as blood slowly stopped pumping, the color of frost as it covered a forest floor and stopped life in its tracks.

More than anything, Kira wondered what it meant. What had happened to her in there that had so fundamentally changed who she was? She didn't feel different, not really.

"Kira!" Tristan yelled from out the window. She dropped the plate, suddenly jolted back to reality. But before walking to the window, Kira couldn't resist pulling the note from her pocket. Slowly, she unrolled the crinkled paper. In elegant, loopy script were the words, "If you want to see your mother, visit my castle any time. Kindly bring Tristan along." Written below was an address in England.

Kira let her back fall against the wall while she thought. Of course she would go. She had to now. Her mother would never be living there willingly, not with someone so evil. Something else was going on, Kira had to believe it.

And maybe it was a trap. Maybe Aldrich did have plans for her like he had said, but what kind of person would she be if she didn't go? Just because she feared him didn't mean she wouldn't fight him.

Maybe something had changed within her—maybe something had awakened inside of her. Regardless, Kira knew one thing—no more playing by other people's rules.

She had gone to Sonnyville because of the council. She was stuck in that hotel room for a week because of Luke and Tristan. She had been playing referee between them and trying to keep everyone from being hurt. But now, Kira was going to do what she wanted when she wanted to, and there would be no stopping her.

If her destiny was to turn into a mindless killing machine, there was only one way she could think to stop it—to do what she felt was right instead of driving herself insane trying to please other people.

"Kira? What's wrong?" Tristan asked again and jumped back up, poking his head through the window.

"Nothing," Kira said and stuffed the note back in her shorts. Nothing at all was wrong. For tonight, everyone was safe and she had gotten exactly what she wanted. Diana was dead and her mother was alive.

Everything was exactly as it should be, which was why Kira felt perfectly comfortable diving out the open window. She knew Tristan was there to catch her. In his arms, Kira felt safe, and he carried her away from the house, only putting her down when they reached the edge of the forest. Kira peered through the branches and searched for the tree she had sat on before.

When she found it, Luke was there waiting for them both. She sat down next to him and Tristan sat down beside her, sandwiching Kira between them.

"Are you okay?" Luke asked without moving.

"I'm alive, aren't I?"

"That doesn't necessarily mean you're okay though."

"I am." Kira sighed and tried to decide how much to tell them both. "Aldrich never tried to hurt me, he really just wanted to talk—about Tristan mostly but also about my mother."

"You can't believe a word he says, Kira, you can't trust him," Tristan urged.

"I know. He's gone anyway," she said. "Aldrich vanished and any hope of finding my mother went with him."

Kira stuck her hand in her pocket to feel the slip of paper hidden there, thinking of the address he had written. She might not be able to trust Aldrich, but she did believe that he had her mother. The look in Diana's eyes at the end when she confessed, when she was terrified to die and begging for her life, that was what told Kira it was the truth. She would never forget Diana's haunted expression—staring death in the face and knowing it was too late to stop its approach. Kira could read in her eyes that Diana knew it was her own fault, that if she had told the truth Kira probably wouldn't have been able to gather the strength to kill her. Aldrich was too smooth and too controlled to believe, but Diana in those last minutes had been completely truthful.

Kira fingered the note again and decided to keep quiet. The boys hadn't seen what she had seen. It would take time for them to understand.

"How's it going in there?" Kira finally asked, realizing that all three of them were just staring straight ahead at the mansion. The windows were broken and glowing orange from the conduit flames.

"We got about half of them, maybe fifteen vampires, definitely more than I expected. They're draining the blood right now, weakening all the vampires so we can transport them to an interrogation house. And then," Luke said with a wide smile, "we're blowing the place apart!"

Kira laughed at his enthusiasm. "The grand entrance was your idea too, right?"

"That was pretty legit, you have to admit. Breaking through the windows with flames a-flying—couldn't have planned it any better."

"As one of the people thrown up against a wall, I beg to differ," Tristan said from her other side.

"But the timing was perfect, you have to admit," Kira said, giving Luke his victory.

"I know," Luke said with mounting excitement. He started talking even faster, letting his hand gestures grow slightly wild. "That blonde woman came in to warn them and Aldrich was like, 'don't interrupt me you insignificant fool', and she was like, 'but but', and then the conduits bust in like, 'too late—you're all fools!'"

"And the look on Bronson's face…" Kira giggled, unable to continue talking.

"No, Aldrich, he was the best. I swear he looked like a little kid playing with a jack-in-the-box for the first time—totally shocked and freaked out. It was great!"

"But Bronson," Kira challenged, "he was so confused. I swear he was looking around like a fish out of water, like 'conduits are not supposed to be here, they weren't invited.'"

"I think it's safe to say he'll never be hosting a red or white rose ball again," Tristan added.

"Yeah, well let's hope no one will," Kira said, instantly feeling a little sorry for bringing the mood back down.

"It's inevitable, though. Conduits and vampires have been fighting for thousands of years. I don't know what would ever stop it." Tristan shrugged.

Us? Kira asked silently, letting herself believe it could be true for a moment.

The fire in the mansion died down, and in the moonlight Kira saw conduits carrying the lifeless bodies of drained vampires out the windows.

"Won't be long now," Luke said quietly.

"And why again are we blowing up the house?" Kira asked.

"Because Luke is a pyromaniac," Tristan responded with a grin.

"While that is totally true," Luke said, also smiling, "it's just standard procedure, at least I think. This way the vampire has to start over. They have no home or supplies to go back to."

At the word *home*, Kira sighed and thought of her family in Charleston. When she got back she would make pancakes. Chloe, Kira imagined, would come running into the kitchen because of the aroma. Then Kira would turn on the coffee machine, easing her parents awake and dragging them out of bed to a fresh cooked meal and caffeine. Just a normal Sunday morning for the Dawson household, something that hadn't happened for a while and something Kira desperately missed.

"I can't wait to get home. All I want is a huge bowl of ice cream, a whole pint maybe. Sweet, creamy Ben and Jerry's Super Chocolate Chunk," Kira said, salivating at the thought.

"You're such a girl," Luke chided and leaned back on his palms, thinking of his own family. "I just want a home-cooked meal, some of my mother's warm and delicious beef stew. Real meat for a real man."

"Oh god," Kira said and rolled her eyes. She turned to Tristan, waiting for him to add something before realizing why he remained silent. He was alone in the world except for Kira. He didn't have anyone or anything to go home to.

"Look," he said instead and motioned to the two last conduits coming out of the house.

They ran under the cover of night to the edge of the forest, a few feet in front of Kira, Luke, and Tristan. One of the conduits pulled out the remote trigger and pressed a button.

After a few completely silent seconds, as if the entire forest were holding its breath, a corner of the house exploded, engulfing the entire building in flames and sending broken pieces everywhere.

Kira watched the wild movements of the flames, felt the wave of heat hit her face, and heard the crackling and crashing of wood as the uncontrollable fire consumed it. The power inside of her responded, gathering in her heart and warming her insides as if the two fires were friends trying to reconnect. Her powers ached to be released, ached to join in on the chaos before her, but she squelched it. Was she like the fire in front of her? Wild and uncontrolled?

But the more she looked at the undulating flames, swishing back and forth and lighting the night sky, the more she saw the beauty in it, like the brilliant golden hues of the flames and the soft glow permeating the yard.

Something had undoubtedly changed in her this night. Like a switch flipped to the on position, her power churned inside of her. But Kira didn't fear it. Killing Diana and breaking through the immunity had given her a taste of her real potential. The hot smoldering burn of her power was a comfort. She didn't fear her strength. There was a purpose for it, something more than all of the killing. She just wasn't sure what that was yet.

And, even though a little voice in the back of her head told her that it was a bad idea, Kira knew Aldrich held the answers. Her gut told her going to his home would solve all of her problems. Finding her mother wasn't the end goal anymore, finding the truth about herself was.

"Hotel?" Luke asked when the fire died down to smoke, and the house was charred beyond recognition.

"Hotel." Kira nodded.

"Hotel," Tristan agreed.

All three of them stood at the same time as though tied together with a string. And maybe they were, Kira thought—maybe they were tied together for some inexplicable reason. She watched the last spark of the fire, saw embers drift through the smoke like fireflies, and waited for one of the boys to make a move.

Luke reached out his hand, tanned and freckled, inviting her to follow him.

On her other side, Tristan reached out his smooth white palm, asking her to move with him.

Kira stared for a moment, looking at the choice before her, small and unimportant, but at the same time symbolic of so much more. She was stuck. Something that had seemed so obvious a choice only days before was somehow difficult now. It was almost as if she were two different people. And like she was cut in half, Kira's hands acted on their own, each taking hold of the hand before them.

On one side, she grasped a hand that was cool and comfortable, a hand she had held a thousand times before, one that enveloped hers and made her feel safe.

On the other side, she gripped a hand that was warm and welcoming, a hand she had held before but never in that way, never with excitement and a twinge of the unknown.

The night may have awakened more than just her powers, Kira realized. She was taking charge of her life. She wouldn't wait for the boys to come up with a plan. For the first time, she stepped forward and pulled both of them behind her, forcing them to follow her lead.

And at that moment, walking through the smoke-filled forest, all Kira wanted to think about was a hot shower and a warm bed—no boys, no conduits, no parents, and no vampires. Just one night to herself, completely free of worry, because the fire inside her was heating up and, like that house, Kira knew she was about to explode.

**Blaze (Midnight Fire Book Three)
is available now!**

Keep reading for a preview of the first chapter!

"Kira gulped, unable to stop the growing sense that everything in her world was about to change."

With Aldrich's note burning a hole in her pocket, Kira is off to England to finally reunite with her birth mother. But what begins as a dream quickly turns to a nightmare, and Kira is left questioning everything she has ever known. Can she be the conduit Luke wants her to be? Can she be the rebel Tristan needs her to be? Or is she something else? Something no one, not even Aldrich, ever saw coming...

Chapter One

Kira ripped another page from her notebook and crumpled the thick paper between her fingers. Frustrated, she threw the ball into her wastebasket.

Quite the collection, she mused as she glanced down at the paper pyramid by her feet. Kira had been sitting at her desk for nearly an hour, but still the right words had eluded her. How could she explain it to Luke, her best friend and ever-faithful protector? No matter what, he would be angry. No matter what, he would feel betrayed. But it was the only way to keep him safe from Aldrich.

Kira sighed and leaned back in her chair, slowly swiveling it from side to side as she thought back a week and a half ago to the night of the Red Rose Ball. Kira could still picture it perfectly—the fear on the vampire Diana's face when she realized she was about to die. The way both of Kira's arms lit entirely on fire, pushing her power further than it had ever gone in order to break through Diana's immunity. The moment Tristan's maker, Aldrich, burst into the room only to be interrupted by a swarm of conduits exploding through the windows. The minutes Aldrich spent calmly evaluating her without any hint of fear, knowing his power to move objects with his mind was unbeatable. And of course, the feel of his hand when he slipped her a note with his address, promising that her birth mother would be there, waiting for the daughter who had been taken away from her more than seventeen years ago.

Kira remembered watching the mansion collapse in on itself after the conduits had set it on fire, remembered holding both Tristan and Luke's hands while the three of them observed in silence. She remembered how the note Aldrich had given her seemed to burn a hole through her pocket and the moment a plan popped into her mind. Most of all, Kira remembered the moment she had decided to act on it.

After destroying the mansion, the conduits retreated to a safe house to question the vampires they had captured. Luke followed, but Kira stayed behind feigning exhaustion. True, she had desperately wanted a shower and a soft bed, but the promise of a few hours alone with Tristan was what she had really needed. That night, while Luke was off on official business, the lie had begun—the lie that made this letter to Luke so difficult to write. Kira and Tristan were going to fight Aldrich, and they were leaving Luke behind.

Kira dropped her pen and glanced at the photo of her and Tristan that sat on the corner of her desk. Taped to the back, hidden behind the blue plastic frame, was the note Aldrich had slipped her before he had escaped. Kira didn't need to look at it to know what it said—she had the address memorized by now. Her mother was waiting in some cold castle in England, and Kira needed to find her. But it wasn't that simple.

When she first told him, Tristan had been furious. It was the night of the ball and they had just gotten back to the hotel room after ditching Luke. Kira tried to casually let it slip that his maker, Aldrich, had invited them to his castle, but Tristan wasn't fooled by her light tone. His eyes had flashed an ice-cold blue that stabbed at Kira's heart and he yelled at her for the first time. Kira knew it was his own fear and insecurities that fueled the outraged response—his own issues with Aldrich—but Kira suspected Luke's response wouldn't be any better, which was why she had decided to keep it a secret.

After calming Tristan down and firmly stating that she would be going to England with or without him, he had finally started listening to her. They worked out a plan to get her birth mother back, but it was a two-person plan. And tomorrow Kira would be ditching Luke at the airport to secretly fly to England with Tristan.

Oh yeah, Kira thought, *this will go over very well… not!*

She had reached for her pen again, ready to finally

write a coherent note, when strong arms enveloped her from behind, circling her shoulders and sending a chill down her spine with the suddenly cool touch.

"Hi," Tristan whispered in her ear as he pressed his cheek against hers and placed a soft kiss on her neck.

"Hi," Kira said, letting her head fall back against his shoulder. Perfect timing, she thought, thankful for the break from writing this note. A little procrastination never hurt anyone.

"Ready for your party, birthday girl?" he asked.

"Crap—no!" Kira shot up, suddenly energetic with surprise. "What time is it?"

"Almost five."

Tristan laughed under his breath, not at all surprised that Kira was running late. Never one for shorts, even in the middle of summer, Tristan had on his classic dark blue jeans and a crisp white button-down. Kira didn't have time to admire how the stark ivory brought out the twinkling blue of his eyes, she was too concentrated on being on time for once in her life.

"No, no, no…" Kira buzzed while pulling her T-shirt off and reaching for the yellow cotton dress hanging on the back of her door. She had been so focused on writing the note that she had completely forgotten about her birthday barbecue—the one happening in roughly five minutes. The only reason she was still at home in Charleston was her birthday, otherwise Luke would have shipped her back to

Sonnyville already. Kira knew he was eager to keep training her in order to see what her stronger powers meant. He had already forced her to light the wooden table in his backyard on fire, so she didn't even want to know what he was preparing back in Sonnyville.

"Don't worry. No one's here yet," Tristan said while he watched Kira tug her shorts off and smooth out her dress. Had Kira been less pressed for time, she may have felt a little self-conscious about changing right in front of her boyfriend, but as it was, she didn't have any time to be insecure.

"Are my parents outside?" Kira asked and bent over to pull the fuzzy socks off of her feet.

"Your dad is starting up the barbecue, and your mom is setting plastic plates on the table with Chloe."

"Perfect," Kira said, yanking one last time on the stubborn sock. Tristan put a hand on her back to keep her from falling over, and she slipped her feet into a pair of sandals. "How do I look?" Kira said while twirling around a few times.

"Beautiful as always," he said, catching her hand and guiding her toward him. Kira spun right into his arms and quickly kissed his lips, loving how familiar yet exciting his touch was. The slow exploration of her body, sexy in its restraint, made Kira feel delicate—something she direly needed when most of the time she felt too powerful, too uncontrolled, too…everything.

Tristan pulled back, breaking the kiss, to say, "I hear Emma's car out front."

"Just when we were getting to the good stuff," Kira cursed, making both of them smirk. Her best girlfriend was nothing if not prompt.

"I'll go get everyone to the backyard." Tristan slipped free of her arms. "You still need to put your contacts on." Kira grimaced, thinking of the bulky, itchy lenses that had become part of her daily routine. She nodded regretfully and pushed Tristan toward the stairs while she stepped into her bathroom.

Only Luke and Tristan knew about the change in her eyes. On their way home after the ball, Kira bought color contacts and had been using them ever since. It wasn't the perfect solution, but it was something.

Looking in the mirror, Kira still had trouble recognizing herself. Bright cobalt blue irises stared back at her. Orange-yellow flames danced around the edges, pushing into the cooler color and fighting for a place, but the shockingly saturated blue overwhelmed everything else. Sometimes, Kira liked how the blue popped against her red-blonde hair, but mostly she missed the warm, comforting green that used to be there. Her hair was already over the top with its bright hues and voluminous curls, she didn't need even crazier eyes to get noticed in a crowd.

Nothing else had physically changed about her since the night of the ball, but something stirred inside Kira, making her feel stronger. Luke and Tristan had no explanation for her new eye color, and Kira didn't want to harp on it when there was so much more to worry about. She had barely used her power since that night, only practicing when Luke forced her. She was more in control of her body and her fire, but the flames she commanded had changed. It was more than just the difference between her softer Protector powers and her rage-filled Punisher flames. Everything was stronger. All of her fire burned brighter, scorched hotter, and practically exploded with heat. When Luke had challenged Kira to light his wooden table on fire, it had come easily, like flipping a switch. The destruction was almost too welcome, too natural to her.

A high-pitched screech pulled Kira from her thoughts.

"Kira!" Her younger sister Chloe yelled from the bottom of the steps, "Where are you?"

"Yeah, Kira, where are you?" A deeper voice laced with mirth called after. *Luke*, Kira thought, hearing his laughter mix with Chloe's a second later.

"Coming!" she yelled and quickly pulled on her eyelid to slip in one contact. More squeals echoed down the empty hallway, and Kira followed the sound after quickly putting in her second contact.

When she looked down the steps, Kira saw the source of the noise. Luke had trapped little Chloe in his arms and was tickling her mercilessly while she giggled and squirmed to get away. Kira raced down the steps two at a time to free her sister.

"Kira!" Chloe yelled again before bursting into a new round of giggles. Kira smiled to herself. She knew exactly what to do. Reaching for Luke's stomach, she squeezed her hands against his abs and gave him a taste of his own medicine.

"No!" Luke laughed against Kira's attack and released Chloe, who followed Kira's lead and jumped on Luke to tickle him. He fell to the ground in mock surrender, chuckling helplessly and begging Chloe to stop.

"I win!" she screeched and raced out the back door, leaving Kira and Luke alone. Suddenly, Kira didn't know where to look. Between his confession of love the night of the Red Rose Ball and her plan to go to England behind his back, things were more than a bit strained. At least, it felt that way to Kira.

She offered her hand, doing her best to ignore the electric jolt his touch caused, and helped pull Luke to his feet. He dusted his khaki shorts off and tugged his navy T-shirt back down below his waist.

"Happy birthday," he said after a moment.

"Thanks," Kira responded, briefly glancing at his disheveled blonde locks and slightly strained gaze.

"So, Sonnyville tomorrow? I challenge you to get through an entire meeting with the council without burning their completely wooden dais to the ground," he joked, trying to lighten the mood.

"Yeah, can't wait," Kira hurriedly replied before heading for the door. She couldn't stand lying to him. At least that would end tomorrow. Even if he hated her for it, at least the lying would finally end. "Everyone's waiting, I better get out there." Kira nodded in the direction of the kitchen window.

Luke followed her gaze to the spot where Dave, Emma's silent but lovable boyfriend, and Miles, their geeky on-his-way-to-Harvard friend, stood next to her father around the grill.

"Yeah," Luke agreed and walked outside behind her.

"Happy birthday!" everyone shouted when Kira stepped into the sunlight. It was a small party, but it was perfect. Kira smiled at the streamers hanging in the trees surrounding her backyard and the freshly painted sign wishing her a happy eighteenth birthday. Chinese lanterns hung from the porch railing, ready for the sun to set so they could sparkle in the darkness, and raspy strains of the local radio station struggled to be heard from an old boom box sitting on the table.

"Thank you!" Kira smiled and stepped lightly down the porch stairs, practically dancing with her movements.

"Now, Kira, we know you're the chef in the family but tonight the men are making steaks," her dad said while standing beside an already smoking grill. Even though Kira knew he was really just her uncle, not even related by blood, the familiar image of him behind their family grill made it seem like old times, before Kira had known anything about the conduits or her real parents. "Luke, did you grab the aprons?"

"Got 'em, Mr. D!" Luke said, stepping past Kira to rush over to the grill.

Kira was more than happy to let the men do the work tonight. She loved cooking, but on her birthday she was allowed to relax. Especially since all she had been doing since she got home was make food—cooking was a serious stress reliever and all of the lying had her pulling her hair out. The Dawson family fridge was currently full to the brim with praline pecans, chocolate mousse, patience-trying risotto, and one of Kira's favorites, homemade spaghetti. Her fingers needed the night off.

Kira turned toward the foldout table her adoptive mother had put up in the backyard. She was really her aunt, her birth father's sister, but Kira tried to forget that sometimes. Especially on a day like today, with everyone around, Kira wanted to feel happy, not anxious about how much her life had changed in less than a year. She had gone from being a normal teenager to a mystical half-breed conduit who could potentially mean the end of the world. And the recent events at the Red Rose Ball had changed her again—she felt that in her bones even if she didn't know what it meant yet.

A moment later Kira blinked, pushing old memories

to the side to look back at the table where Emma was setting out the silverware and her mother was arranging a vase filled with fresh flowers. She stepped forward to help.

"Luke, you didn't!" Kira's mother gasped and put a hand to her mouth to cover her laughter. Kira stopped walking and turned just in time to see Luke finish tying an apron around his waist—the apron no one in her family ever used, the one her mother bought her father as a joke years ago, the one that had a life-sized photograph of Michelangelo's *David*... in the nude.

"Luke," Kira whined with a grimace, but the semblance of a smirk tugged at her lips.

"Just trying to get this party started." Luke grinned. He reached for the raw steaks and started dropping them on the grill.

Kira shook her head, but couldn't shake the small curve of her smile.

She looked around for Tristan, noticing he wasn't grill-side with the other men, and spotted him at the far side of the yard with Chloe. The two of them sat in the middle of a ring of Barbie toys, and Tristan was pretending to listen intently to whatever Chloe was trying to explain about her dolls. He looked up, as if sensing Kira's gaze, and flashed her a dimple-filled grin followed by a roll of his eyes.

"Should we go save him?" Kira's mother whispered in her ear, but Kira shrugged.

"Let him suffer." She laughed and out of the corner

of her eye, she saw Tristan shake his head at her. He had definitely overheard. *Good,* Kira thought, *let him know I'm totally calling the shots.* But her brief moment of power passed when a wad of napkins was shoved in her face.

"I'm going inside to work on the potato salad and coleslaw. Can you girls finish setting the table?"

"Sure, Mom," Kira said and took the napkins from her mother's arms before walking over to Emma.

"How is it possible that I'm wearing a dress and you're not?" Kira asked, eyeing her blonde friend's relaxed shorts and polo shirt attire.

"You're allowed to out-dress me one day a year— consider it my gift to you." Emma smiled and sat down in one of the vacant seats around the table. Kira sat next to her and dropped the napkins onto an empty plate.

"Want to learn how to fold these?" Kira asked. Years of working in a restaurant had taught her this nifty trick, and she quickly folded the first napkin into a simple, yet elegant, pyramid. Kira spent a few minutes showing Emma the steps, but it became obvious that there was something on her friend's mind.

"Is everything okay, Emma?"

"Of course," she said, but Kira didn't buy it.

"Really?" she pressed.

"Yeah… I was just thinking about how sweet it was that everyone came back for your birthday. I mean, Tristan came all the way back from backpacking around Europe just for the weekend—talk about dedication! I'm going to miss this…you know, having the gang together." She ended softly, concentrating on her napkin rather than the people around her. Kira pulled the linen from her friend's fingers, forcing Emma to concentrate on her words.

"I thought we got all of that talk out at graduation! We're still going to be 'the gang' no matter what."

"I know, but it won't be the same. You and Luke were only gone for what? Three weeks? And still, things felt off. Sometimes I just don't want things to change, you know? Like I don't really want to grow up."

You're telling me, Kira thought but quelled her inner monologue. Emma was almost never like this. Sure, she was emotional at times. But normally she was the calm, collected one—not the vulnerable, nervous one. Only one thing would bring this side out in her.

"Did something happen with Dave?" Kira asked, taking Emma's hand to comfort her. Dave and Emma were the perfect couple—they were classic southern sweethearts and they would both be going to college in Texas come fall. Kira couldn't even imagine them apart.

"No…I don't know. I'm just nervous I guess. People always say that when you grow up you grow apart, but what if I don't want that to happen?"

Kira couldn't suppress a sidelong glance at Tristan, who was still trapped by her sister, Chloe. She couldn't deny that her birthday had made her think the very same question—for her and Tristan, growing up literally meant growing apart.

"If you don't want to grow apart, you won't," Kira urged, turning her attention back to Emma and leaving her own thoughts for another time. "Nothing will change if you don't want it to. I mean, Dave is head over heels for you! You're all he ever thinks about and that won't change."

Both girls took a moment to look toward the grill where all four boys—yes, including Kira's fully adult father—were taking turns dropping lighter fluid into the flames to make them explode. Definitely Luke's idea, Kira assumed. "Well, when he's not playing with lighter fluid, all he does is think about you…"

"I know that," Emma said, "it's just that we'll be going to different colleges… they're only two hours away from each other, but still, it'll be different. And people always say that high school relationships never last, that they are sort of your first taste of love before the real thing comes around."

A sudden tingle stirred at the base of Kira's neck and she knew, before shifting to meet his gaze, that Tristan was watching her. His eyes were hidden beneath the shadow of his hair, but the tense muscles in his neck told Kira he was listening—waiting to hear what her response would be. She loved him and he her, but both of them had sensed the change in their relationship. He was a vampire. She was a conduit. They were supposed to be enemies, and the more prominent Kira's powers became, the more impossible their future seemed. That wasn't enough for Kira to give up on them and forget her feelings, but it was enough of a crack for a few small, almost imperceptible doubts to seep through.

"I don't believe that," she finally answered her friend. "Love is love, no matter how old or young you are."

"You're right," Emma said and let a slow smile spread across her face, lighting her features. She broke her long stare in Dave's direction, ready to tackle napkin folding again, but saw the gloomy expression on Kira's face. "Oh god, I've totally ruined your birthday! I don't know what came over me!"

"You haven't ruined anything," Kira said, casually waving the air away. "It's my party and I can cry if I want to!"

"Cry?" Luke's voice interjected from above Kira's shoulder. Kira spun in her seat, completely forgetting the apron Luke had on, and came face to face with the exact part of a nude male she did not want to be staring at.

Quickly shielding her eyes, Kira muttered, "Can you take that thing off? I can't take you seriously."

"You never take me seriously." Luke laughed, stepping even closer to Kira, who leaned further away. *Do not blush*, she thought, *do not blush*.

"Luke."

"Fine, fine. Ruin my fun," he said and untied the

apron before slipping it over his head. "I came over here to talk anyway."

"And that's my cue," Emma said, ducking out of the way and over toward Dave and Miles by the grill. Luke took her vacant seat and Kira instantly felt the space around them thicken. Her throat tightened and she took a deep breath, letting the air out slowly to calm her speeding pulse. She felt nervous around him—something she had never felt, not even since the first time they had met.

"What's up?" Kira said, hoping her voice had come out calm and strong.

Luke reached into his pocket and pulled out a small black box decorated with a white satin ribbon. "It's not much, but I got you a birthday present," he said and clumsily shoved his arm in her direction.

Slowly, Kira reached out and lifted the box from his hand. Using the power Kira had only discovered a few weeks before, she skimmed his thoughts, unable to stop the impulse to dip into his mind. The buzz of his nerves calmed her. His mind was hesitant, stopped on a breath and waiting. An expectation hung in the background, surrounded by a glimmer of hope and a tinge of excitement. But Kira could tell by the bright green hint in his eyes that he was energized—she didn't need the mind reading for that, and she retreated from his thoughts to tug the ribbon free from its bow.

Kira lifted the lid and sitting inside, gently resting on a

white satin cushion, was a tiny golden sun sparkling in the daylight.

"Luke," Kira said, breathing the word out like a sigh.

"I saw it in a store and thought you might like it." He shrugged.

"It's perfect," Kira said and set the box down on the table. Reaching around her neck, she unclasped the thin chain holding her father's wedding ring, an heirloom her adoptive mother had given her months ago when Kira had found out the truth about her star-crossed parents. The locket with her family portrait was still with her grandmother back in Sonnyville and the chain had felt uncomfortably light recently.

Kira untied the charm and slipped it through the chain, letting it fall to the bottom where it easily landed inside her father's ring. The two golden trinkets fit together perfectly, one slightly more aged than the other, but both brilliant against the late afternoon sky.

"So, you like it?" Luke asked quietly. His head was bent toward the ground and he looked at her under hooded eyebrows.

"I love it," Kira told him and pulled him in for a hug.

Maybe things can get better between us, she thought hopefully.

He wrapped his arms around her, holding her close, and breathed deeply into her hair. Kira willed herself to ignore it and not ruin the moment, but when she opened her eyes they met a hard, blue stare and she instantly retreated from Luke.

Kira knew Tristan couldn't help overhearing. His magnified senses were hard to turn off, but sometimes she wished he wouldn't listen in on conversations he knew would hurt him. The downturn of his eyes and straight line of his mouth told her all she needed to know, even if they disappeared a moment later when Chloe pulled him back to her toys.

"Food's ready!" Kira's mother called from the kitchen.

"The steak is being taken off the grill as we speak," her father added.

Luke quickly stood and put the apron back on to help her father, and Tristan walked over to take his place. She grabbed his hand, lacing her fingers through his, and pulled him down into the seat next to her.

"Everything okay?" she whispered.

Tristan nodded, turning away from her to smile at her mother who had just plopped a bowl of potato salad on the table in front of him. "Looks delicious, Mrs. Dawson."

Kira grinned at the formal use of her mother's name. He was a hundred years older than her, but he still wouldn't call her by her first name.

"Delicious enough for you to eat?" her mother asked hopefully.

"Not today," he apologized. "I ate before I came.

Special gluten-free diet and all." Tristan peered at Kira in his peripheral vision, meeting her gaze with a grin. It still amazed Kira that her mother didn't realize what Tristan was, having grown up around conduits. But it seemed like she had truly blocked out that entire part of her past and was choosing not to notice what was right in front of her.

"One of these days you will eat something I cook, Tristan, one—"

"Mom," Kira interjected, changing the topic.

"Right, right. Let me run inside to grab the coleslaw."

"She might force feed you, you know," Kira joked once her mom was out of earshot.

"I can handle it," Tristan said and placed his arm around her, hugging her to his chest.

Kira let her head rest on his shoulder. Soon enough, things would go back to normal between them. There was no telling how long they would be in England and some time away from Luke would be good, even if it was in Aldrich's castle.

She missed being alone with Tristan. He made her feel at peace and helped her step away from the conduits. With Luke it was always about conduits—teaching her how to be one and teaching her about them. He was a constant reminder of the future she couldn't walk away from—one supposedly full of death and destruction. But with Tristan, even though he was a vampire, she felt human. He let her escape her powers, so that even if only for a small moment in time, she was just a girl with a boy—nothing more, nothing less. *And when you're seventeen*, Kira thought, *sometimes that is all you need.*

But she was eighteen now, and Kira wasn't quite sure what that meant yet.

About The Author

Kaitlyn Davis graduated Phi Beta Kappa from Johns Hopkins University with a B.A. in Writing Seminars. She's been writing ever since she picked up her first crayon and is overjoyed to share her work with the world. She currently lives in New York City and dreams of having a puppy of her own.

Connect with the Author Online:

Website:
KaitlynDavisBooks.com
Facebook:
Facebook.com/KaitlynDavisBooks
Twitter:
@DavisKaitlyn
Tumblr:
KaitlynDavisBooks.tumblr.com
Wattpad:
Wattpad.com/KaitlynDavisBooks
Goodreads:
Goodreads.com/author/show/5276341.Kaitlyn_Davis